Family Blood:
Tales from the Whitestone Chronicles

by

Joseph Hanzlik

TELEMACHUS PRESS

Cover Graphic Design by Matthew J. Pogue
Cover Illustrator Ed W. Wendt

Back cover photograph by justzoilaphotography.com

Published by Telemachus Press, LLC
http://www.telemachuspress.com

Visit the author at:
http://joehanzlik.com

ISBN: 978-1-937698-43-0 (eBook)
ISBN: 978-1-937698-44-7 (Paperback)

Version 2012.04.23

Printed in the United States of America

10 9 8 7 6 5 4 3 2 1

To Janeen Spencer,
who knew I could do anything I put my mind toward.
Thanks Mom.

To Judith, who waited patiently for me to do just that.
Git her done.

Acknowledgement Page

Writing a book is a journey one takes alone, locked in a comfortable embrace with Imagination on one side and a blank computer screen on the other side. Once the story is done, several more people are involved in the process.

This book couldn't have been done without the help of the people from the Editorial Department, especially R.J. Cavender for his help, guidance, and suggestions; and Jane Ryder for her eagle eyes in the process.

In addition, the book wouldn't be what it is today without the awesome team at Telemachus Press which includes Steve Jackson, Steve Himes, and Karen Lieberman as well as all the other people who made publishing a book so effortless. Thank you.

A story needs a cover and a cover needs an artist and a graphic designer, both of which were found in the persons of Ed and Matt. Thanks to you both for coming up with great work on short notice and then enhancing that work. A bow of thanks to Ed W. Wendt, cover illustrator, and Matthew J. Pogue, graphic designer. You guys are great.

Family Blood:

Tales from the Whitestone Chronicles

Chapter One

THE NIGHTMARE WAS always the same.

Jared stood in a large cave at night with soldiers around him. He gripped his sword in his meaty hand as orders were issued and men started fighting. The creatures rallied against them, coming out of the darkness of the cave with a force and vigor that frightened and awed him. All that naked power, now unleashed, was beautiful and terrifying.

They crawled out of stone and from the roof, from the corners of hard packed earth and the structures they lived in. Then, with speed and economy, they gathered together hissing and moved closer to the soldiers armed against them. Battle ensued as shouts and curses filled the air. The soldiers fought and kept their fear in check as the vampires, eager for battle, rushed forward like madmen delirious for anarchy to spill human blood with fangs and claws.

The vampires were massing.

She was there.

Her slender face was framed by long blonde hair and her dark eyes looked out in terror as she hunted for a place to run; someplace to hide away from the battle that waged all around her, someplace where she could forget about the dangers that circled her on all sides.

"Christina!" he shouted.

She turned toward his voice eagerly searching for him when a river of flame coughed and spewed forth, cascading between them. The winding inferno cut a wide swath of heat, smoke, and noxious fumes that drove them apart. The flames snaked across the cave dividing them. He and the soldiers were on one side. On the other side, Christina stood rooted in place, her white dress flowing around her, hands pressed together and her face a portrait of fear. She was all alone.

The vampires swarmed about her, engaging the soldiers as she heard her name being shouted in the cave.

She turned toward Jared, her eyes searching for his voice. He saw a reflection from her, a bright sparkle of copper light, from her chest. It was from the brooch he had given her. The piece of jewelry reflected the nearby light. His heart thumped inside his chest and then she locked eyes with him.

She stopped moving, her eyes pleading for help.

"Christina!"

Something hard and metallic struck him in the head. A sharp pain exploded on the side of his head as he hit the ground. His head felt on fire and his eyes stung from the smoke. He pushed away the pain, tears coming to his eyes and streaming down his face. He grunted. He climbed slowly to his feet, taking several ragged breaths and steadied himself on the back of his heels, his boots firmly planted in the earth, his fists balled up as he did so.

When he lifted his head and his vision had cleared, she was gone.

He brushed against a soldier and took a step toward the deadly river of flames, to try and cross it, but the soldier reached out and stopped him.

"No, my liege. You mustn't. It is dangerous."

"She's over there."

"Then she's *dead*, my liege. Forget her."

He backed away from the wall of flames, the heat threatening to sear his lungs if he got closer. "I promised I would bring her home."

"You're a dead man if you do, sir."

He lowered his head and realized she was beyond his reach. Jared remembered the vow he made to bring her back and because he failed, he felt a hollowness grow inside. It ate away at the best part of him. He had gone to great lengths to rescue her. To fail was more than he could handle. A mad crazy impulse to dash into the wall of flames seized him for one moment, so that when he looked at the dancing tendrils of orange colored fire it seemed perfectly natural and such an easy way, to step into the flames and let them swallow him whole.

He fought against the self destructive urge to leap into the fire and cleared his head.

The fighting continued all around him and then he heard a clear and piercing scream—

Jared jerked awake immediately, hurriedly pushing back the blankets and leaves that covered him just as the nightmare that haunted him did time and again. He stood up, and reached down between the massive tree roots and grabbed his gear: a sword, and bow and quiver. His hand brushed against his chest and he felt the chain mail underneath his tunic.

A scream cut through the night. It came from behind him.

His mind alert, his heart beating wildly, he raced past the trees and over the hilly ground. The moonlight sprinkled light through the tree branches. It was enough to see by.

A small hut appeared before him. A figure swayed and started moaning in the night. When he got closer, he saw a woman with a shawl wrapped around her shoulders, a torch clutched in her hand.

Her sad and worried eyes told him what he feared.

"My children are gone. A foulness took them."

"Which way did they go?"

Her bony fingers shook as she pointed down the road. He took the torch from her and headed off in the same direction.

With his mind racing at what he might face, Jared was alert for any signs of the attacker.

The loud snap of a twig ahead of him in the dark told him he was getting closer.

Jared rushed forward, crashing through shrub and branches, enduring scratches across his face and forearms. He ignored the pain, and found his way through to a clearing with hard packed ground. A shape was moving ahead.

The figure stopped and hissed and bent forward to pick something up from the ground. It hissed again.

Sword in one hand, torch in the other, Jared redoubled his efforts and ran. He had a promise to keep and he was good to his word. It was all he had left.

The torch cast enough light for him to see by. A man was bent and reaching out with one arm toward a frightened boy. The boy kicked at the man's outstretched hand. The man hissed again.

Under the man's other arm, tucked close to the side, was a smaller boy. They looked like brothers. The free boy sat on his buttocks, hands and feet flat on the ground. He moved away from the hissing man the way a crab would move: awkward, jerky, uncoordinated movements.

The boy kicked at the outstretched hand whenever it came near.

The man turned toward him and Jared clearly noticed the red eyes and the fangs of the foul creature.

It looked up at him in wide-eyed surprise.

"Leave the boy alone," Jared said. "There is nowhere to go."

The vampire stepped toward the child on the ground, and with reflexes as quick as a snake, he reached out and caught the child's ankle and gripped it tightly. He lifted the child up, dangling him upside down.

The vampire said, "We mean you no harm, hunter."

"Put the child down."

"Step closer and both will die."

"Take a step away and you will die," Jared said firmly, feeling the grip of his sword in his meaty hand.

A brief smile flashed across the vampire's face and then disappeared. There was a change in the creature's eyes as a hardness washed over him.

"Catch this one, hunter."

With sudden speed and deftness, the vampire tossed the child high into the moonlit night.

Jared gasped and then focused on what was important; track the child. He saw, out of the corner of his vision, the vampire take off in the opposite direction, running away from him down the hard packed ground. Jared had no time to chase the vampire while still protecting the child from harm.

The child came first.

He saw where the child was headed and changed direction automatically, his feet moving quickly over the ground. At the last moment he dropped the sword and torch to stand beneath the falling child. He opened his arms and a body as heavy as a sack of grain with twirling arms and legs dropped in. The boy's screaming continued until the boy looked at Jared and climbed down safely out his arms.

Jared looked down at the child.

The child set his jaw defiantly and said, "He was a nasty man. He had a foul breath. And he was scary. And his hands were icy. Yuck!"

Jared picked up his sword and torch. With the light still burning thoroughly and brightly, he ran after the vampire. His only hope was to catch it and to save the other child still in its clutches, but he was already too far behind and the vampire had too big a lead on him. And then he noticed the overhanging branches. Trees dotted both sides of the lane and the branches formed a canopy overhead. The branches extended down the road, encompassing both where Jared stood, and where the vampire was, going even further beyond that.

He might just make it.

He lowered his sword, readied his bow and drew an arrow from his quiver. He notched the arrow and drew back on the string, feeling the tight pull of his mighty bow. He placed the arrow tip into the fire and when it was burning he pulled back his bow and let the arrow fly. He prayed that his aim was far enough and high enough to work.

He was a better swordsman than an archer.

He lit another arrow and let it follow the first one.

And he fired three more arrows, all a flame, into the canopy of tree branches.

The fire caught and moved quicker than he could hope for, jumping from dry branch to withered bark. The darkness slipped away as flames spread quickly, covering the branches and providing a canopy of flames over the lane.

The night creature ran, the child still in his clutches.

Jared picked up his sword and gave chase. He was making progress, but he was still too far back.

The vampire leapt skyward changing its form. A leathery creature with a large wing span lifted off the ground, carrying the kid in its talons. The flames from the branches leapt across its path.

An angry screech filled the night air as flames touched its body. The creature careened and turned not skyward but toward the hard dirt-packed road. It nose-dived and screamed in pain as its talons opened up and it dropped the child. The wobbly winged creature crashed, lying in a lump in the middle of the road.

Dazed from the crash, the child groaned and lay on the ground. Jared surveyed the child quickly. The legs weren't bent at weird angles, there were no bones sticking out past skin through his shoulders or arms, no bloody gashes across his forehead. The child looked worn and tired, but no worse for his experiences.

Jared knelt and touched the child's forehead. "You'll be all right. Stay here."

"Okay," the boy said, lifting his head up to get a better look at Jared.

With his sword drawn, Jared moved carefully until he stood over the vampire, blade ready to slice downward and take away the life of the kidnapper. But then something caught his eye. Something was pinned to its jacket, and it looked familiar.

The creature stirred and Jared pressed his sword into the vampire's windpipe. "Where did you get that brooch?"

A dirty long fingernail tapped the brooch. "This?" the vampire said. With slits for eyes, he carefully regarded Jared for a moment.

"Tell me true," Jared said.

"Look into my eyes. You can see the truth for yourself."

Jared steeled himself and fought against the powerful suggestion but he couldn't help himself. He found his eyes drawn toward the crimson eyes and he felt his willpower seep away from him.

He saw the creature get up and stand on its feet. But Jared was unable to move.

His mind was screaming: *Do something. Stab him. Kill it.*

And then something clicked inside. He closed his mind from the vampire and instantly remembered the nightmare (it always ran through his mind, haunting him) where Christina was trapped on the other side of a wall of flame. He cried out to her and swung his sword.

He broke through whatever control the night creature had over him and opened his eyes, swinging his sword at the dark shape in front of him.

The night creature ducked underneath the blade and swiped his claws at Jared's chest, raking him with both hands.

Jared fell, thankful for the chain mail across his chest and stomach. It had provided ample protection in the past and it saved his life again tonight.

The night creature leaned over him.

With tremendous strength and speed, Jared put one leg up and kicked out at it.

The vampire fell back, the wind knocked out of him.

With sword firmly in hand, Jared got to his feet, pressing the blade into the vampire's chest.

Jared pointed at the piece of jewelry on its coat. "Now, you vicious creature, you will tell me where you got that brooch or you'll never see another nightfall."

The vampire hissed.

"Then *you* are the one who killed her and I am too late."

He plunged the sword into the night creature, putting his weight into it, but not letting it cut all the way through its body.

Not yet.

"I want you to experience great pain before you die. Like the pain I felt for her."

He twisted the blade slowly, turning left and right, the blade chewing up the creature's heart.

The vampire sucked in air, and then hissed, its fangs and red tongue prominent.

"You. Don't. Frighten. Me."

With a two handed swing, the sword blade struck the neck, cutting through muscles and bones and spine, severing the head.

Jared reached down and grabbed the brooch just as the body dusted away. It always amazed him how quickly the body of a dead vampire would crumble on itself and quickly be converted to its base elements.

He picked up the head, looked at the face, and then placed it in a sack that he carried just for this purpose.

He lifted up the torch and turned. The children stared at him open mouthed, fear shining brightly in their eyes.

"Children?"

They backed away from him, as new footsteps approached.

"My children. My children."

The children turned and ran into their mother's arms.

There was shouting and muffled cries of joy as they hugged each other. He watched them from a distance, feeling intrusive on their privacy. The branches above, aglow with flames only moments ago, started dying out.

The shawled woman, with her arms around her two sons, came up to him. "Your courage saved my children. I am in your debt."

"Then according to your means," Jared said.

"What do you want?"

He held the brooch out to her. "Have you ever seen this before?"

"No. But it is very beautiful. Maybe the next village over might help you."

He raised the sack to her, the one that contained the head of the vampire. "Show this as proof to others. I do what I say."

Chapter Two

THE WHEAT FIELDS stretched before him, an inviting and pleasant tapestry. Beyond that was a small village where farmers and field hands worked together harvesting the wheat crop. They bent their bodies and scythed the wheat and bundled the crop into short stacks and laid them on the ground.

Separated by a narrow river that ran the length of the fields, the nearby village bustled with people setting up their stalls for the day's activities. Together the fields and the little village stirred with life. Jared examined the beginning of the day. Maybe this would be a good place to forget about the past and to begin a new life.

His rough fingers tightened around the brooch.

"Come on, girl," Jared said to his horse, eager to see the village up close.

His horse clip-clopped down the road past the workers in the wheat fields until they stopped in the middle of the small bridge. The thick planks were sturdy enough to hold his horse and him without bowing or bending under the pressure. Jared glanced about and breathed in deeply. This placed offered everything: nature on one hand and civilization on the other.

But Jared had to check something out. He looked down at the brooch in his fist. He had to know if anybody had seen this before. Probably nobody had and he was wrong in continuing his vow.

The water lapped against the shore, making gurgling sounds and then it moved past and the river widened out. A convenient place to wash. He took in a deep breath and scratched his head. He could just leap off his horse, find a cozy place to sleep and forget about the whole world for a year or two. He felt worn and used up. The best part of him had been gone for a while now.

Since his vow, he had changed.

He urged his horse on and clip-clopped over the wooden beams of the bridge and entered into the small mouth of the village. In front of him was a collection of tattered vendor's stalls and tents. Close to those were better stalls and larger tents and following these were rough buildings and the start of cobbled streets.

He dismounted and tied his horse to the post near the tavern.

The tavern owner couldn't help him—they didn't provide food before noon, and more importantly, they didn't know who in the village would be interested in looking at a piece of jewelry.

Jared nodded thanks and left. Outside the tavern, the first thing to catch his attention was the scent of roasted pork.

He ambled in front of the stall, looking at the pig on the spit. The fire licked at the smallish beast already gutted and dressed and being cooked right now before him. His stomach gurgled and his mouth started to water. It was an unconscious act that he suddenly became very aware of.

"How much for a plate of your food, misses?"

The woman wiped her copper tinted hair out of her face and said, "It'll be ready soon. How much did you want?"

"A plate full."

"Do you have coin?"

Jared reached into his tunic and held out the coin bag for her to see. "Aye."

"Pay now and you'll have your food in half an hour."

"Gladly," Jared said, pulling open the drawstring, he upended the bag until a single coin tumbled into his palm. He handed it to her. "Is that enough?"

The woman took the coin and examined it with eager green eyes and inquisitive fingers. "Would you like a second plate with that, sir?"

"Maybe for the road."

"Aye. I'll have it for you. Come back in half an hour when the food's ready."

Jared nodded. The rumble of his stomach alerted him to how hungry he really was and how much he was looking forward to his meal. He walked away to visit the market. In half an hour he would be eating. Right now he enjoyed walking past the various market stalls. Vendors of all kinds were lined up. He breathed in deeply filling his lungs with cool air and listened to the laughter of children running through the marketplace, to the sounds of birds in the nearby trees, to the talk of young women as they passed him. It had been a lifetime since he was around people.

Two years was a lifetime.

A lot of things had changed since then.

Twice in the past he came across men he had recognized and had avoided them. Better they don't know, and it was better if everyone thought he was either dead or missing.

He stepped into the throng that was the marketplace, turning only once to look back at his horse. A tall man with his face hidden under a wide-brimmed hat brushed by his horse only briefly and was then gone. It was nothing out of the ordinary. Jared turned and wandered, biding his time for when his food would be ready.

Jared strolled into a courtyard and found himself off to one side away from the people, watching a game of chance with dice. Three men bent over eagerly while another man blew on his hands and rolled the dice against the stone wall. Eager eyes followed the dice.

"Bad luck there son," the big man with a broken nose said. He took the dice and held out his hand. "Pay up."

"The dice are weighted," the lean, wiry man blurted out.

"The dice are fine. Pay up now or we'll take it out of your hide."

"That's not very smart thinking now, is it?" Jared stood behind them, his arms crossed over his chest.

The tall man was heavy and stocky, his short black hair combed forward. His dark eyes regarded Jared carefully, his broken nose set off to one side of his face. Broken Nose had pudgy, fleshy hands that cupped the dice easily in his palm. The hands, Jared noticed, were made for squishing things together into a pulpy substance like birds, rabbits, or small and desperate people like the young man here. Broken Nose wore stained, dirty clothes.

He had with him two companions, one a bald man with a missing front tooth in the middle of his leering smile; and the other a man with almost no chin at all under his mouth and mousy colored hair that shot out in nearly every direction. No Chin glanced over at Jared. He was being measured and weighed, assumptions being made and the amount of risk was being scrutinized.

The young man was boxed in between No Chin and Missing Tooth. With his back against the wall, he stared up at Broken Nose; he had nowhere to go.

Broken Nose swiveled his head and rolled his shoulders at Jared. "You're not the law."

"Correct. But beating him up won't get you what you want. How much does he owe you?"

"Two coppers," Broken Nose said.

"How about a wager?" Jared saw the interest in their eyes and behind that interest he saw the plain hand of greed rattling their cages.

Jared moved closer and looked at the young man. "Why gamble like this?"

"We need food. I thought I could make my money go further, sir."

"Do you gamble like this regularly?"

"First time. My sister is hungry."

"And what will she be if you don't come home with food tonight?"

"Even worse off, sir."

"So no more gambling."

"No, sir."

Broken Nose smiled, showing uneven teeth and said, "You mentioned something about a wager. Are you a gambling man?"

Jared reached into his belt and pulled out his money bag. For the second time that day he reached into it for coin. When he did the men looked down at his hand and their eyes went wider with naked greed.

Broken Nose said, "Lad, get out of here. You're off my hook till next time you come back and make a losing wager."

Jared watched as the boy scampered off. He then looked up to see himself surrounded by Broken Nose and his two companions. All avenues of escape were blocked. The large fleshy fist

from Broken Nose struck him in the stomach, right under the rib cage.

Jared bent over, coughing.

The moneybag dropped to the ground and the men scrambled for it, but Broken Nose grabbed first and curled his greedy fingers around the purse. The men started arguing and cursing as Broken Nose stuffed the coin purse inside his shirt.

Jared got to his feet and started toward the men when a shout went up.

Guards rushed them. Jared breathed a sigh of relief and staggered forward, focused on Broken Nose.

But before he could get closer, the man grabbed one of his companions, the bald one with the missing teeth, and threw him into the oncoming guards. There was cursing and a great deal of noise as the guards staggered into each other to get out of the way, a few of them tripping and falling to the ground.

Broken Nose and No Chin slammed him against the wall as they ran past, down the alley, with his money.

Jared looked up at the guards. "They've stolen my coins," he said, pointing at Broken Nose.

"They're long gone," the Captain of the Guard said.

"But my money—"

"Isn't important," the Captain of the Guard said.

"Isn't important? It is to me," Jared said.

"But not when it's compared to murder it isn't."

Chapter Three

JARED FOUGHT TO break free of the confusion that threatened to swallow him whole. What kind of place did he land in? He came into the village just minutes ago, and now he was involved in a murder. How was that possible?

"I'm a stranger here. I just rode into town. If I murdered somebody why would I stay around?"

The Captain of the Guard looked at him with level eyes and said, "That's what we want to know."

"But I just arrived here," Jared said. "I have no quarrel with any man here."

"Is that your horse over there?" The Captain of the Guard pointed toward his animal, still standing right in front of the tavern.

"Yes."

"Come with us."

It wasn't a suggestion, not with his hands already bound with leather, and one guard standing on his left, another positioned on his right. The last guard following him three steps behind. If he was to jackrabbit away, it would be both incredibly difficult to do, and it would be the luckiest of all escapes. He'd have to work at his bonds to loosen the leather strappings. Maybe with enough slack in the leather, he could wiggle his hands free and run away. It was no good running if his hands weren't free to defend himself it he needed to. If he had to choose between spending time in a jail cell or somewhere out in the wild, he'd prefer the latter. Obviously, he didn't murder anybody, so how was he involved in something he never did?

They walked toward his horse.

He recalled the events of this morning. He was innocent. Surely, they would see that and then they would laugh and joke with him. Obviously, this was a cruel joke and when he found out who was responsible for it he'd strangle them.

They must have the wrong man. But why did they ask him about his horse?

They stopped in front of the tavern and the Captain of the Guard turned toward him.

"Just to be clear: is this your horse?"

Jared nodded. "Yes." What was going on?

The captain motioned to a guard. The guard stepped closer to the horse, one hand resting on top of the saddle, the other hand fishing beneath, between blanket and saddle. The guard's face was determined and then he made an O shape with his mouth. His eyes grew wide. "I have something here."

"What do you have?"

The guard pulled a large sword out from beneath the saddle, the kind that was curved and rarely seen in these parts. The handle was made of pearl and the cross guard was studded with small precious stones. The blade was curved and wide at the end, measuring the width of a large man's hand.

A sinking feeling came over Jared. This was no joke. He felt his throat tighten. He was in a nightmare, caught up in something that was beyond his understanding. He shook his head and without even thinking the words tumbled out. "That's not my sword."

Another guard approached the captain, pointing across the field he had traveled. "The drunk. He's been hacked up in the ditch."

"Hacked up?" The captain looked grimly at Jared and then to the guard. "How so?"

"His body and face were butchered, blood everywhere. Whoever did it was angry."

"Not a dagger?"

"No."

"Not an arrow?"

"No."

"Not a lance?"

"No." The guard looked at the sword. "The killing was done with a sword, with an especially wide blade, and before you ask, I know because the depth of the wounds is very deep where the flesh is pulled back. Deeper and wider than what you would get with a normal sword."

The Captain of the Guard turned to Jared. "Who would want to kill the drunk and then frame you for it?"

"I don't know," Jared said.

"Neither do I." The captain exhaled and said, "Bring the body to the undertaker. I want his opinion."

"I didn't do it."

"I believe you." The captain looked at the ground, his brow furrowed. "But I have a witness who said you did. He pointed you out to us."

"It stands to reason I didn't do it, but he set you on me, so he was involved," Jared said.

"We are already looking into that," the Captain of the Guard said.

"That's not good enough."

A voice said, "Hey, sir. Your plate of hot food is ready."

Jared turned and the woman with the coppery hair, the one he had paid for his food, was standing there, her hands on her hips.

The Captain of the Guard said, "Good morning, Maggie. He won't be coming for sup. We have him."

"What happened?"

"He's wanted for murder."

"Murder?"

"We have him under control, Maggie. Nothing to worry about."

Everything swam before Jared's eyes with a startling clarity. He could stand here and let them corral him, accuse him of a murder he didn't commit and possibly kill him for it. Or he could run.

He had worked some slack into his wrist bonds. The guards were close but their eyes were elsewhere. The Captain of the Guard was deep in thought looking across the field where one of his guards knelt by a hidden body. Everybody around him was momentarily distracted.

The time was now.

That or stay here and be condemned for a murder he didn't commit, in a village he had never visited before today.

Taking a deep breath, Jared bolted.

Chapter Four

THE SLACK IN his wrist bonds was enough to allow Jared his freedom, but he had gotten two feet away when a hand clamped down on his shoulder. With a savagery he thought was burned out of him, he turned around, faced the guard, and kicked him straight up into the soft sack of his groin. The guard fell down, his face contorted in pain. Groaning on the ground, and rolling on his back and side, he blocked the other guards from getting at Jared.

It was enough time for him to run through the marketplace where the shoppers were present and disappear into the crowd.

Jared heard the whistles behind him and forced himself to slow down and take a deep breath. If he ran he would look guilty. He was innocent. If he had to give up, he wanted it on his own terms; he didn't want to be forced into it.

It was a matter of pride.

Three days ago Jared might have let them take him, sentence him for a crime he didn't commit, and hang him. Or whatever they did with criminals in these parts. And he still had half a mind to do just that. But attacking and running away from the guards had sealed his fate. He ran, therefore he was guilty. They'd hang him.

He worked the last of the leather straps off his wrists and pocketed them. He never knew when they would turn out to be useful. Jared looked over his shoulder. Down the street the guards moved slowly toward him. They weren t looking at him; rather they were checking all the crevices and nooks that a person could hide in on both sides of the marketplace. They were conducting a thorough sweep of the area and moving slowly in his general direction.

He hoped for a less diligent pursuer, but that was not to be. The captain of the guard was a thorough and efficient man.

Jared rounded a corner and bumped into a large oaf and his fellows. Jared looked up and Broken Nose stared back at him.

Jared raised his fists. "It's you," Jared said, as he bared his teeth and leaped at Broken Nose, his hands already around the big man's thick neck.

He clamped both hands tight and forced Broken Nose to his knees. The others struck and kicked at Jared, but he didn't let go.

The sound of a shrill whistle grew closer.

The fellows, one of them the bald man that Jared recognized from before, stopped attacking and scattered.

"You took my money, you thief!"

Broken Nose's face turned a deep shade of scarlet and then pale. His eyes fluttered and he fell to the ground.

Jared released his grip and blood immediately flowed back into Broken Nose's face.

Jared reached forward and patted him down. He found the bag of coins in Broken Nose's shirt pocket and stuffed it inside his own waistband. He looked down at the unconscious man and waited.

The Captain of the Guard reached him first, with his sword drawn.

"Running makes you look guilty."

"I thought the same thing."

"Who's he?" The Captain of the Guard kept his sword aimed at Jared, while pointing with his free hand to Broken Nose.

"He's the guy who stole from me. Took my money."

"If you run, I'll give my men orders to kill you on sight."

"Nope. I'm not running. Do with me what you will. What do I care?"

The guards swarmed over Jared, pressed him against the wall, and tied up his wrists.

Jared marched past the courtyard, with the guards surrounding him. He saw the angry faces and the raised fists directed at him with such venom that even a snake would slither away and hide.

Jared kept his eyes lowered but when he saw his horse being taken by one of the guards, he took notice. Leading the horse by the reins, the guard tugged and the horse followed obediently.

Jared's caravan of shame was now complete: his escort, two guards on either side of him, with the Captain of the Guard in front leading them all, guard following them with his own horse clip-clopping along the pavement behind him. They moved through the courtyard and headed toward a tiny building at the end of the village.

The door was shoved open and Jared was ushered into the building. He stood in a small office ten paces deep and five paces across. There was another door in the back of the room that opened to a small corridor that barely allowed two men abreast that led to another door twenty paces away. At the end of the hallway was a jailer seated at a small desk. The jailer looked at him and his escorts and placed a key into the lock and twisted it to open the door.

Jared stepped out of the narrow hallway and through the door and found himself in a large room with three distinct cells against the outer wall. Each of the cells contained criminals and cast-offs.

In one cell, the one closest to Jared, two men were in the middle of an argument. A tall slender man with a shock of short, black hair and wearing a brown colored robe that fell to his knees argued with a thin, smallish boy, someone who, Jared guessed, could get into tight places if he really needed to.

They stopped arguing and looked at Jared as his guard stepped up to the cell door, inserted a key, and opened it.

Jared was shoved past the two men and into the middle of the cell. The guard slammed the cell door shut behind him.

"I'm innocent," the tall man said, moving past Jared with an angry look on his face. He gripped the bars of his cell and pressed his thin face against the cold iron barriers.

"You're innocent as a fat whore," the smallish young man said. "You did the crime. I, on the other hand, *am* innocent."

Jared ignored their continued rants and protestations and stepped onto the pallet shoved against the corner. He was in trouble, that was all there was to it. He went over the course of events that led him here and wished he could find a way out.

On the other hand, if he were dead then all of his problems would be solved.

Maybe, he thought, this was God's way of punishing him for his failure. Maybe he would find peace in death. Death would certainly be better than listening to the racket caused by these two.

The pallet was hard against his back. His cell mates continued bickering and he was hearing no end of it.

"I've seen you with your magic," said the smallish man. "You call yourself a wizard. I call you a fake."

"I will turn you into a toad!" The wizard faced the smallish man, looking down at him with his hard grey eyes.

"Yeah. When? You talk large, but you're a fake."

The tall man reached out for the smaller man, his hands ready to throttle his short neck.

"Stop it," Jared said, getting to his feet. "I won't have this bickering going on."

Both of them stopped and looked over at him.

"Finally," Jared said. "You two have been going at it like dogs fighting over a bone. Stop it and have a rest or, by God, I'll take care of you both."

"And who are you?" The smaller man looked up at him with dark penetrating eyes.

Jared took in the smallish figure. He was a lad, maybe eighteen or nineteen years of age, with brown curly unkempt hair. The boy, for that was how Jared thought of him, had large brown eyes quick with intelligence. He was short, maybe five six, but he wasn't stocky. He was thin and lanky, dressed in brown leggings and a gray tunic. Over the tunic he wore a brown vest. It gave the impression of being nondescript, somebody who wouldn't draw attention to himself. It was the appearance of nearly anybody in the marketplace.

Jared felt as if the lad was trying to remember his face, soaking in every detail of his features.

"My name is Jared," he said, not wanting to reveal any more about himself. "And I can take care of you easily enough."

"Ah, yes sir. You are a mighty bag of bloated wind, like the wizard here. You should both join up and start your own club. I suppose you are like him?"

"How?"

"You are innocent, of course. Isn't that the way of criminals: we are all innocent. None of us deserve to be here. Isn't that what we all say?"

"Get back, get away from the door," bellowed the guard, jabbing a stick through the bars and hitting the smallish man with it.

"Owww!"

"Back." the guard warned.

The cell door opened again and the guard, with help from two others, shoved a new prisoner into the cell. The large man with an ugly face and a broken nose looked around the cell.

Broken Nose regarded the lad, and then turned and noticed the wizard. He kept turning until he faced Jared.

The eyes grew hard as he looked and grinned.

Jared looked up at Broken Nose and shook his head. "Not you?"

Chapter Five

BEFORE JARED COULD move, Broken Nose reached down with powerful cable-like arms, picked Jared up, and slammed him against the wall.

The cell door clanked shut and the guard started laughing. "Fighting again. This is entertaining."

Jared brushed away the stars from his vision and ignored the pain. He crouched in front of Broken Nose. "You want to learn a lesson, huh? I can teach you to have better manners."

Arms outstretched, Broken Nose rushed forward. Jared ducked, stepped to one side, and with all the force he could put behind it, gutted Broken Nose in the ribs with the point of his elbow.

A violent rush of air escaped from Broken Nose. Jared backed away. "Had enough, big guy?"

Broken Nose favored his left side, his hand pressed against his flank, his mouth open wide. He tried to breathe deeply but had trouble doing so.

"You caused me a lot of grief," Broken Nose said in a fitful way, the air wheezing out of him in spurts.

"You stole from me. You shouldn't have."

"I'll give you that." Broken Nose stepped back. "Where did you learn to fight?"

"From fighters, of course."

"Could you be more specific?"

"I could, but I won't. I don't have to tell you anything. You're a menace. If we were children I'd label you a bully."

"So?"

"You leave me alone, or you'll get more of the same from me," he said pointing at the big man's ribs.

"I don't see how. I'm bigger and stronger than you."

"You're also uglier than me."

"You're a pretty boy, that's all you are."

"Have it your way. Most fights can be avoided, but some have to be endured."

"Huh?"

Jared took a step closer and stood in front of Broken Nose. The large man's expression changed from a puzzled look to a satisfied one. Broken Nose grabbed Jared by the collar, but before he could do anything, Jared turned a half step away, grabbed Broken Nose's wrist and kept turning it until Broken Nose bent over, his face near the ground.

He screamed in pain. "Oowwww!"

"I can break your wrist. Do you want that?"

"No."

"Will you stop bothering me?"

"No."

"Stubborn."

"Yes. Owwww!"

Jared applied pressure to the wrist lock, driving the big man all the way to the ground. "I am losing my patience with you. Surrender now."

"No."

"Surrender twice."

"No."

Jared exhaled and applied more pressure to the bony structure. Broken Nose screamed even louder and fell to the floor. Loud cracking sounds came from his wrist, followed by a pop. Broken Nose yelped and held his forearm close to his body.

The wrist flopped over to one side.

"You broke my hand!"

"No, I didn't."

"What do you call this?"

"Actually, it is your wrist. But to you it must be the same thing."

The guard on the other side of the bars started laughing.

"Would you look at that! The smaller one bested the big one. Wouldn't have thought that was possible. That was a good move."

Jared watched as Broken Nose stood up and gasped in pain, holding his hand close to him. He tried to move it and wiggle his fingers. He scrunched his eyes closed and yelped. Broken Nose took some deep breaths and cradled his injured wrist, resting it against his body. "I can't move it without incredible pain."

"No more trouble from you, correct?"

"Not here. Not now."

Jared said, "I could kill you, but that would be a waste. Why not be agreeable with me? You can't go around thinking you can steal from everyone and get away with it. Someday somebody will stand up to you and be better than you. Like I did just now."

"Are you always this polite?" the lad said, clearly amazed by what he'd witnessed.

"Words first, fists and swords second."

"Well spoken," the wizard said. He stepped forward and clapped Jared on the shoulder. "My name is Naveen."

The lad turned to Jared. "And friends call me Nix. What are you going to do with him?"

Nix pointed at the large man sitting in the middle of the cell floor, who cradled his damaged wrist in his lap.

"He needs to have his bones set. Some bracing would be good for his wrist, and then some cloth to tie and bind his wrist bones. It should be better in a month or two," Jared said.

He glanced over at the smiling guard. "Do you have anything for him?"

The guard clucked. "This is a jail, not a healer's place."

"But if we had it here, we could help him."

"Not my problem."

"Do you sleep here?" Jared asked the guard.

"Huh?"

"Who guards us at night, in case we try to escape?"

"I do."

Jared stepped toward the bars and addressed the guard. "You just saw the fight, correct?"

"Yeah. Good move."

"Thanks. I broke his bones. That means he's in pain."

"Of course, but not my pain."

"Correct, but his pain will keep you up all night. If we don't do something for him now, he'll be wailing in pain, grow feverish, maybe start yelling in the middle of the night. I don't want that, you don't want that."

"I could just shut him up then."

"You could, but there is a better way. There are laws. The judge might frown on how you treat him."

"What do you want?"

"Some splints and some herbs to calm the body and the mind. He needs some cloth to tie the splints down and make them secure."

"No. I'm not doing any of that. That's too much work."

"You'll be up all night then, your loss."

The guard's face worked through the choices available to him and then he said, "Would a healer help?"

"Yes. That would be good."

"I'll have one fetched for you."

"Thank you."

"I'll do it because I don't want to be woken in the middle of the night by scum."

Jared watched as the guard left the room, the jail keys dangling from his thick leather belt.

"I'll kill you," Broken Nose snarled.

"Maybe. But not today and not in your condition." Jared picked up a small pebble off the floor and tossed it. "Here. Catch."

Broken Nose reached out with his right hand and immediately yelped in pain.

"I thought as much. You won't be any problem to anybody tonight. You're right handed."

"Yeah."

"That means you're not left handed, so figure it out for yourself, you dumb ox."

Jared moved to the corner of the cell where the pallet waited for him. He considered it his corner. Nix stood next to him. Naveen gathered to the other side of Jared.

"Since we are cell mates," Naveen said, "I just want it declared that I shouldn't be here. I was falsely accused and imprisoned."

Jared laughed. "That is what every criminal says when they are caught and are hanging upside down by their feet, or worse." Jared turned to Nix. "Does that sentiment go for you as well? Are you also innocent?"

Nix scowled. "I'm a thief, so I am not innocent or clean as others. But of this crime, I did no thieving; no blemish, no sin. I am innocent."

Jared nodded. "I see. And you stand by your innocence, Naveen?"

"I am a wizard. I tell people that and they think I can do all sorts of strange and magical things that will wow and awe them. Like disappearing, or shooting flames out of my hands, communicating long distances through air. I can do none of those things."

A slight smile lifted the corners of Jared's mouth as he sat down on the pallet. "Sit, gentlemen. We'll swap stories. What was your crime and why are you in this jail cell? We will judge each man's story, for we are honest men, after a fashion."

Jared listened as Nix told his story, his hands expressive and in the air. Nix had stumbled upon guards who were stealing the harvest crop from local farmers, and the guards planned to take the crop and keep the money for themselves.

Nix discovered the plot and he set off to tell some official what was going on, when a guard came up to him, sword at the ready. Because he had uncovered what the guards were up to, Nix was beaten and tossed in jail.

The guards accused Nix of what they, the guards, had done. The farmers never saw their crop or the profits from its sale.

Nix bowed and said, "In short, I was innocent."

Jared clapped and said, "Well told. Good story."

Naveen said, "All nicely laid out, but a little too pat."

"You're a critic now," Nix said. "But are you a storyteller as well?" Nix leaned back and Naveen stood up and adjusted his robes.

Nix leaned in to Jared and whispered, "He's probably as bad a wizard as he is a storyteller."

Naveen heard Nix's 'whisper' and gave the young lad a reproachful look. Naveen cleared his throat. "I am not a very good wizard. I am, in fact, a poor wizard. I barely manage to make spells work, much less foretell the future."

Nix grinned. "What did I warn you about?"

"I was short of funds," Naveen said. "That's all I'll say in my defense."

Nix hissed and booed and Naveen held up his hands to quiet the lad.

"I was approached by a wealthy young woman one day while in the market. She noticed that I was a wizard, by my staff, and wanted to procure my esoteric knowledge. Did she want me to do some spells for her? No.

"Did she wish for some love potions to make her lover stay in her arms longer? No, (and in her case it wouldn't have helped in any regard). Rather, she pressed up against me, her round belly and small nose and beady little black eyes and said she wanted her fortune told."

Naveen gasped. "What was I to do? I needed money but I didn't do fortunes. And I told her as such. The more I said I couldn't do it, the more she insisted I do it for her. She gave me, at first, two gold coins. Then four. Then eight. Then to seal the arrangement, she gave me a small bag of gold coins. A small bag of gold coins can go a long way. This lady knew how to count; I'll give her that."

"So I took the money and worked on her fortune. When she came back the next day I had it all figured out. She was there with her future husband. I told her all the things young couples want to hear: he loves you deeply, you'll both be happy together, you'll have many children, that sort of stuff."

"At the end of the fortune telling the man was looking at me as if weighing my words in his mind. The next day the bride to be came back and pointed a finger at me. I lied. I told her one thing and the unexpected happened instead."

Jared leaned forward. "What was that?"

"Her husband to be left her. He got a taste of what life would be like with her, and he vanished. The bride-to-be, with her hurt feelings, went to her father. The father went to the captain of the guard. The captain of the guard arrested me for being a lousy fortune teller. I never did say that I was a good one. I find myself in jail, gold coins back in her possession, and here I suffer mightily because of this lad. He thinks he's better than me; he isn't."

Jared threw his head back and laughed. "That was a good story, Naveen. Funny. Nix's was too serious."

Nix said, "We live in serious times."

Two guards approached their cell, a slight balding man next to them. The balding man carried a satchel. One of the guards pointed at Broken Nose and said, "Heard it snap clear across the room. Can you help him?"

The man nodded. "If you want my help with him then I need some place private, so I may inspect his injuries."

The guard nodded. "I have just the spot." Then he addressed Broken Nose. "Hey, you. Get up. I brought somebody here to look at your wrist."

Broken Nose groaned and got to his feet.

The guard opened the door and the slender man, thirty years older than everyone else, stepped into the cell and stood before Broken Nose, looking carefully at the damaged wrist. "Who did this?"

Broken Nose pointed to Jared.

The guard said, "He did. Stupid here tried to do something and the other man snapped it as quick as taking a drink of water. Never seen anything like it before."

The older man turned to the guard. "Get him to a room. I'll be right behind you."

One of the guards escorted Broken Nose out of the cell. The older man, slightly stooped, looked down at Jared. "If you did that, then you are an expert at dealing out pain to other people. Do you do that all the time?"

"Only when I have to. I gave him three chances to surrender. If I didn't stop him, he'd keep hounding me. Otherwise, I might have gone to sleep tonight and never woken up again."

The older man nodded. "I appreciate the skill it took to stop him. Remind me to never make you mad at me, young man. I agree with your young friend here. We do live in serious times."

"Times are always serious, it's how you handle them that counts," Jared said.

The old man stepped out of the cell and the guard closed the door behind him. The old man following him out of the room.

Naveen nodded to Jared. "Now it's your turn for a story."

Jared thought. Tomorrow would take care of itself. Why borrow trouble from the future? He would have to face the prospect of dying in this small, forsaken village, but tonight he had a story to tell.

He cleared his throat and he spoke on how he rode long distances, seeking a treasure that was elusive, hoping to find it, but never could, no matter how hard he searched. He finally came to this village, letting his horse rest at a tavern.

Whatever tomorrow may bring, he would face it bravely. For now, he had the company of two fine people, criminals like he was, and they weren't any worse than others he had been around before.

Chapter Six

BOUND IN CHAINS, Jared shuffled forward, following the tall wizard in front of him, the thief trailing after them. The guards watched their every movement, the slow line inching forward into the low squat building. The guards prodded them with pikes until they stood assembled before a raised platform.

To one side of them were stairs. A man, Jared noticed, watched them from the side of the building in the shadows. A wide brimmed hat concealed the man's features. Jared got the sense the man was watching them, for what reason he didn't know.

A door opened and three men in robes moved across the raised platform, walking toward the center of the stage floor. The tallest of the three men stood behind the podium.

One of the guards said, "Kneel before the sword and shield of the village."

Jared paused, turned around to look at the guard, and was struck in the face.

"I said *kneel!*"

Naveen and Nix each grabbed Jared and pulled him down, their heads lowered.

"Don't resist," Naveen whispered. "He can have us killed with only a word."

"I love the abuse of power, don't you?" Nix shot a dark look at the guards around them. "I'd like to see them alone in the dark, without help or friends."

Jared touched his tender mouth and wiped away the blood. "Who is the sword and shield in these parts?"

"Grinbell, the wizard," Naveen whispered. "Now kneel."

With chains rattling, all three kneeled, keeping their heads bowed in submission and their eyes downcast.

"Rise," said a commanding voice filled with power.

Jared lifted his eyes and saw three men on the platform. Two of them he dismissed immediately: they were older, with white fringe around their scalps and obviously in positions of authority, but the man in the middle was in the prime of his life. He stood behind the lectern, one hand resting on the top of the podium, the other hand wrapped around a staff.

The source of the wizard's strength, his staff, hummed with power, or so it seemed to Jared. A golden light pulsed through the symbols and runes etched in the wood of the staff. Grinbell's right hand gripped the wooden staff and each finger wore a ring; some were plain bands of gold and others had bright colored gemstones.

Jared had never seen the strange markings on the staff before and couldn't make out what they said or meant, but when he looked into the hard blue eyes of the wizard, he shivered. A coldness, like that of stone, came out of the man.

The wizard looked down at them, through hardened eyes, past a hooked nose, with red hair worn long down to the man's shoulders. He was the tallest man in the room; but Jared realized it wasn't the imposing height, or the cold stone look from those blue eyes that made others wary of him. Rather, it was the obvious power he had and the arrogance to use it that made him dangerous.

"Bollix," Naveen whispered, averting his face from the judges.

"What's wrong?" Jared asked.

Naveen lowered his gaze and remained silent.

"These are the criminals you have locked up?" Grinbell asked the other judges standing next to him. They nodded their heads. "I see. Do any of you want to be free?"

Jared said, "I've been accused of murdering a man. A bloody sword was found on my horse. I have never seen that sword before, and I didn't use it to kill a man. So what is the cost of this freedom you offer?"

Grinbell appraised Jared and said, "You may not escape any killing, but you may lengthen the time before your death."

Nix muttered under his breath, "Unjustly accused."

Grinbell nodded to the other judges. "A popular refrain among captured criminals." Grinbell pointed to Naveen. "Did you commit your crime?"

Naveen straightened up. "I am innocent. I explained to the young lady that I was never a fortune teller but she wouldn't hear any of it."

"And yet you took money from her and promised her a fairy tale. When the fairy tale broke, she demanded satisfaction," Grinbell said.

Naveen bowed. "Yes, my lord."

Grinbell pointed with his chin at Nix. "And you. You look familiar. Have we met? What is your crime?"

Nix raised his eyes and looked defiantly at the wizard. "Guards accused me of stealing wheat from the farmers. When in fact they stole it for themselves. When they saw that I discovered what they were doing, they beat me up and put me in jail. I am innocent of that charge."

Grinbell chuckled and turned to the other judges. "You see how they all claim to be innocent. If they were all innocent, we would have peace everywhere and nobody would ever break the law."

The other men murmured agreement.

Jared looked up, his lips tight. "If that is your law, I think I prefer death."

Naveen hissed and grabbed Jared by the collar. "No you don't. Hear him out at least."

Grinbell looked down and smiled. "He is correct in that matter, criminal. You will die, if that is what you want. But the time of your death can be delayed for several days or weeks or months. If that suits you and me."

"It does suit him, milord," Naveen said, giving Jared a dark look. "Besides, we are all in this together, are we not?" Naveen raised the chains that held him.

Jared glanced at Naveen and then back to Nix. "It seems that we are, doesn't it?"

"Indeed, you are all in the same tough spot." Grinbell said. "Criminals should be rounded up and executed, it saves time and trouble, and it gives a peaceful resolution to the ills of society. Or they can serve society."

"What service are you speaking about, milord?" Nix asked.

Grinbell looked at the dirt on his sleeve and brushed it away in three swipes. "Children have been kidnapped from the village. Vampires are responsible for it. The captain of the guard and his men are charged with protecting the village, so they cannot go after the children. The king's men haven't responded back yet, so the children are still in danger. We need to search for them. We want somebody to bring the children back to us safely. Are you the men who can do this?"

"Are you crazy?" Nix said. "Go into Vampire Nation?"

A guard was about to strike Nix with the end of a pike but Grinbell gestured for the guard to stop.

Naveen said, "Vampires. Isn't that for a specialist?"

Grinbell shook his head. "It is for anyone with the guts and courage to try to rescue them from the vile creatures that took them."

Jared nodded. "I'll do it. I'll go and rescue the children from the vampires."

Grinbell smiled. "Splendid."

Naveen stared into Jared's dark eyes. "A moment ago you wanted to die. Why the change?"

"I don't like vampires," Jared said.

Nix said, "My last holiday: a bit of travel, meet new people, and die in the process."

Jared said, "I know vampires. I'm not afraid of them."

Grinbell looked down at them. "Is it settled then?"

Nix glanced at Jared. "If you can fight vampires, then I'll come with you. It's better than rotting in a cell or getting shanked by a guard some night."

Jared faced Naveen. "What about you, wizard?"

"I'm not good with combat magic, but a wizard might be helpful, don't you think?"

Jared looked up. "It seems we're in agreement. So, to be clear, my companions and I are free to go, given provisions by you and the village, to hunt down the vampires and to bring back the children."

"That sums it up perfectly." Grinbell smiled and then nodded at the guards. "But there is one more thing that needs special attention."

The guards herded them into a smaller, private room. Jared stood there with one of them behind him.

The blue eyed wizard faced them. There was a slight smile around the corners of the man's mouth, but there was no warmth from him.

"You three have volunteered to find and return the children to us. But if we let you go, how do we know that you'll carry out your mission? For that reason, Bruce and Rygil are going to accompany you. Further more, you will each have a Death Spell placed upon you."

"I protest." Naveen shook loose his guard and stood before Grinbell. "They don't know what that means. Please, anything but that."

"It is a serious thing I place upon you, because our children are special to us. It would be easier to submit and be done with it."

"But it is deadly," Naveen said. "And there is no known way to remove it."

"You call yourself a wizard? Go back to your studies! There are two ways to remove this spell: one is to die in the performance of the task. Once death has visited, the spell is broken."

"And the second way?" Naveen asked.

Grinbell's thin lips turned into a cruel smile as he looked them over. "Who shall be first?"

Chapter Seven

"ISN'T THAT ENOUGH?" Jared had his arms around Nix's shoulders. The smaller man had choked and fell to the ground in reaction to the Death Spell placed around him. So far, it had an unpleasant effect on first Naveen and now Nix.

Naveen sat in the corner of the room, head down, eyes distant. The experience had changed him, Jared noticed, in much the same way it had changed Nix. Jared was next.

"Come now," Grinbell said. "Don't make this hard on yourself."

Jared looked at the two spent figures. "You said the Death Spell wasn't permanent. It looks permanent to me, Grinbell. If you want us to find the children, if you want us to return here with them, I need my men and myself to be fully capable. Look at them. The life has gone out of them."

Grinbell scratched his jaw with his pointed nails. "What you are witnessing is what occurs when they meet their death. It is not pretty, not a very uplifting sight. It is usually something that haunts a man or woman the rest of their life. It is not easily forgotten, but it does pass."

"You killed them before they even started!" Jared said. "You don't care about the children, all you care about is your hide and you get to say that you've done your best!"

"Have a care with your words, stranger. Men, mightier than you, have died for less than what you have said."

Jared balled his fists in frustration. He wished for a sword in his hand. He could kill the wizard from this distance. A quick run straight at him, the point of his sword aimed at Grinbell and then a slice through the air at the soft part of his neck, the blade cutting through muscle and bone and nerves. It would be a quick kill.

A satisfied smile played across Jared's face.

"Enough of this stalling." Grinbell nodded to a guard.

The guard behind Jared yanked him to his feet.

Jared started toward the guard and then stopped. It was useless to fight.

Grinbell was across the room, with armed soldiers on either side of him. Before Jared could take two steps, the guards would put him down.

Jared gave Grinbell a hard look and said, "I'm ready."

Grinbell motioned with his head and the guard moved away.

Jared found himself alone, next to the wall, when Grinbell rose to a great height, towering over him.

The two previous Death Spells had been spoken, but this time, Grinbell closed his eyes and concentrated. He gripped the staff firmly as sigils glowed with orange light and thrummed with deep powerful sounds, filling up the small, oblong room.

The light went away and a darkness stretched over Jared.

Jared noticed the guards standing behind Grinbell. He turned and saw Nix lying on his side, curled in a tight ball, and Naveen sat slouched with his back to the wall, his knees drawn close, his hands gripping his lower legs.

His eyesight grew dim and shrank until he focused only on Grinbell's face. The longer chin, the red hair over the angular face, the blue eyes. Suddenly his vision was sucked into the blue eyes; he felt himself falling.

Whether he was spinning or the room was, he didn't know. All he knew was that he couldn't stand anymore. He wobbled and reached out to hold onto something, but he fell down, landing on his right buttock, feeling the sudden jolt from the cold, stone floor.

The tightness around his throat increased. It was like he couldn't breathe. Of course, he could breathe. It was easy to breathe. He'd done it all his life.

But his lungs wouldn't obey.

Breathe.

Panic screamed in the hallway of his mind. As hard as he tried to breathe, he couldn't. He opened a steel door in his mind and shoved his panic hard into the darkness. He didn't have time for panic. Not now. He stayed calm and raced through his mind, recalling how easy it had been to breathe in the past. This time he tried it again.

Take a breath of air.

Inhale.

Suck in air.

None of that worked.

He was getting dizzy, ready to black out.

Jared looked up at Grinbell's icy blue eyes and couldn't find any mercy in them.

Darkness laughed and swooped down over him, claimed him as its own, and it crawled over his body. Then, his skin was ripped from his body.

He tried to pull his skin back, but stronger arms than his pulled the flesh out of his hands and he stood naked. With or without body, he didn't know. In this new state, he felt incredibly light, and suddenly the darkness was gone.

He stood in the middle of a white room, with mist rolling along the floor. He looked out the window and saw a man, a woman, and three children together. The laughter of the small family carried over to him and filled his heart with light. He wanted to hug them.

But then suddenly he was thrust back into the darkness, grasping for air. And then he was awake, lying face down next to Naveen and Nix.

Jared rolled over on his back and saw Grinbell, or what he thought was Grinbell looking down at him with contempt.

"The spells are around each of you. I know this for certain. If you do not progress toward the goal you will die. If you waver off course, you will die. If you take two steps in the opposite direction, you will die."

And then the image of Grinbell vanished. Jared was alone except for the thief and the wizard next to him.

Jared got to his feet and struggled to Nix. "You okay?"

Nix nodded. "You?"

"I guess."

Jared went over to Naveen.

Before Jared could say anything, Naveen said, "Let's get out of here."

Jared nodded. "I couldn't agree with you more."

Who did that wizard think he was?

All Jared could think about was how unfair it had all been. He had been outmaneuvered and trapped. Now he was bound to fulfill his part of this crazy scheme. He would make sure, to the best of his ability, that the children came back, safe and sound. He didn't mind rescuing the children. What he didn't like was being forced to do something.

Ever since his failure, he had been searching for ways to redeem himself. Rescuing the children would be another step closer to redemption.

Jared looked around the room and saw Grinbell's men, Bruce and Rygel, leaning against the back wall and acting as Grinbell's eyes and ears.

Jared shouted, "We'll need supplies. We'll need horses, swords, warm clothes and blankets. We'll need money as we journey."

"Do you think we follow your orders?" Bruce sneered at him.

Jared got to his feet and padded across the room and stood in front of Bruce. Jared leaned close and whispered, "Just because I have the Death Spell on me doesn't mean I can't kill you right now, or anytime I see fit. Since what we asked for is in keeping with our quest, and you represent the wizard, go tell him our needs and be quick about it. If Grinbell comes around and asks why we haven't gone yet, I'll tell him very, clearly and loudly, that his two asses wouldn't move when they were told to move. That the two asses hindered us in our quest. See how he likes that."

The two pairs of eyes widened in recognition of the threat and then they both nodded and disappeared.

After they were gone, Nix came forward.

"That was brave of you."

Jared shook his head. "Bravery had nothing to do with it. We can't go out on our quest without good supplies. It was strictly common sense."

"Then I wish more people had common sense."

"People do have common sense," Naveen said. "Rather it is usually wizards who lack it because they know magic and because of that arrogance they think the whole world is theirs for the taking."

Jared smiled. "And does that apply to you?"

"Sometimes. But I'm modest enough to know that I don't know everything."

"I guess we'll wait until our supplies are ready. Shall we all meet back tomorrow morning?"

"No," Nix said. "If we go, we should go today. Tomorrow something bad may come up and prevent us from doing our job."

"Superstitious?"

"Covering all angles." Nix looked at them both. "But a couple of hours from now and I'll be ready to go, after I settle some minor affairs."

"That is very wise coming from you, thief," Naveen said, his grey eyes sweeping past the smallish man and settling in on Jared. "In fact, a couple of hours would give us all time to get ready. Shall we meet back in the courtyard at noon?"

Jared nodded. "We meet at noon."

Chapter Eight

NIX SHUDDERED AND tugged at his neck. He felt the slight constriction of the collar and panicked; obviously, the result of Grinbell's Death Spell. He wanted to spit in the wizard's blue eyes. How dare he use his authority, how dare he act like a god, and push others around to do his bidding. What made him any better than the vampires?

Grinbell could feel the sharp end of his dagger, for all Nix cared, but he had things to collect. Revenge whispered in his ears. He shook it off, for now, and brought himself back.

The sooner he collected the items, the better it would be.

He hated the abuse of authority, had seen its effects up close. Only the cool breeze on his face reminded him to take control. He couldn't let his emotions run riot. He focused as he leaned against the stone wall.

The marketplace was open but the crowds were dwindling in size. The morning rush was over and it was a couple of hours before lunch. There was plenty of time to accomplish what he needed to do.

His clothing was bland, making it easy for him to walk in the crowd, nearly any crowd, and go away unnoticed. He wore a gray tunic with the sleeves ending an inch before his wrists. Over the tunic he wore a brown vest special made with pockets sewn on the inside, large enough to carry items of importance. His brown leggings and shoes completed his uniform. And with his curly hair combed forward he looked like somebody's apprentice or assistant in a shop.

Nobody would figure him out to be a thief.

He searched for the spot where he dropped the stone before being confronted by the guards. A thief had to be careful. It wouldn't make for a long career if he got caught carrying stolen property on his person.

With the sun breaking through the cloudy skies, Nix pushed away from the wall and scanned the marketplace. He shut out the noise of the vendors calling to him and gathered his attention together like a fine pointed light. Where was the building he'd jumped down?

He mingled in the crowd, smiled at the enthusiastic vendors vying for his coin, and scanned the rooftops with his clear brown eyes. He had jumped from one roof to another, landed on a balcony, and then jumped to a passing haystack. Had he landed here?

The building didn't feel right to him.

He paused and remained quiet. No use getting mad at himself. After all, he was being chased at the time.

The really useful marketplace, at least for his trade, was in another section of the village. It was where his contacts got in touch with him. Discrete services for clients who needed items that only a really good thief could provide: jewelry and coins were easy. But intelligence always paid the best and there was never anything to carry, except in his memory. Certain intelligence, intelligence that could topple authorities and governments and shift the balance of power in the surrounding kingdoms always had a market to select, interested parties. Chloe brokered connections to people from all over, inside and outside the kingdom. Damix was another broker who needed unique, one of a kind, fulfillments that were more specialized and secretive in nature.

Nix made a slow turn around the plaza and saw the building. He retraced his path, his eyes covering the ground with an easy movement, spotting the area where he stashed the stone. He walked across the wide avenue and stood in front of the vendor, a tiny, small boned woman. She looked up, her bright brown eyes smiling at him.

"Yes, young master."

"Hello. I wanted to purchase that sack," Nix said. He pointed at the familiar burlap sack that had a purple cord tied around its neck.

"Really," the woman said guardedly. "What's it worth to you?"

"What would you like for it?"

The old woman frowned.

Nix knew what was going through her mind. How could she sell him something that she never had any knowledge of? The burlap sack was half-buried in her wares, just the neck of the bag sticking out, the tell-tale purple cord wrapped tightly around the neck of the bag sticking out, dirty from the dust and mud of the recent rains.

She scratched her chin. "I've never seen this before. I wonder what it is."

Her aged hands untied the simple knot and opened up the burlap sack. She reached in and pulled out the stone. She laid it on the table.

"It's rough on the hands," she said.

They both stared at it for a moment.

"It's a particular stone that I'd like to show my friends."

The vendor drew a knife from her waist belt and poked the stone with the edge of her blade. Sparks flew off when blade met stone and there was a snapping sound. The woman looked in disbelief at the broken blade.

"It was old anyway," the woman said. "Now, let's get to the real heart of this. Why do you want it? Tell me truthfully."

"If I tell you the truth, you may be in danger. The less you know the better off you'll be. Name a price for the stone and I'll give it to you."

"I have a mighty imagination."

"It's a stone," Nix said. "How valuable can it be?"

"Three gold coins, for a mighty stone like that, able to break a blade in half, with barely a jab put to it. Is there magic to this stone, something you're not telling me?"

"I'm not telling you things about the stone for two reasons," Nix said; leaning closer to the old woman, they were almost eye to eye.

Her skin was as leathery as a farmer's face, from constant exposure to the sun and years working outside in the fields. He admired people who worked for their living.

Nix said, "Reason one: It's stolen and I don't want any trouble to land upon your frail shoulders. Reason two: with this gone, big people get to suffer for their arrogance and the little people, you and I, get ahead with no harm done to us." He winked at her and held out two gold coins for her.

The old woman held out her hand. "Three gold coins and it's yours."

Nix smiled and bundled the stone into the burlap sack, tied the purple cord around the neck and gave the burlap sack back to the old woman. "You'll have your money. Three gold coins."

Nix handed her two gold coins.

"What? We agreed upon three." The woman looked surprised.

"I don't carry a lot of money on me. I'll be back," Nix turned and scanned the crowd around him, saw the people out to purchase items on a fine day, "In an hour I'll be back." He leaned forward. "For your sake, old woman, don't tell anybody. The anxious party would probably pay you back in bruises and pain, if you know the kind I speak of."

"This transaction will be honored for two hours," the old woman said, a smile picking up her face. "It was never my stone to begin with, but you want to be able to say you purchased this from a vendor and to be able to tell the truth about it. A truth to cover a falsehood. Don't run into any mind tellers now." The woman cackled and slapped her hand on the table. "Two hours you have now."

Nix nodded and turned to spot his next opportunity. He searched the crowd for people who dressed rich, had an air of arrogance about them, and shoved or pushed their way through the crowd, knocking the small or unfortunate out of their way without concern for their well being.

Stealing money would be easy. But first he had to find help.

The fat fingered man looked startled as the children swarmed all around him. The kids were on the skinny side, but they were eager for the promise of money. "Get away from me," the man said.

They circled him, yelling and laughing. The fat fingered man tried to strike one of the children, but the girl ducked just in time. The big man dressed in fine silks and a rich cloak turned, keeping an eye on one child he thought was the leader.

Nix spotted the bulge on the man's waistband and moved in.

Nix came up behind the man; his hand snaked in and he grabbed the bag of coins.

The fat fingered man turned and faced Nix. "Thief!"

"No. Here is your money, sir." Nix upended the money purse and gold coins fell into his hand. He tossed the gold coins into the air while keeping a small handful for himself. The gold coins rained down on the fat man as he turned away from Nix and tried to shoo away the children who scrambled after the glittering money in the dirt.

The fat man shouted at the children. "Give me my money. Give me my money. Stop!"

The fat man turned around in desperation and Nix was gone.

An old man ambled up to the table and smiled at the old woman vendor. He was dressed in a brown vest that covered a gray tunic. The sleeves were long and almost swallowed the man's old arthritic hands. He pointed a crooked finger at the burlap bag with a purple cord tight around it. "You promised a friend three gold coins for that sack. He wanted me to collect it for him."

"Do you have the three gold coins?"

"Two have already been paid, have they not?"

The woman's eyes widened and then she drew in a deep breath and stared at the old man before her. He was bald with a fringe of white hair around his head. His nose was large and the ears drooped a little, the effects of old age. But the woman looked at the man's brown eyes: they sparkled with youth and mischief.

The old man withdrew a leathered pouch and brought out three gold coins. He tossed them on the table. "That's for you and your service."

The woman looked carefully at the coins. "Three was agreed upon. I have been given two already. You have overpaid me for a simple service."

"It is enough to insure good meals for many months, am I right?"

"My lucky day." The old woman nodded and looked at him carefully. "A younger man than you was here less than an hour ago. He wore the same clothes you do now. Old man, do you have a potion that would give me a younger face?"

"Alas, I don't. Money is a poor substitute for health and youth." The old man tossed her five additional coins and reached to pick up the burlap sack.

"If you ever want me to hold more things for you remember my name. Alicia."

"A beautiful name for a beautiful woman."

The old woman cackled. "Your honey-tongued words are sweet, but go. I have to put these sweet ten coins away; you can never be too careful."

"Careful?" the old man said.

"Thieves, you can never trust them."

The spyglass was next. He had spotted the carpenter and his daughter.

Still in his old man's face, the result of a magic potion that he swallowed, Nix ambled up to the carpenter and his daughter. "Hello."

"Good day, sir. What can I do for you?"

"A few days ago I was robbed."

"I'm sorry to hear that, what was the object?"

"A bronze colored spyglass."

"I don't want any trouble. Talk gets out and business dries up."

"Understandable. Your daughter was traded the spyglass for a pony doll. I don't have a pony doll on me, but will some gold help transfer the object back to its rightful owner?"

The carpenter looked down at his daughter. "Honey, go fetch your new toy."

The little girl nodded and ran down the marketplace to her house. A moment later she returned holding the spyglass in her hand. The carpenter took it from her and looked at it.

"I don't want your money. Here. I'm an honest man and I do honest work. I want nothing to do with stolen goods and thieves. Thieves are the worst; they take things that don't belong to them, robbing people of their livelihood."

The old man shook his head. "You suffered from thieves?"

"Years ago. My tools were taken from me. It took me a winter and a spring to replace them. It was the worst time of my life. Do you know who did it?"

"Sadly, I don't," said Nix, feeling the magic fading from his face. "May I have it, please?"

The carpenter handed the spyglass to the old man. Nix looked down at the ground. He knew his face had started changing, the magic was slowly undoing itself; he half-turned from the carpenter and the little girl. His heart went out to them. "Not for this, but for her, for another doll." He tossed some coins into the air and walked away, feeling his face reassemble itself back to its original shape and condition.

"Daddy, coins. Look."

With the stone and spyglass in his possession, Nix breathed deeply. Now he could set off on his suicide adventure. He started laughing. Who needed money when it was all around? He liked stealing money from the arrogant and passing it on to those grateful to have it. As long as there were arrogant people, money would never be a problem for him. He smiled and wondered what the spyglass could do. And what did he make of this stone?

Runes and words of power! What was he supposed to do? As soon as Naveen got out of jail, a message was delivered to him. He sat at his almost bare table, the surface of the table empty except for the half burnt candle in the middle and the small tin cup next to it. His staff was set in the corner, near the door.

Who was the leak? And how did it work?

Naveen looked up at the white-washed wall and seemingly looked through it.

A fine line existed between being something and not being something. A mixture of truth and lies, carefully massaged into place. It was easy for him to pretend to be an inept wizard. The truth was he stuttered and that gave a very convincing impression that he was inept. Truth and lie. The other truth was equally simple: he had a brilliant mind. Truth concealed and truth revealed.

And he worked as a spy for the wizard council.

His mission was simple—find any connection to the old magic in his area and report back. The old magic had reappeared months ago, first as rumors and then as unexplained occurrences that he wasn't allowed to know the details about. He was tasked with looking for any connections in this area. His cover as an inept wizard served him well, although it bruised his ego as much as anything.

Maybe the old magic was coming from the vampires? He frowned. Magic was unknown to them. He drummed his fingers across the top of the table.

The message would be delivered shortly and then he would be ready to go.

Naveen, the bumbler.

Naveen, the inept wizard.

He *hated* this assignment.

He stretched out his hand and looked at his staff leaning in the corner. "D-dal ven-to."

The staff lifted up and moved toward him in a jerky manner. If he concentrated really hard, the staff would move smoothly to him. But he was tired and he didn't care about how good his magic was right now.

His fingers curled around the hard Mallor wood, a special tree that only wizards knew about and cultivated for their magical properties. He traced the sigils etched into the wood. The staff hummed with power and he felt the sound slide into him, comfort him, reassure him. The sound had been with him for six years now, since he gained adulthood, since he gained his wizard's staff.

He breathed in the sound.

It accompanied him and he heard it all the more clearly when he held the staff in his hands.

What the sound meant he didn't know. When he questioned other wizards about the sound he heard, they all looked at him with a blank expression. None of them knew what he was talking about. Apparently, in all of wizardry, he was the only one who heard this piercing sound. It came from his staff, and maybe it came from the power it represented. Whatever it was, it shifted something inside him. Maybe it was making deeper inroads into his being. He shrugged. Maybe he was a fool for doing this assignment and he was deceiving himself?

Maybe he was a fool.

He sighed and swept away foolish thoughts and closed his eyes. He focused on the Death Spell around his neck. The sound grew louder and he felt his body start to vibrate. His body grew still and he closed his eyes and he seemed to shift. He slid out of his body and then he slid back and then he slid out again. He willed himself to stand on the opposite side of the room. He turned, the sound louder now than ever in his ears, and he considered his physical body sitting at the desk.

He never liked how he looked. He was angular and tall, not skinny, but lean and muscular. His hair was short cropped and combed forward. His face, with its high cheekbones, made him look very severe, almost skull-like. And his grey eyes—at times as hard as granite—and other times as soft as inviting water for a swim—unnerved people. People liked green eyes, blue eyes, brown eyes, even black. But nobody liked grey eyes.

Naveen leaned closer and inspected his neck, focusing closely with his wizard senses. He cleared his mind and opened it, willing himself to see what had happened to his body. Energy streams appeared and flowed around and through his neck, flexing itself in a green band of iridescent light that sparkled with diamond brightness. Naveen circled his body and followed the green band. A small portion of the green band traveled from his neck and snaked up into his brain, wrapping itself around his grey matter.

"Ohmygod," Naveen said.

He focused again and looked down and saw another tendril, this one thicker, had traveled down into his torso and burrowed into his heart. The Death Spell consisted of tendrils to the brain and to the heart. Either one would be enough to kill. Both of them would be a certainty.

Only death or the removal of the curse would free them.

Naveen closed his eyes and shifted back inside his body.

It felt jarring to be standing up one moment and then finding yourself sitting the next.

He looked around the room and stood. He staggered to his feet and caught his hand on the table, balancing himself.

Naveen walked to the doorway and wondered who was pulling the invisible strings.

Chapter Nine

JARED SURVEYED THE company.

The horses and supplies were ready, courtesy of the Sword and Shield of the village, and with the assistance of the captain of the guard and his men.

Nix grabbed the reins of the horse and put his foot securely into the stirrup. He had fallen twice already and Grinbell's men, Bruce and Rygil, snickered as Nix tried again. Nix pulled himself successfully over the horse's back and sat in the saddle. With both feet in the stirrups, his hand clutching the horn of the saddle, and a satchel worn over his shoulder he said, "I hate horses. I prefer walking. I like my feet to be on the ground."

Jared turned and noticed how Naveen walked up to his horse and gently patted its face. The wizard leaned forward and said something softly into the horse's ear. Then he grabbed the saddle and leapt onto it. The wizard and horse were one.

"Horses are fine animals," Naveen said. "You can walk all day, Nix, but a horse can get you there faster."

"I prefer my feet on the ground. I trust the ground."

With the five present, they were ready. In Jared's mind he trusted Naveen and Nix. It was an odd combination to trust a thief and a wizard. The other two, Bruce and Rygil, were a problem. They were eyes for Grinbell. Jared didn't trust them and he'd have to figure a way to be rid of them.

Jared glanced at his company. "Let's move out," he said, kicking his horse in the flank with the heel of his boots. The horse moved along and the others pulled out and followed.

A knot of people stood on the opposite side of the clearing, in the direction they were headed, and glanced their way. The group consisted of younger women and older women and some men who were too old to work in the fields, and too small to handle a sword. All of them curious.

When they were even with the ring of people, a young woman stepped out from the crowd. With her body held erect, she looked up into Jared's face, the auburn hair a nimbus of flame around her head. Her large green eyes burned with an intensity that Jared found over-whelming. Her voice was clear and powerful. "Take me with you."

Jared considered the woman for a moment. Her hair was fair to look at and he marveled at how she took his breath away. Her eyes struck him in the heart with their open honesty. He, for a moment, would give up everything to stay with her for the rest of his life.

He shook his head and discarded the fantasy. "You have no idea where we go," he said and moved past her.

She ran to keep even with him, her hand grabbing the reins of his horse. "You go to rescue the children, right?"

"Aye," Jared said.

"Then I can help."

He leaned forward and took the reins from her. "This journey isn't for women. You need to stay home. Protect your children."

She squared her shoulders and resolve grew in her eyes; behind them Jared saw sparks and flame. This kind of resolve was rarely seen in others, except those who faced battle and death. She would go anywhere and do anything for what she wanted.

"My son is one of the missing ones."

"I'm sorry for your loss."

"His father would have torn out the lungs of any man who denied him the right to help his child."

"Where is he?"

"Dead."

"I'm sorry for your loss, doubly so because of your son."

"My son isn't dead."

"How do you know that?" Naveen asked, looking with sudden interest at the woman.

"Because if he was dead I would know. A mother has that kind of connection with her children."

Nix said, "My mother gave me up when I was small. Not all are like you."

She turned to Nix and said forthrightly, "Nonetheless, he is still alive and I wish to come with you."

"No," Jared said. "It's too dangerous. It's dangerous for man or woman. We would be defending you if you came, and that would take us away from our job."

"Your job?"

"To find the children and bring them back."

"Or die trying," Naveen said.

"A woman is bad luck," Nix said.

"I don't believe in bad luck or good luck," Naveen said, "but this is a dangerous journey and it would be better without another person."

The woman said sharply, glancing at Naveen, "I always thought the opposite: the more eyes open at night the better to keep watch for the vampires. You know they're going to come, so why not be prepared for them? As for luck, I've been taught to make my own."

Bruce and Rygil exchanged nervous glances. Jared wondered how long they would stay in the company.

Jared leaned over the side of his horse and whispered to the woman, "What is your name?"

"Men call me Rowena."

"Rowena, stay here. It will be safer for you. We all … we'll be lucky if we come back alive." His voice trailed off and he left her alone in the middle of the road.

Jared felt angry. Rowena had no right to put herself upon him. They were on a dangerous mission to bring back the children. Did she think it was going to be a picnic? In fact, it was a suicide mission and the woman didn't need to come along for that.

But, her large green eyes and auburn hair had made an impression on him. Jared pushed away any silly notions he'd had. He felt angry at her for asking to come along, such a strong woman would be killed, and that would be a waste. Any man who had her would consider himself lucky. She had so much life. It would be a shame for her to cut it short by joining them on this quest. He caught himself and swept away those thoughts of her.

He was on an insane quest. The more he thought about it, he knew they didn't have a chance. They were going into Vampire Nation, to rescue kidnapped children and have them back in a week's time. If they didn't, they would be dead.

So, how many ways could they die? They could die on the road from an attack by bandits and highwaymen. They could die from vampire attacks before they reached their destination. Finally, they could die while rescuing the children.

It was good that he refused her.

Only a fool would join them.

Or, Jared thought, she was a woman who truly loved her son and wanted him home safe and sound and would go through heaven and hell to get him back.

He hadn't met a mother's love like that in his life. What passions must flow through her veins? What desperation and hope must swim in her blood and enliven her hope.

Jared shook his head.

He acted like he was already dead.

He remembered the wall of flame in the cave and his sister's scream. He died that night, and every night since then.

With the wizard and thief out in front and the two spies from Grinbell behind, Jared and his group journeyed slowly out of the village, the clop-clop-clop sounds of the horse's hooves marking their steady progress. Even the animals sensed their destination and lowered their heads, moving toward Vampire Nation, a piece of land and myth that lay to the east several days ride from here.

They were traveling along the road outside the village when something tugged at Jared's awareness. He saw a glimpse of an indistinct shape moving parallel with them. Whenever he looked toward the tree line and vegetation, he saw nothing out of the ordinary.

But they were being followed.

The overcast sky opened up its cold gray arms and the wind blew upon them, forcing them to wrap their cloaks around their bodies for warmth and protection.

"I hate this foul weather," Bruce said. "It chills me to my toes."

"You can always leave us," Nix said. "Happy to let you go."

"We have our orders, thief," Rygil said. "He wants us to go, we go."

Jared looked up at the sky.

It didn't feel like it would rain. But he'd been wrong before about the weather. If they had a weather witch with them then they'd know. But since they didn't have one in their company, he'd have to go without. But the weather was the least of his concerns right now.

Jared knew two things: they were being followed and the weather had made a turn for the worse. One he could do something about. The other he'd have to suffer through it.

If there was to be trouble, better to be alerted than to be caught unaware. Jared kicked the flanks of his horse and rode forward to the wizard and thief up front.

Before Jared could say a word, Nix said, "Have you seen it?"

"You too?"

Nix nodded. "Following us since the village. Last three miles or so."

Naveen looked at them wide eyed with surprise. "What? We're being followed? Were you going to tell us this bit of intelligence?"

"I just did," Jared said.

"I meant him," Naveen said, indicating Nix.

"Doesn't slack away, doesn't come closer." Nix gave Naveen a blank look. "Keeping an eye out. No harm yet, but it will be night soon enough and I don't fancy my throat being slit and blood pouring out of my veins."

"What do we do?" The wizard looked upset.

Jared glanced around. The open fields laid to the right. "Let's ride into the open. Whoever is behind us will have to break away to follow us."

"I got it," Naveen said.

"Then we turn the tables on him." Nix said grimly.

"Exactly."

They crossed the road and entered the open field and moved eastward. The overhead sun was blanketed with thick clouds making the dim warmth barely noticeable. Their shadows were pale and weak against the grassy fields.

They traveled like that for an hour or so, going up and down the grassy landscape. After passing the crest of one high bank, Jared got off his horse and staked the reins to the ground. He didn't want his animal to wander off without him on his back. The wilderness was no place to be without a horse.

Jared approached Naveen and Nix. He looked up at them. A rough voice said, "What's going on? Why are you stopping?"

Jared ignored Bruce's question and said to Nix, "We set the trap now. I'll backtrack and circle to the side and outflank him. When I give you the signal, ride like all hell has broken loose and charge at our stranger. Do you understand?"

Nix nodded. "What will you do?"

"With the attention focused on you two, I will sneak up and ask him what his business is."

Naveen said, "What if he doesn't tell you?"

"I have a great motivator," Jared said, patting the sword at his side.

Nix rubbed his chin. "What about Dog and Cat?" He indicated Bruce and Rygil with a nod of his head.

"Tell them what we know and to have them stay low."

Jared crouched down and ran to the far slope of the hilly mound and laid flat on his stomach. He looked back and saw Nix getting ready.

Jared inhaled and felt his heartbeat racing through him. His throat went dry as he waited for the stranger to appear.

Jared lay still for half an hour, scanning the hilly terrain in front of him when something moved.

Across the distance, a dark shape crested a small hill. Alone, padding softly, a man dressed in forest green clothing, with a hood and cape, followed their trail. He carried a bow and was armed with a sword. The man looked small, but strong.

Jared waited until Hood and Cape was positioned in the valley between the two hilltops. Jared rolled to one side and stood up. He raised his arm, being careful that Hood and Cape didn't see him, and gave Nix the signal.

Nix nodded his head, and got on the saddle.

Nix waited as Naveen mounted his horse, then they both charged the top of the hill, yelling and shouting as they came up to the crest.

Jared rolled back into position.

He watched Hood and Cape stop in his tracks, swiftly pull an arrow from his quiver, and notch it. The bow was ready, with the deadly arrow primed for death.

It wasn't supposed to happen this way.

Nix and Naveen crested the hill and charged over to the other side, shouting and looking down at Hood and Cape.

Jared saw the tension in the bow. The arrow was pulled back and the bow string hummed with power as the arrow sliced through the air, traveling with deadly accuracy at Naveen.

Naveen waved his hand in front of him and Jared heard him mumble strange words very quickly.

And then something struck Naveen in the shoulder.

Nix yelled and Naveen looked up and jerked himself to the right.

The arrow landed, with the force of a rock slide, into Naveen's left shoulder. Naveen was knocked off his horse and to the ground.

This was happening too fast, Jared thought. Who was this man?

Jared was too far away to launch an attack. He would have to circle around and come up on the man's back side. He ducked behind the next hilly ravine and moved closer.

He heard Nix's voice carried on the wind.

"Master Bowman, why do you follow us? We mean you no harm."

Jared crouched low and ran along Hood and Cape's right flank, keeping out of sight. Jared felt his heavy breathing, and wished he wasn't wearing the chain mail. The armor offered protection, but the weight made his running slower.

Hood and Cape looked straight across at Nix.

Nix continued. "We can't have somebody like you trailing us. You could kill me with that arrow, from that distance, but ..." Nix brought a bronze colored spyglass to his eye and looked out through the telescope at the figure. Then he lowered it and said, "It wouldn't suit you, would it?"

Jared moved until he was in a straight line behind Hood and Cape. He was fifty feet and closing the distance. If he drew his sword, the sound of metal against scabbard might alert him and he didn't want that to happen.

"I mean you no harm," said an oddly deep voice.

Surprise was going to be Jared's best weapon. If the stranger got sight of him, he could turn around and kill Jared with an arrow as easily as taking a breath.

Hood and Cape spoke. "I mean you no harm. My arrows do not have their pointy tips on today."

The voice was roughly deep, but the choice of words struck Jared wrong. Pointy tips?

Jared moved closer, now within ten feet of Hood and Cape. The bowman didn't hear or know that he was being hunted.

Now that he was this close, Jared saw the bowman was somewhat smaller than himself, but certainly no less dangerous because of the size. He studied the bowman for a second, waiting for an opportunity to take him by surprise, and then rushed forward. "We are not for you."

With a loud and startled gasp, Hood and Cape pivoted and faced Jared.

Jared hurried forward and, with his upraised hand, grabbed the bow and slammed it down. He drew Hood and Cape's bow arm down until it was pointing earthward. Their bodies clashed and dangled. Grunts and shouts erupted as they grappled and fell hard to the grass.

Jared rolled several times, holding onto Hood and Cape. They rolled to a stop and Jared found himself on top, breathing heavily, his hands pinning Hood and Cape to the ground.

Naveen, nursing his shoulder, stepped closer and watched. "Be careful. He's tricky." Naveen touched his shoulder and grimaced in pain.

"I think you're wrong, Naveen" Jared said. He worked off the cape and it fell away. "There's more than meets the eye here, isn't there?"

Hood and Cape, exerting all the strength possible, finally collapsed and lost all energy. Hood and Cape stopped struggling and was breathing hard, still pinned to the ground by Jared.

Naveen stared at the two of them. "What?"

Jared leaned closer. "Take off the hood. Let us see your face."

Jared got up, moving carefully away from Hood and Cape.

The figure sat up and carefully pulled off the hood. Long auburn hair tumbled around the shoulders.

"You?" Naveen said, surprise in his voice.

"You are good," Nix said, admiration in his voice.

Jared looked down at Rowena, dressed in the forest green woodman's outfit.

Jared said, "You cannot come with us. I told you before; this isn't a place for a woman."

In one fluid movement, Rowena was on her feet, her hand coming up to Jared's throat, a tiny, sharp blade pressed against his flesh. "My child needs me."

Jared felt the steel against his neck and fell backwards. He grabbed hold of Rowena's knife hand, pulling it away from his body, and dragged her down to the ground with him.

Rowena felt the knife slip from her grasp.

Then Jared rolled away from her and gained his feet in seconds.

Rowena grabbed an arrow from her quiver and held it like a small sword, the sharp end aimed toward Jared.

Her reach, with the arrow, failed to counter the reach of the sword, as the cold and hard blade pressed against her throat.

They froze, all four of them looking at the tableau. Nix had his arms folded across his chest, admiration on his face; Naveen stood close by, a hand rubbing his sore shoulder; Jared breathing hard, the sword tip pressed against Rowena's throat, and Rowena with her arm outstretched, the arrow clasped tightly in her hand. If she had three more feet, she'd be in better striking distance.

Naveen quietly said, "She has heart. And she's got skill with the bow and arrow." He rubbed his shoulder.

Nix nodded. "She's bold and unafraid. She came after us as an equal. One against three, I find that fair odds."

"Hey," Bruce said behind them. "What about us?"

Nix glanced back and shrugged and turned his attention forward.

Jared said, "Drop your weapon."

Rowena dropped her arrow. She showed her empty hands, the dark leather fingerless gloves covered her palms but left her fingers free to operate her weapon with skill and precision.

Jared slid his eyes away from Rowena and over to Nix and Naveen. Out of the corner of his eye, he saw a blur. He instinctively held up his sword and turned to face her again, this time not letting his eyes leave her.

Rowena's dagger traveled along the blade of Jared's sword and stopped at the hilt of his sword. The tip of her blade was inches from his throat.

Everyone froze again.

Jared saw the look of determination and brimstone in her eyes, saw the lengths to which he surmised this woman would go to achieve her goal. He didn't know what to do, perplexed by her actions. He'd never been tested like this before. Just then, laughter suddenly broke out.

It disarmed him as much as her actions.

The sounds echoed off the hilltops as Nix, a hand over his stomach, leaned back trying to catch his breath. He kept laughing as if letting go of all the tension he could.

Then Naveen joined in.

"What are they laughing at?" Rowena asked.

Jared stepped back and withdrew his sword, sheathing it. "I think it means you can join us. I'd rather have you with us than fighting you all the way."

Rowena nodded and stood up from her crouching position. She got to her feet and studied the men around her for several seconds. With a look of satisfaction on her face, she sheathed her blade.

Chapter Ten

STRETCHED OUT ON his blanket, Jared stared into the fire. It was growing lower by the minute.

Nix sat the first watch.

Jared shivered. The fire reminded him of long ago.

He stared into the orange flames, his mouth tight. When he realized he was holding his breath, he consciously forced air in and out of his lungs.

He died—a long time ago in a wall of flame and an echo of screams. He shuddered at the memory.

He twitched. His right eyelid twitched again. He rubbed his face, trying to work away the nervous energy inside him.

"Are you okay, Jared?" said a voice.

The words pulled him back from the memory he was facing. He blinked and looked up. Rowena sat down next to him.

"What?"

"You were staring at the fire like a man who's lost everything."

"You know why I'm here? Why I'm doing this?" Jared said.

Rowena shook her head. "No."

"Because I hate vampires. I hate what they do to families. I hate how they destroy families and wreck lives. And the death they cause isn't just to one person, but it affects everyone who knew that person."

"Who did you lose?"

Jared shook his head. "It was a long time ago."

"You might feel better if you get it off your chest. Your burdens might be lighter."

He looked at her, and frankly he didn't know what to make of her. He had refused her help, but now she was here. She didn't seem strong on the outside, the way she had an attractive face with bright, intelligent eyes looking out at him. But maybe she was made of sterner stuff.

People came in different packages. Some people looked strong on the outside and they were strong on the inside too, and others were the opposite of that. They looked weak on the outside and were just as weak on the inside. There were combinations of both inner and outer strength. Was she as strong on the inside as she appeared on the outside?

"What happened to make you hate vampires?"

"They killed my sister and brother. I tried to save them but I was too late. There was nothing I could do but swing my sword in rage and kill as many of them as I could. I didn't bring them back, but I avenged their deaths."

His fingers curled around the blanket.

"Did it help?"

He suddenly wanted everything to cease. He sighed, and a weary smile crossed his face. He welcomed the day when he wouldn't remember the screams or pain from that event.

He wanted to be awake. Now.

Jared blinked and instantly caught the scent of burnt wood and ashes from the camp fire.

He tensed his hand muscles and felt the sword beside him. He lifted the blanket away and scanned the darkness around them, sensing it with his mind. To his right and left people were sleeping.

But they weren't alone.

Quietly, Jared got to his feet and shook off the cold. It was closer to dawn than night, but still it was dark out. Daylight would be here soon.

But something else was here, now.

He moved around the smoldering camp fire and noticed Nix resting on his side and Rowena lay on her back, the bow at her side. Bruce and Rygil were on the opposite side of the fire.

Naveen perched on a rock, his head jerked to the left. He caught himself in mid-motion and jerked away. He looked around the camp and righted himself.

Jared tapped Naveen's shoulder. "Rest. I'll take watch."

Naveen opened his eyes and said, "It's been quiet."

"Something is near."

Naveen narrowed his eyes. "How?"

"Feeling."

A sharp undulating scream rent the night. It came from their right. The sound was a mixture of bear and jaguar and something human all combined into one. The tone was laced with jagged hopelessness and soulful misery. Then another scream, a cousin to the first one, joined in from the left. And this song sang of futility and uselessness. A third scream came from behind them, and its song was the most painful one of all: one of certain death, a welcoming of the deep and dark velvet warmth of the void.

"What was that?" Bruce said, sitting up. Rygil rolled awake instantly, sputtering grass out of his mouth.

"I'm awake," Nix said, breathing heavily, his dagger in hand.

Rowena drew her bow and peered out into the darkness all around them. "Same here."

Naveen stood and gripped his wizard's staff. The runes came alive with an orange and green light. He held the staff like a weapon, ready to use it to strike the unseen enemies down.

Jared raised an eyebrow. "You have skill?"

"For a beginner," Naveen said. "Listen."

Jared strained his ears and there was a quick sound of running footsteps pounding dirt. They heard the sound first of something very fast coming closer, coming faster, growing louder.

A figure raced toward them, arms and legs pumping. It charged straight at them. A suicide run, thought Jared. He stood braced, sword raised, body half turned to the figure, so that he presented the smallest target possible.

The figure hissed and leaped toward Jared, over the logs that had served as an outer barrier. The leap was inhuman, the attacker gliding right at Jared, fangs glistened, nails as long as talons extended and ready to slice him open. Arms and legs pumped furiously through the air.

In the instant before contact, Jared looked at his attacker. The strangeness caught him off guard. The man was dressed in a dark coat, open with nothing underneath. His dark pants were torn and ragged down by the ankles and he ran incredibly fast for someone wearing no shoes.

Jared marveled at the thirty foot leap over the logs that served as their camp boundary and knew he was facing a supernatural enemy. The jumper raced toward him easily. His dark red eyes, crazed and full of blood lust, chilled Jared.

Jared wished he had the same raw power of their attacker, but he didn't.

He gripped his sword.

Wait for it.

Snap out of it.

Don't look at the eyes.

Jared inhaled, opened his eyes, and swung his body, trailing the sword behind him until the jumper almost knocked him down.

Almost.

He thrust the sword tip into the creature's stomach, the point of the sword slicing all the way through to the bones in its spine. Jared yanked the sword out and dug it in a second time, but not as deep. With both hands on the hilt, he plowed the sword upward to the sternum. He twisted the blade and shoved it brutally down toward the pelvis.

When he was done, he had carved two deep lines that opened up the flesh of its stomach. The creature screamed in agony and looked down at his destroyed body. Organs and guts were clearly visible, as blood pumped out of the torso and spilled down his legs. The attacker hissed at Jared, showing two sharp fangs, ready to bite him and then he collapsed to the ground.

Quickly, Jared raised his sword and brought it crashing down on the creature's neck, at the intersection between the top of the shoulder and the bottom of the head.

Blood gushed from the neck and within three slices, the head toppled free from the body.

Jared picked up the vampire's head and said, "Go back foul creatures or face this." He shoved the head high into the night air.

The others looked at him dumbfounded.

"We heard three different screams, not one. There are more creatures out there."

A beheaded monster lay at his feet and a head was gripped in his hand.

"We need fire," Jared said, sweeping the perimeter of the camp with his vision, looking for telltale signs of the next attack. "Get it higher. Our lives may depend upon it."

Rowena stirred herself to action, and gathered up some sticks and placed it on the dying fire. Naveen stepped forward and, without a word, aimed the tip of his staff toward the embers. Fire bloomed instantly to life, licking eagerly at the wood, growing larger until it was the size of a bonfire.

Jared said, "Face outward. Backs to the fire."

They each turned and faced the surrounding darkness.

Rowena fingered her bow. "I'm scared."

Almost as a whisper Nix said, "I hate darkness."

Rygil shivered. "What are we doing here?"

Naveen shifted the staff from hand to hand, the runes burning brightly in the night. "Courage all. We killed one of them. We can kill all of them."

"Stand fast," Jared said. He strained to hear any movements and wondered how many were out there. Three was a logical assumption. But there could just as easily be a lot more of them. If there were more they would have been overrun by now, so it had to be a small party of vampires. How could they travel so far out from Vampire Nation?

Naveen said, "Something's coming."

"What?" Rowena strained to listen.

"I don't see a th—yowwww." Nix bent over and Jared saw Nix clutching his stomach as a hand sized rock slipped to the ground.

As everyone went to help Nix, three vampires leaped out of the darkness and into the camp.

"Attack!" Jared screamed. He swung his sword and it struck hard against the opposing sword from the vampire.

"Why attack us?"

"We do what we want." The vampire, lean in the face and slender, looked back at him with bright crimson eyes.

"Who is your leader?"

"You mean the vampire king?" Lean Face laughed. "We bow to no one. We are free vampires, and we do as we please. Nobody can stop us."

Out of the corner of his vision, Jared saw Naveen let loose some kind of spell. The spell zoomed toward the vampire and engulfed it and then suddenly the vampire ignited. The vampire, its body aflame, ran madly in a circle. The creature fell to the ground, screaming in pain.

Madness consumed it until Rowena took aim and shot. The arrow penetrated its head. The creature laid still, its face contorted in pain, and its body crumbled into dust. With no body to burn, the fire died down and then flickered out.

Nix and Naveen fought another vampire. And now Rowena joined in.

A sword flashed in front of him. Jared back tracked, and blocked the downward path of the sword with his own.

"Stand down," Jared said. "We mean you no harm."

"You wish to come into our lands, take what is ours."

"The children do not belong to you."

"Our might, our right. The children are ours."

Jared charged forward, his sword cutting viciously at the air, missing the vampire by mere heartbeats. Wherever the vampire was his sword went. But always a second late.

The vampire pulled back his mouth, showed his fangs and charged at him. Jared felt a battle cry issue from his lips as he raced forward. Sword to sword, they clashed.

The vampire head-butted Jared against the side of his face.

Jared staggered back, his vision exploding into bright tiny clusters of light, alongside a dull throbbing pain. He brought up his sword, working on pure instinct, guessing where the vampire might attack next.

He felt a nick on his arm. It was a thin cut. He brought his hand up and covered the wound on his left arm.

The vampire stopped and sniffed the air. "Daylight approaches," he said, stepping away from the fire. "See you later human, if you survive."

The vampire turned and leaped out of the camp site.

Rowena tracked the vampire, fitted an arrow, and let it fly.

The arrow sailed toward the creature, ready to strike him hard in the middle of the back, but at the last minute the vampire feinted to the right and the arrow passed him.

The creature turned his head to look behind him and locked eyes with Rowena. She readied another arrow. He disappeared while there was still night. Daylight would be here shortly.

"We made it," Rowena said.

Nix looked at his torn shirt. "We barely survived."

"Look. It's not over yet," Naveen said, looking at Jared.

Jared stood before them, sword on the ground, hand over the wounded arm. Blood ran down his flesh and turned his white shirt into a blood soaked mess.

Jared fell to his knees. "What's wrong with me? He only nicked me, that's all."

Rowena said, "Jared!" They rushed to his side.

"The wound isn't deep," Nix said.

Rowena looked at the thin slice of flesh. "Agreed. It's a flesh wound, but he's been poisoned."

Jared looked sideways at her. "I don't feel well."

Naveen said, "This is not good."

"What can we do?" Rowena said.

"I have nothing for poison. In our journey, I didn't think that would be important."

Rowena pressed a cloth against the wound. "Neither did I. It takes weeks to stopper a potion."

Jared looked at her, his face profusely sweating, he was panting, his eyes looked puffy. "My vision …"

Nix looked around. "What can we do?"

Naveen stood up. "It's far away, but maybe."

Rowena turned toward him. "If you have something better, spit it out, wizard."

"The Lady of the Lake may help us. If we petition her …" he let his voice drop.

Jared looked up at him, his head tilted to one side. "Lady of the Lake?"

Naveen rushed toward Jared. "Get the horses ready. We break camp now."

"How far is it?"

"If one knows the lands around here, the distance isn't very far."

A fever grew inside him. He wanted to peel back his skin and let the cool air refresh him. Instead, he kept getting hotter and sweating more. His vision, in one eye, was already blurry, and now the other eye was getting affected.

What happened?

He remembered—the sword fight with the vampires.

He reached out and gripped a forearm.

Rowena looked down at him, her face grim and resolute.

"Did we win the fight?"

"We drove them off," Rowena said, and that was the last Jared heard as he hung his head down and fell into a fevered sleep.

Chapter Eleven

AFTER DECIDING TO take Jared to the Lady of the Lake, they quickly readied the horses and rode hard, although to Rowena the ride itself could have been anywhere from five minutes to over an hour in duration.

Time, on this particular ride, had a way of slipping past her. Whether it was because they had a wizard with them or because somehow the Lady of the Lake was involved, she didn't know. Time, to Rowena, seemed to bend and twist during their ride to rescue Jared from the vampire's poison.

Rowena loved and valued the quick intelligence and sturdy endurance of the horses they rode on, but this day, for this time, it seemed to her that each gallop, each stride, had the combined effect of multiplying the actual length the horses covered. The distances the horses traveled had a supernatural assistance given to them. A normal horse would cover X amount of space with each gallop, but their horses, now, covered ten times the distance.

It seemed to her, as they journeyed to seek the assistance of the Lady of the Lake, that they were in a bewitched state, and in such a state anything was possible.

Immediately after Naveen had talked about the Lady of the Lake, he picked up their fallen companion and threw him sideways over the horse. Then Naveen swung into the saddle and rode off at a gallop, with Jared laid across the horse in a feverish and unconscious state.

She and Nix hurried to catch up, stowing their gear quickly.

Now the funny thing was simple: they rode hard and fast, the clip-clop of the hooves pounding hard on the earth. She rode in the saddle and the bruise on her right inner thigh was evidence of her ride. But this ride had been long, and yet it seemed short.

Again, the trip was strange.

At one point while going full speed across a field, Naveen raised his wizard's staff and muttered some words that she failed to catch. There was a bright light from the tip of his staff, or was that a falling star? She tried to remember and even her memory was fuzzy. She had trouble focusing on what exactly happened. Her recollection of events was a chaotic mish-mash of jumbled activities.

She thought, and she would have sworn to it and fought men to the death for her conviction, that they jumped through a portal of some kind. It was large enough to encompass all of them and the spare horse that belonged to Jared.

But it was also very, very cold and Rowena could have sworn that she fell asleep while riding.

It was very confusing.

And then, before she knew it, they raced to the edge of the lake shore and stopped. She blinked her eyes and was surprised that they were already there. She had a strong urge to go to sleep but then Naveen leapt down from the horse and pulled Jared with him into the waters of the lake.

With the sound of splashing waters reaching her ears, with the unconscious form of Jared carried into the cold lake waters, Rowena suddenly felt awake—as if a jolt went through her body.

Rowena cried out: "Naveen, what are you doing?"

She jumped from the horse and rushed toward the shoreline. She started to go in when a hand stopped her.

Nix held her back.

"What are you doing?"

"He's a wizard," Nix said.

"He can't drown him."

"He's not. He's calling the Lady of the Lake."

"The what?"

Nix ignored her searching eyes and looked past her. "See."

She turned and her heart beat wildly in her chest and it seemed to climb up into her throat. She started to speak, but Nix held up his hand.

"Listen," Nix said.

Standing waist deep in the lake water, Naveen gently placed the man on his back, his hands supporting the poisoned man's body. Naveen was beseeching the lady of the lake.

"From time before time, from the highest sky to the deepest earth, I call upon you Lady of the Lake."

Naveen bowed his head for a second and then, raising his eyes, he gently pushed the body deeper into the water. "Please have compassion, and help this man. He is on a quest to save children from creatures of the night."

Next to her, Nix shivered. "I am superstitious and I do not like calling upon powers we do not understand or know."

Rowena said, "He's as good as dead. What chance did we have against that poison?"

"If he doesn't survive, we are all dead."

"No. My son is still alive."

"If he doesn't survive then your son might as well be dead."

Rowena turned away and fought down the panic in her thoughts. She raced to the only conclusion that would mar her life and make her the most cursed woman of all of creation: her son would be dead and there was nothing she could do about it.

"No!" Rowena said with vehemence. She wanted to strike Nix in the face, but Nix was only speaking from his own heart.

Her own heart spoke differently to her. Her heart—a mother's heart—said, 'your son is alive.'

She took comfort from that belief. After all, she had sacrificed, she had laughed, she had loved and cared for her son. For years she loved him and took joy in his simple existence. She thrilled with each new discovery he made of life and of his environment around him. He was all she had, since his father died. If her son, Steen, were to die, her world would close up and become as dark as night.

Rowena couldn't face that kind of bleak future.

She ignored Nix, shook off his hand and watched as Naveen gently pushed Jared deeper into the lake.

From the depths of the lake came a shimmering light. The light was two, no three times larger than the measurement of her arms if she were to extend them in opposite directions.

In fact, the light was revealed to be a sphere and it rose from the lake's floor and swallowed up Jared's body. The sphere stayed on the surface of the lake, pulsating with crystal lights. Inside the sphere was Jared.

With her mouth open, with her mind numb from what she had witnessed, Rowena stood hip deep in the cold lake water, her world turned upside down. She was in the middle of a bewitching. What was going on?

Jared opened his eyes and found himself lying on grass. He looked up and there was a lady dressed in white. She smiled at him.

"You are safe," the lady said before he could question her.

"Where am I?"

She looked at him for a second—but it was unlike any second he had ever experienced before. It seemed filled with answers even before he asked the questions. An answer formed in his mind. He found himself smiling before she could answer him.

And then she said, "In between. Beats of your heart. Your friends thought you dead. The fast acting poison would have killed you."

Jared nodded. "You took it away? Thank you. But why?"

The Lady displayed a faint smile across her thin lips. "Nobody protects the weak anymore. They need a champion. Are you that champion?"

"I've failed in the past."

"I see that. But you've tried and—"

"Yeah, I know."

"You wear a death mask, but there is a way out of that. If I remove it, it may upset balances that cannot be measured."

"Can you remove it?" Jared asked.

"Yes. Mortals think they know so much. When the time comes, this could be given back to its owner."

Jared nodded. "So I'm free?"

"You always have choice. If you exercise it."

"So the spell is gone?"

"Unfortunately, no. You have a Death Spell hanging over you."

Jared rose from deep sleep, drawn upward to the crackling sounds of twigs burning in fire. Next he caught the scent of burning wood as it rolled over him and assaulted his sense of smell. He shook his head, breathed deeply and opened his eyes.

He lay on the ground, a small fire built next to him. On the other side of the fire was Rowena, busy tending to the boiling water in the pot. She glanced across at him.

"How are you feeling?"

"Tired and refreshed, at the same time."

"There was poison in you. Did she help?"

She? Jared blinked and searched his memory. He should know who she is. She? She. A sharp piercing light struck deep in his memory and the sudden flash of her face showed up in his mind's eye.

"I am free."

"Of what?"

Jared said, "I'm free of the poison. I feel tired."

"You should. You've been cut almost all day."

Naveen stepped forward and looked down at him. "The Lady is a strong force for those who believe."

"But I never heard of her," Jared said.

"It doesn't matter."

"But doesn't belief require a believer and something to believe in?"

Naveen nodded. "Ordinarily, I would agree. But sometimes faith is all that is required."

Jared stared at him for a second. "I wasn't aware of wizards believing in faith."

"We don't. We believe in ourselves and energy and imagination. But even those pale in comparison to other things to believe in."

Rowena poured hot water into a cup and added some crushed leaves to it. She handed the cup to him. "What things are more precious than family and friends?"

Naveen bowed. "Exactly. Sometimes nothing is more precious than family and friends."

Jared sipped the brewed tea and felt the warmth of the liquid spread out into his chest and then to the rest of his body. His head suddenly came into focus and he glanced to his right. "What are those?"

Jared stared at a shield, a sword, and a small leather bag.

Nix said with disgust, "He wouldn't let me touch them. He said they were for you."

Rowena hugged herself. "She came up out of the water bearing these as gifts to you. I think you're meant to have them."

"We'd better press on with our journey then," Jared said. He turned to get up and stopped.

"What's wrong?" Rowena asked.

Jared lowered himself, clutching the blanket in his hands. "Everything is spinning around. I'm afraid I can't stand. Not yet anyway."

Naveen frowned. "We should be going, but I think we can stay here."

Nix impatiently tapped his foot on the ground. "But what about our death curse? I mean, shouldn't we be moving on?"

Everybody turned to Nix.

Nix stared back at them. "That's why he cursed us, so we'd always be making progress, right?"

"We'll make progress," Jared said. "Besides we have a time limit as well. We have to rest. Tomorrow I should be as good as new and then we ride toward Vampire Nation."

"Then it's settled," Naveen said. "I'll take first watch."

Jared looked sideways at the lake shore and a woman walked toward him. The others didn't seem to notice her, so Jared didn't tell them what he saw. She was a tall woman, fair to look upon, a pleasant smile and deep green eyes, the whole earth was in those eyes, and he felt safe and warm just looking at her.

"Who are you?"

"I am what you call the Lady of the Lake."

"Thank you for saving my life."

"The poison almost overwhelmed you, but now it's gone."

"My gifts. Thank you for them."

"Yes. They are interesting. A sword to be borne with courage and strength. A shield to help defend the powerless and the poor from those who think they know better."

"And why a coin bag?"

"There are no coins in that bag."

"No?"

"Rather, when you have lost all hope, and when everything seems to be in darkness and you're at your end, open up that bag and let hope grow inside you again."

"Hope?"

"It is the one characteristic in people that helps them to move forward against all forces, real or imagined."

"Thank you, my lady."

She bowed her head. "Remember, you are free to do whatever is necessary and true, even if that is terrible to you."

Jared shivered. He watched as she walked back to the shoreline and then waded deeper into the water. First, she was up to her knees in water. He blinked and looked again. The water line came up to her waist. She continued moving deeper until she disappeared under the surface; a small ripple traveled across the surface of the lake, her only evidence of being here.

Jared turned on his side and racked his brain.

Her answer disturbed him and made him look inward. What would be necessary and true for him to do? And what terrible consequences would he face?

He searched his memory and came back empty. He gripped the blanket with his hands and closed his eyes. Her words troubled him as he slipped into sleep.

Chapter Twelve

THEY TRAVELED SLOWLY toward Vampire Nation, the
sun beating down on them as Jared felt a ringing headache with every
step and jolt of the horse. He couldn't take it anymore. He was tired
of riding on the make-shift litter dragged by Rowena's horse. Naveen
and Nix were in the lead and Rowena pulled him along, a decision
they made out of necessity. Bruce and Rygil rode behind him. Jared
was tired of looking at the smirks on their faces.

"Stop!" Jared shouted. "Hey, Rowena, stop."

"We have to keep going," she said. "You know that."

"I'm ready to stand up. I'm ready to ride again."

"You said that in the beginning of the day and you couldn't.
Why should now be any different?"

"Because I'm better. Because I can ride now. Because if I don't
get off this makeshift litter I'll go mad. My body is sore. You may
think this helps me, but you have no idea how this is driving me
crazy. Please, stop the horse."

"We can't."

"Have pity, please, and stop the horse. I can ride."

Rowena stopped the horse. "Naveen. Nix. Hold up. He wants to
ride."

Naveen and Nix circled back. They looked down at Jared, who
was strapped to the plank. Earlier that morning when they set out,
Jared was still too weak to move, so they made provisions for him
and set out on their journey, with him bound to the plant and
Rowena's horse pulling him along the way.

"Are you sure?" Naveen pulled the reins tight on his horse. "Because we can't take any chances. We have to keep moving forward."

"I know," Jared said, feeling the bite of the straps against his flesh. The ride was bumpy, the back of his head was sore from striking the plank whenever they rode over a large bump or divot in the road. "I know. But I can ride a horse."

"Not a bit weak, are you? Not like yesterday and this morning?" Nix gave a weary look and glanced sideways at the wizard. "Can't you give him something to make him stronger?"

Naveen glared at Nix. "Why should I be able to do that?"

"Because you're a wizard."

"And what, in your expert opinion, does a wizard do?"

"A wizard is somebody who," Nix closed his eyes and said, "Slays dragons and helps princesses."

"Neither is present."

"As well as help people when they're in need."

"Yes," Naveen said grudgingly.

Nix pointed at Jared. "He is in need."

"Wizards do not stop people from getting into fights, drinking, singing off key when drunk, or making bad decisions."

"Who said anything about singing off key?"

The exasperated look from Naveen made Nix smile. The baiting Nix had done seemed to brighten up his day.

Rygil looked down at Jared. "He looks green around the gills. You'd think he's been drinking all day."

Bruce jumped in. "I'll bet you he can't get on the horsey."

Rygil nodded. "I'll take your wager! How much? Five?"

Bruce said, "Make it ten."

Rygil nodded. "I think he can get on the horsey. I just don't think he'll stay on it all day."

Bruce added, "I'll cover that bet too."

Jared glowered at them. "To hell with you two."

Rowena stood in front of him. She leaned forward and undid the straps. "If I have to bury you, then at least stand up like a man."

Her green eyes widened in surprise as Jared pushed her back and climbed to his feet. He saw the flecks of gold in her surprised eyes. Rowena was impressed by his actions.

Jared wobbled a bit and glanced over at Rowena. She frowned at him. He ignored her look and took in a deep breath, feeling the cool air fill up his lungs. It felt good.

He started coughing.

Bruce and Rygil laughed.

Naveen rode closer and leaned down toward him. "Can you function?" Naveen asked, looking carefully at Jared and taking the measure of him.

"I can," Jared said.

"And can you ride a horse for hours at a time?"

"Yes."

"And endure the hot sun?"

"Yes."

"And can you—"

"Enough!"

Nix nodded encouragingly at Jared: "It's good to see you back in the saddle."

"I'm not there yet," Jared said, "but thanks."

Jared turned from Rowena and, taking his knife, cut the straps away from her horse that held up the makeshift lean-to that carried Jared for the half day.

He cut through one strap, then moved to the other side and cut through the last strap and then overturned the plank that carried him.

He was glad to see it go.

Rowena climbed on her horse and watched, along with the others, as Jared tottered over to his horse.

Jared held the reins of his horse in one hand, grabbed the pommel with the other, and putting one foot in the stirrup tried to lift himself up. He fell to the ground. The horse looked down at him and then pulled up some grass and munched on it.

"He can't ride." Naveen looked annoyed.

"He's not strong enough," Nix said, looking away.

"You owe me ten," Bruce said, holding out his hand.

Rygil shook his head and slipped his hand inside his tunic and brought out his coin purse. He paid off his debt.

"He's strong enough," Rowena said, ignoring the two louts. "Ride with me." She held out her hand and waited as Jared got up, brushed the dirt from his clothes, and walked over to her.

He took her hand. "I owe you."

He climbed onto Rowena's horse, making it the very first time, his face scrunched up in equal amounts of pain and determination, and sat behind her.

Rowena turned and whispered to Jared so none of the others could hear her. "Put your hands anywhere else than on my waist and I'll stick you. Is that clear?"

"Of course," Jared said quietly.

Jared watched as Nix gathered up the reins of Jared's horse and wrapped them around his saddle horn. Nix looked over at Naveen. "I'm ready."

"Now that we're clear on the matter." Rowena looked over at Naveen and Nix. "Let's go."

They road across the grassy fields and headed down near the riverbed.

The saddle was hard against his backside and he wasn't used to the rhythm of this horse. He preferred to be on his own horse. The stride was different, and so was the saddle. The only good thing about what happened was he was able to wrap his arms around Rowena's waist.

He smiled.

He remembered her warning and made sure his hands didn't stray. It would have been so easy but he promised. And if anything he made sure, to the very best of his ability, to keep his promises.

"Jared, can I ask you a question?"

Jared leaned away from her and wondered about her question. "What?"

"It's a simple one."

He thought he knew her question. It was the one thing that was driving her throughout this whole journey. "Will you get your son back?"

"Yes. Will we get him back?"

"It is—" he inhaled deeply, "my hope to make sure your child comes back safely. And the other children as well."

"You say that because of the Death Spell?"

"Yes—"

"Because I would say anything, as well, if I had a sword blade hanging over my neck. You can trust me. I won't break. I've faced worse. Tell me. What do you really think?"

"I was going to say—and because I don't like vampires."

"I'm sorry. I should let you finish your sentences."

Jared inhaled and said softly, "Vampires are evil, but they're like you and me. They can bleed and they can die. But they're awfully quick and hypnotic. Also they're dangerous like a wounded animal in the wild. Never turn your back on one."

"But you haven't answered my question."

"I thought I did," Jared said. "I can tell you that the sun will come up tomorrow and it will. But I cannot tell you what I'll have for breakfast. There are too many variables for that."

"So you cannot give a yes or no answer."

"I thought I did."

"You didn't. You're being perfectly vague."

Jared frowned. "Let me say I believe this: with all my might and skill I can bring the children back."

"But how do you know?"

"Because I said I would."

"Just because I say I can fly in the air like a bird doesn't make it so." Rowena turned and looked at him.

"Have you killed vampires before?"

"No."

"I have," he said in a low voice so others wouldn't hear them. "It won't be easy, but it's not impossible. At least, I don't think it is impossible. Is that good enough for you?"

"I don't know how to take that."

"Take it with kindness. This journey is a dangerous one. It is filled with menace, the vagaries of vampires, and the stink of death. And rapture."

"Rapture?"

"When the children are safe."

"You're confident then?"

"I'm confident in that I know what I want."

Rowena stopped the horse and turned around in the saddle, looking at him for a very long time. "Can't you give me a straight answer?"

The others also stopped and looked at them.

Jared said, "The sun will rise tomorrow. The moon will rise later. I know that for a fact. I know we go to Vampire Nation to take back what is ours: children stolen from the village. That is all I know.

What I am prepared for is this: to weld my sword, to demand the children be set free, to fight for them if necessary and to die if that is the only and last resort for them to be free. If you want to know the future, you should ask Naveen. He knows how to foretell the future."

Naveen glanced sideways and said, "He speaks both true and false, Rowena. I have no power of prophecy in my bag of tricks, but the words he spoke are as true as you could ask of any warrior ready to raise up his sword and lay down his life for a cause greater than himself."

"Well spoken, both of you," Nix said.

Naveen continued, "We have Death Collars around our necks. We die whether we stay here or go forward. Why not help save children from a dark fate?"

Nix chimed in, "I'd rather enjoy the sunshine and be in a market place, but if this was the last thing I ever do in this life, then helping children escape from a bunch of nasty vampires is fine by me. Maybe the children we rescue will have a better life than us." Nix then pointed a finger at Naveen, "They'll certainly have a better life than that poor fool."

Rowena lowered her eyes and smiled briefly. "Is that the best you can say?"

"My life to help others," Nix said, "I dare any other thief to say the same thing."

"Then it is hope that guides us."

"Hope," Naveen said, "is what drives all people everywhere to make a better life for themselves."

Jared said, "We have a general direction. We know Vampire Nation is to the east of us. I'm sure the signposts will spring up along the way ..."

"To hit us in the face," Nix added.

Jared raised an eyebrow at Nix, "... to aid us in our journey."

Rowena rolled her shoulders, loosening the tension in them and said, "Why do you believe that, Jared?"

"It is my way to take a situation, whatever state it is in, and to elevate it into the best state possible for that situation."

Naveen looked sideways at Jared. "That's magic. Taking something, rearranging it, and coming up with something better."

"I am no magi or wizard," Jared said. "Nor have I any skills in the arcane arts. But I have one thing in my favor: I do not back down. I go after the target. More than anything else, that counts heavily in my favor. And if it counts in my favor it counts in your favor; and by extension, it counts in the children's favor as well.

"We are company, except for two people," Jared glanced briefly at Bruce and Rygil and then looked back at Rowena, "on a sacred mission to bring missing children back home. Do you disagree?"

Rowena shook her head sideways and felt a small lump in her throat. A small sound escaped her lips. "No."

"No. So let's go."

Jared felt hope rise in him and he saw the resolution upon Rowena's face as she turned around and continued riding forward. Naveen and Nix glanced at each other and then Nix started whistling a tune. The light tune turned into a ribald song as Nix sang to them about a trio of sisters by a wishing well.

Naveen smiled several times and laughed. Rowena kept shaking her head at Nix's nonsense and Jared felt in control instead of being a puppet for the local village government and local wizard who either didn't have enough courage or didn't want to face death going up against vampires.

Rowena's gentle laughter at Nix's song descended and filled Jared with life as it could be for him, if he had chosen another path. He smiled and turned away from the others.

Later that day, they found a grove of trees and settled into the clearing before them, away from inquisitive eyes and travelers on the road. They made camp.

Jared slid off the horse that Rowena was on, his legs giving a little as he lowered himself all the way to the ground. His legs weren't strong enough to leap off a horse and walk. He rose to his feet and moved over to Nix. He grabbed his horse's reins from Nix and staked the reins to the ground. He unhitched the saddle, making it easier for the horse to move, and grabbed his bedding from the horse.

He turned and saw a space between two large rocks and placed his bedding between them, rolled it out and lay on top of the bedding. He soon fell asleep.

It was night and a small fire was going when Naveen said, "He is still gaining his strength."

"But at least he is stronger. We have the Lady of the Lake to thank for that."

Nix set his tin of food down. "I wish I could sleep like that."

Naveen frowned. "Why can't you?"

"Because he's afraid," Bruce said.

"Yeah. He's a small weasel, getting into tight spaces and that's all he's good for," Rygil said.

Nix bristled against their comments.

"Ignore them," Rowena said. "They wouldn't know courage if it rose up on its hind legs and bit them in the backside."

Dark looks were exchanged between the two groups but neither side moved as Bruce and Rygil laid down on their mats, quickly falling asleep.

Naveen turned to Nix. "Before we get sidetracked, why do you have trouble falling asleep?"

"I'm not good with making plans up on the go. If I were to steal from you it wouldn't be an impulse. I'd watch you, your house and see the best way to take what I want. Then I'd figure out where your valuables are and go straight for them. But this," Nix gestured with his arms, indicating the camp, "is all against my nature. I'd rather know where we're going and then plan it out. As it is, we're going into a great unknown and there's nothing I can plan for. I have to react to the situation. So how can I sleep when danger may be surrounding us all the time?"

Rowena pushed a stick into the fire and said, "A journey starts with a single footstep."

Nix smiled at Rowena and glanced across to Naveen. "Do you think we'll make it?"

A clear, solemn voice broke through from the darkness surrounding them and said, "No."

Chapter Thirteen

ALARMS RANG INSIDE Jared's mind as he swam out of a deep sleep, moving toward the surface, with a desperate sense of urgency. He opened his eyes. He noticed Bruce and Rygil standing far behind the rest of them, their weapons drawn.

In front of them was a lone man. The man had dark shoulder-length hair, parted down the middle, and he wore dark pants and boots, with a white shirt; over that was a coat that reached down to his knees. The coat had a brooch on it.

This piece of jewelry caught his attention. It looked similar to the brooch he had collected from the previous vampire. Was that possible?

Jared stood up quickly and laid his hand to rest on the hilt of his sword. He pulled the sword out and held it against his leg. "What do you want, creature?"

The vampire bowed and lifted up his dark eyes and said, "My name is Champion. I am commanded to challenge each of you to the death, so to speak."

To Jared's left Nix said, "We can just kill you and have done with it right now."

Champion frowned and tilted his head to one side. "Can you?"

Nix let his hand rest on top of his dagger. "My steel wants to taste your dead flesh."

Before Champion could respond, Rowena blurted out, "Where is my son?"

Champion leveled his eyes at Rowena. After a moment, he smiled. "Your son is safe. For now. We have plans for the children and wish them no harm."

Naveen said, "Who else is with you?"

"That," Champion said, a slight curl to his lips, "is a perceptive question, wizard. I am not alone. If I am killed before my message is delivered or I am killed against the terms of our engagement, my brothers will see what you have done and they will descend upon this camp and stir up the dirt and mix your bones with it."

The heaviness in the air descended upon Jared and the rest of them.

Champion continued, "There will never be a trace of you, your bodies, or this camp site ever again." Naveen bristled and the humming power of his staff was growing louder with each second.

Jared stepped forward and said, "We will hear you out."

Nix spat in disgust. "He toys with us."

"The battle is never won being hot headed. Control yourself, Nix."

Nix blinked and stepped sideways.

"That goes for all of you. Including you, Naveen."

"I am just preparing for any actions that may come our way."

"Don't any of you initiate the fight. Let's hear what he has to say," Jared said quietly. Nix nodded, Rowena bit her lower lip, and Naveen kept looking at Champion for any sudden movements.

Jared turned around and raised his voice. "Your threats are nothing." Jared gripped his sword. "So what?"

"I am to issue a challenge—of single combat—with each of you. One at a time. Who is your bravest warrior?"

Before Jared could respond, Nix stepped forward, his dagger in his hand. "Prepare to look up from the ground at your better."

Rowena said, "Nix!"

"Are you crazy?" Naveen said. "I was to be first."

"Beat you to it, slow wand."

Nix stepped forward, and faced the vampire. It was out of character for him to push himself forward like this but a chill of death and fear traveled down his spine and threatened to immobilize him unless he acted fast. If he didn't move, Nix knew he'd be stuck, fear anchoring him to the ground. Nix looked at his small dagger and then over at the tall vampire.

It was a classic battle of a mouse versus lion. And Nix wasn't the lion. He had no doubt who would win, but if he could wound the vampire then the others could take over and finish what he started.

Unlike Naveen, he had no magical incantations to throw at enemies, and he certainly didn't have a wizard's magical staff in his satchel. Nor did he have the training and sense of tactics that Jared seemed to possess. The only person who awed him was Rowena. To Nix's way of thinking she was a shining example of courage. She had the resolve to set out and save her son from vampires, whereas his own mother gave him up for adoption.

He glanced at the vampire and hoped his actions could buy them the precious seconds needed to turn defeat into victory. "Hey fangs. Come and get me."

Champion bowed. "Before we engage, thief, I honor your courage. I want you to know that this isn't personal. And I ask that you abide by the ancient rules of the contest."

Nix looked at Champion and then looked back at his companions. Naveen gripped his wizard's staff. Rowena was fitting an arrow to the string. Jared's dark eyes anchored Nix to the here and now: Jared's concerned expression told Nix to be careful. Jared nodded.

Nix turned, coughed, and faced a supremely confident vampire. "I agree."

"Then let us begin."

Nix crouched low and rushed forward, the dagger close to his side, ready to raise it up and strike home in the creature's cold heart. Death to the vampire.

Nix screamed and raised the blade—

Champion leapt over Nix and struck him across the face and throat with his sharp, pointed nails.

Nix ducked but was too late. Pain and heat throbbed across his forehead and the side of his face. Nix brought his hand to his forehead and it came back covered with blood.

Champion breathed in deeply. "I love the scent of fresh blood. Thank you for this gift of yours."

Nix stumbled and fell to the ground, but he caught himself at the last moment, his left hand braced against the earth. Lightheaded, blood seeping into his eyes, Nix staggered to his feet.

"This isn't over yet, fangs." Nix teetered, his legs rubbery. He jabbed the air in front of him with the dagger's sharp point. He crouched and edged closer to the vampire. When he was within striking distance, he aimed as best he could for the vampire's heart, he reached forward, the steel tip of the blade at the farthest point of his reach, and lunged.

Champion deftly moved aside, grabbed Nix's wrist, and pulled him forward, the dagger falling from Nix's hand.

Nix stumbled off balance, whirled and tried to catch himself, but he fell. His chin hit the ground with a jarring impact and he found his head throbbing with pain and his teeth ached from the impact.

Nix rolled onto his back, groaning, his eyes shut because of the pain and he felt something press down on his hand.

Nix opened his eyes and discovered Champion standing on his hand. The vampire applied more pressure, pinning him to the ground.

Nix screamed.

The vampire hissed at him.

Nix felt cold all over.

Nix looked on as Champion took a length of rope from around his waist.

The vampire quickly bound Nix's hands together and lifted him up over one shoulder as easily as lifting a small child. He carried Nix to a large nearby tree; along the way the vampire picked up Nix's dagger.

Champion pressed Nix against the hard bark of the tree, one hand pinning him against the trunk easily. The other hand raised the dagger at him. The dagger sliced through the gray tunic and brown vest Nix wore, pinning him to the large tree. Nix felt weak and helpless, his strength all spent, as Champion moved closer and pressed his finger across Nix's bloody forehead.

Champion pulled back his bloodstained fingertip and licked it. The vampire shivered and said in a low voice, "Do you surrender?"

"You already have me," Nix said.

"Nobody likes defeat. Between you and I, I accept that you would have 'died.' Rest, brave fool. I go to take care of the rest of your companions."

Nix lowered his head, afraid to look at the others as Champion turned and said, "Who is next?"

Rowena watched at how easily Nix was handled by the vampire and grew angry. She couldn't help but see her son handled the same way and it made her blood boil. She bristled at the one-sided fight, raised her bow and notched an arrow.

Before she could reach maximum tension on the string, a hand reached in front of her and pushed down the bow. "We don't know how many are out there," Jared said.

"But we can't do nothing."

"If Champion wanted to kill Nix, it would have already happened. We made an agreement, and we'll abide by it. Besides, something else is going on here."

Rowena gave him a dark stare.

What were words in the face of her son taken from her? What words did the vampires trust and obey? Rowena clutched her fist. What words was her son saying right now? Was he worried? Or angry? Was he frightened?

There was only one vampire here. Rowena didn't see any others in the darkness around them, didn't sense them.

She could, with cool certainty, strike the vampire in the heart with her arrow and kill it. Right here. The vampire stepped away from the oak tree, leaving Nix pinned to the tree. "Who is next?"

Rowena stepped forward and, pulling back on the string with all of her might, sighted the vampire's heart and she let go of the string and watched as her arrow took flight.

It flew straight and true and deadly. She had been a woodsman's daughter and a soldier's wife. She recognized the desperate chance Nix took against the vampire. She loved him for the courage and the pluck he showed, and that monster was one of the monsters that had taken her son. They had no right to take away Steen. No man or vampire could take away what was hers. Not by force or cunning.

Her arrow traveled the space of fifty feet and still the monster didn't look up to see what was coming straight at him.

Whether it was acute hearing or some supernatural sense that she did not know, Rowena watched as Champion collapsed to the ground at the last moment, hugging the dirt as the arrow passed harmlessly over him, narrowly escaping the deadly shaft.

He let out a low growl and got into a crouch. He raised his head and red eyes locked on her.

Rowena felt her heart thump loudly in her chest. Did everybody else hear her heart beating wildly? She wasn't going to be afraid. She wasn't going to let this monster dictate how she would respond. She lost her son and this one may have taken her son for all she knew. She wouldn't back down.

She raised her bow, tracking him as he moved in a zigzag pattern—left and then right—on the ground. From this distance, her arrows would finish him. She wasn't frightened by him.

And the closer the creature came, the more deadly her arrows would be. As fast as the creature was Rowena knew he couldn't out run her arrows.

The vampire pressed closer, continuing the zigzag pattern.

She led him with her aim and at the right moment, she released the arrow.

Champion hissed and, with powerful leg muscles, he leapt straight up into the darkness, the shaft whistling between his legs.

In a blur, Champion was out of sight.

Rowena looked up into the tree branches above and lost track of him. She automatically fitted another arrow, and was pulling back on the string when Champion crashed down upon her, knocked the bow out of her hands and, grabbing an arrow from her, he broke it in half.

He threw away the pieces of wood and hissed at her. With his red eyes covering her, Champion moved quickly and got right in her face: red eyes staring straight at her green eyes.

She went for the knife at her side.

He grabbed her wrist and squeezed it until she dropped the weapon.

She went for her other knife, hidden in her boot.

He knocked it with a vicious backhand out of her grasp.

She raised her knee to strike him in the groin.

He sensed the attack and sidestepped her. He swept his feet toward her legs and with his arm, he pushed her back. Rowena fell to the ground, landing hard on her back, moans of pain escaped her lips.

The monster jumped on her, his hands pinning her shoulders to the ground. He straddled her and pressed his face close.

Hot breath sliced across her face as she tried to buck him off, but he had more weight and she had no leverage.

She took in his red eyes and the rancid foul odor that breathed upon her. She wanted to retch but didn't. She found the strength to stare back at him, to look into those merciless red eyes.

She willed it. She looked back at him, for herself and for her son. She had the courage to look the monster in the face and not be scared. She was the master of this situation. What could the monster do to her?

And then, as if reading her mind, the monster answered by a subtle shift of his weight. With her arms pinned down by his knees, and with his hands now free, he took her face roughly in his hands. He bent low until his nose was almost pressed against hers.

He hissed at her, the menace and the intent behind it all: *I own you and you are mine.*

He revealed his glistening fangs.

The open mouth was death incarnate.

Rowena stared at the fangs and then something inside started to slide away from her control—a pebble at first, and then more—as her resolute attitude began to crumble and dissolve away.

Her lower lips trembled.

She forced herself to look at the monster. The damn monster— the same that took her son away—she forced herself to look at him and her eyes started stinging. She blinked back the tears and found herself coughing. The monster wasn't fair. Dammit.

"I'm not afraid of you," she said in a low voice. But all she thought about was the vision of her son dead and curled up on his side. Her son was dead and gone.

The monsters had taken him away and she would never be able to hug him, never be able to hear his laughter, never be able to smell him as she hugged him close.

They took him away from her.

Forever.

She turned her face away and cried.

The monster rose up and peered down at the broken woman.

Rowena curled up into a small ball and laid on her side weeping.

The sigils on Naveen's staff glowed brightly; the runes flared and showed the mystical symbols clearly to all concerned. The energy running through the magical staff, powered by his will, vibrated with power and the faint sound could be heard clearly by all around.

Naveen stepped forward and held the staff across his chest with both hands. "Vampire, y-you will not get a-away from me."

Champion stepped away from Rowena's sobbing form and stared across the distance at him. "Others have tried and failed. Why should you be any different, wizard?"

"Because they don't know how to put you away."

Champion stiffened and walked carefully away from the crumbled form of Rowena, never taking his eyes from the wizard. He walked backwards slowly. Naveen noticed the subtle distance the vampire was putting between them. The vampire kept moving away, increasing the distance, and increasing his ability to escape, until he came to rest against a tree. "Your move, wizard."

Naveen stepped forward until he was standing next to Rowena. He looked down and saw the uncontrollable shaking and heard muffled sobs escape from her lips. He paced two more steps beyond her, keeping his body between Rowena and the vampire.

He would do everything in his power to protect her.

That was what wizards do.

He had the power to protect those who needed protecting, to serve those who were unable to help themselves in times of need.

By runes and words of power, he faced the vampire and stretched out his arms, the staff held overhead in both hands. He felt the power generate inside him, he felt it flow and connect with his staff. The runes glowed even brighter than before; the orange and fiery symbols shimmered in the heat. The thrumming sound from the wood grew higher.

Naveen said, "In all that is holy: earth, wind, fire, and water, dal vento! Dal vento!"

The blue nimbus around his staff erupted and a loud cracking sound hurt his ears as a cyclone appeared at the edge of his staff. The winds blew hard buffeting him. The force of a cyclone, controlled and held in place by his thoughts and the use of his own power, was barely contained.

Naveen strained to keep the cyclone in place.

The cyclone wanted to leap out at Champion the way a pet dog would leap out at a stranger to protect its owner. Naveen directed the destructive energies of the cyclone straight at Champion.

The wind shrieked.

Let the wind knock him off his feet, pull him down and lay him out helpless.

Naveen felt a wolfish smile play across his face.

"Go," Naveen said.

The cyclone jumped across the space eager to hone in on its target.

Champion looked wide eyed at the approaching cyclone.

Naveen moved sideways to better see the collision between vampire and cyclone.

Champion looked for a means of escape.

Naveen didn't want the vampire to escape. If he made it past the cyclone then all would be lost. He couldn't have that. In fact, Naveen would make sure the vampire would never walk another day.

Naveen raised his wizard's staff and aimed the tip at Champion and said, "F-fucco! Fucco! F-fucco!"

A small fireball the size of a man's shoulder raced toward Champion, closing the gap. Two more fireballs followed the first one. All three sped toward the cyclone and the vampire.

Champion turned and spotted the approaching fireballs out of the corner of his eyes. With shock registering on his face and caught unaware, Champion watched helplessly as the first speeding fireball slammed into him and exploded in a wall of fire.

The fireball hit his feet and ankles and the spell knocked him to the ground.

Naveen watched as the flames circled the feet of the vampire.

The vampire struggled and tried to put out the flames.

The fireball engulfed his ankles and started crawling up his legs.

The second and third fireballs barely missed the vampire and exploded against the tree trunk. The fire spread quickly and the tree bark popped and sizzled under the intense heat. The dry tree caught fire, the flames spreading to the branches overhead.

The cyclone moved toward Champion and suddenly Naveen realized his error. The fireballs were being extinguished. The force of the wind was snapping away any fuel the fire would need to continue.

Naveen groaned.

In his over anxious state, he had used too many magic spells to bring down the vampire.

He was impatient to get the job done and now it was being turned against him. The cyclone was closer to the vampire and the fire spell he used on the vampire was being sucked away by the force of the cyclone. The wind was strong and it picked up the loose branches and leaves, blinding Naveen temporarily as he turned away from the wind.

With a wave of his staff, Naveen dismissed the magic-induced winds. When the winds died down, Naveen looked carefully at the tree, looking for a body. He frowned at first, and then the idea that he won grew until he turned and gave Jared a triumphant smile.

It was obvious to Naveen the fire had consumed the vampire and it had been dusted away, leaving no trace of its existence behind.

Naveen walked toward the burning tree, wanting a closer inspection of where the vampire died. He searched the ground. "Where is the body?" He searched for traces of dust on the ground. He had heard that an outline of a vampire's body would be left behind—the only evidence that a vampire had ever existed. Something rustled in the tree branches above.

Naveen glanced upward and a boot slammed against his head, pushing him to the ground. Blackness rushed toward him with an angry hammer slammed against his head. The last thought Naveen had was: He failed his magic and his magic failed him.

Champion landed on top of Naveen and drove the wizard to the ground, knocking him out. Champion hissed and reached for the wizard's staff. When he touched it, the wood burned him. He yelled in pain, and left it alone. The vampire stood up and surveyed his work.

Jared watched as the vampire glanced sideways at the tree where Nix was still pinned, looked sideways at the still form of Rowena on her side, and looked contemptuously down at Naveen sprawled on his back unconscious.

The meaning wasn't lost on Jared.

Champion turned and faced him.

"I am told there is something special about you."

"Who would say that?" asked Jared.

"I cannot say."

"Cannot say or am commanded not to say?"

Champion shrugged his shoulders. "Either way, the result is the same."

Jared stepped forward, glancing at all three of his fallen companions. "What about them?"

"There is nothing special about them," Champion said.

Champion walked closer. "You are special, or so it would seem."

"I am nothing special."

"You are too modest."

"You could've killed them, any of them. Why didn't you?"

Champion stopped and tilted his head to one side, allowing a brief smile to flash across his face.

"Because," Jared said, finally understanding the gambit, "it was all a ruse."

Champion shook his head. "My king sends his apologies. You were never meant to be poisoned. The rogue vampire and his band are still on the loose—he will be taken care of, sooner or later."

"Minus three of his kind."

Champion bowed, "If you are to fight against vampires, more training is needed, especially if one lonely vampire can disrupt four wayward travelers."

"How many days to your kingdom?"

"Three nights, maybe four depending upon your speed." Champion stepped back.

"What? Aren't we going to fight?"

Champion moved quickly away, rushing past Naveen and Nix and then stopped. He turned and said in a low voice, pitched just so. "See you later, Jared."

Jared inhaled slowly and watched as Champion stepped into the surrounding darkness and disappeared, neither sight nor sound betraying him. In a low voice, he said in a whisper, "How did he know my name?"

Chapter Fourteen

NIX STRUGGLED HELPLESSLY against his own dagger that kept him pinned against the tree. He tried to reach the handle and yank it, but the blade was embedded too deeply into the bark and he was at such an odd angle that he couldn't properly get leverage on it. He raised his hands to try to pull the dagger out of the tree, for the tenth time.

"I got you," Jared said. With knife in hand, he cut through the clothes that held Nix pinned to the tree. Nix fell to the ground.

Nix got to his feet quickly, but it was awkward, his wrists tied in front of him. "My clothes are ripped."

"Besides your clothes, are you okay?" Jared asked.

"Yeah, I guess."

"You were brave. Not many people would have done what you did, throwing yourself out there with only a small blade to defend yourself and vanquish an enemy." Jared sheathed his knife and helped Nix back to the camp fire.

"Why didn't he k-kill us?" Naveen sat in front of the fire, his head in his hands.

"He did," Jared said.

Nix glanced down at Rowena, knees drawn up, arms wrapped around her legs, staring into the fire. He kneeled and warmed his hands against the fire.

They all sat around the fire, each lost in their thoughts.

Nix glanced at Rowena and reached out to touch her, but she brushed away his hand and stared into the fire. Let her be, he thought. They were all hurt.

Nix shook his head.

The vampire defeated them as easily as if Nix were to walk into a diamond seller to steal a diamond studded necklace.

Nix took a stick and poked the burning wood. He didn't have a chance against the vampire and knew it. It went against everything he had done before now. He had never sacrificed himself for others before

But what Rowena was willing to do, to give up her life for her son, stirred something inside him. His life didn't seem all that important. Not as important as Rowena traveling to retrieve her son and gaining back her family.

He didn't have family.

He stared at the point where wood turned to ash.

He inhaled deeply and something settled into him: he would sacrifice himself again, for her. He glanced at her. Why? Was it love? No. He didn't love her. It was her sacrifice for her son that made him want her to succeed. If he had a mother, he would want her to be like Rowena.

He settled easily and inhaled the cool air and then exhaled and felt comfortable with his realization. He wouldn't sacrifice himself for the damn wizard. And Jared could more than handle himself in a fight. But the woman had courage and fire. He liked that.

He looked over at her and smiled.

Rowena kept her hands wrapped around her, the blanket hiding her face. Her panting breath an aftermath of her breakdown.

If she closed her eyes, she could still see the vampire looking at her with its red eyes, the lips stretched wide revealing the fangs that were ready to devour her. The fangs came closer with each second.

There was violence and intent behind those eyes. And there was that other something that was alien and wild that leapt through her and wiggled into her brain and slid down her spine and made her want to run away.

She faced worse.

The real horror was imagining seeing her son at the hands of a monster like him. She failed to protect him. She could easily see the blood drained from him, the life crashed out of him.

She had failed to protect him, and she had failed to save him.

She was a mother and she failed to save Steen, her son.

Death was coming or had already come and she was helpless to stop it. Helpless and frightened, she couldn't save him. She was on a fool's mission. She was inches from death and she knew it. And the monster knew it. She balled her fists and thought of her son—and the hope she had in her—dwindled and slipped through her fingers.

If he died, then she would die.

And if she died, then her son was dead and what was the use of living if there wasn't any hope?

In a black well in her mind, she fell a long distance and landed hard. She lost all control and cried. She hid the sobs deep inside herself, closing her eyes. She wasn't a mother anymore. Rather, she was a child who had just lost her father; his strong arms had sheltered her, but now she was naked to the elements.

She inhaled and opened her eyes, looking out from the blanket wrapped around her and into the fire.

"You okay?" Nix sat next to her. He offered her a cup of liquid.

She shook her head and stared at the fire.

She had to gather up her strength. Her father would be ashamed of her. Her dead husband would also shake his head at her. And her son? What kind of mother was she to abandon him just because a monster stared her down? She grew angry at herself for giving up so easily. She rocked back and forth, flexing her fingers, open, close, open, close.

She stared into the fire. She prided herself on her toughness; and she prided herself on being a mother-wolf to her son. A mother-wolf would never back down. She might hide, she might be cunning, she might follow after the enemy, but she would never give up.

She had a son to rescue and she had no time for her fear.

And then she remembered: Champion said, "*Your son is safe. For now. We have plans for the children and wish them no harm.*"

She pulled a knife out of her sheath and felt the handle in her hand. She closed the fingers of her other hand around the blade.

Feel the cold, she thought. Feel the sharpness. Your son needs you to be like this knife: you are steel, you are sharp and you are death to any that get in your way.

She removed the sharp edge of the knife from her hand and, looking down at her bloody hand, she wrapped it up in cloth.

She had a son to rescue.

Naveen turned from the fire, and looked out into the darkness. His head hurt like hell. He felt stupid for thinking he had the vampire where he wanted him. He wasn't good at combat magic; that was true. Near the end he thought he had the vampire, but he was obviously wrong.

"W-why d-didn't he k-kill us?"

The words rang in his head, circling around his mind and he didn't feel any solace in them. Why did the vampire defeat them and yet leave them untouched.

He had seen the mere shadow of something up there and before he could react it was too late. He had only a second to react and his mind was filled with four thoughts all crowding together on him. The thoughts shoved and pushed against him as he tried to order them as best he could and then the words tripped and spilled over his tongue and he couldn't say a word.

He was never any good in combat magic.

Combat magic required thinking on your feet. Naveen could do that. In fact, he was one of the best students in his class. But whenever he opened his mouth, especially under stress, he stuttered and the words would trip out of him.

Words were important to magic.

If he didn't get the words right, then the spell was damaged before he even started.

What could he do? He had to do something, but what?

He stared at his wizard's staff. It represented several years of study and, for the staff itself, six months of hard work to fashion it. He had to find the right tree. A Mallor tree. Then he had to cut it down and select the right piece of wood from the tree. Then he blessed the wood with energy and made plans for it.

All the things he loved about being a wizard, about being able to channel the energy of the earth, air, water and fire, now left him frustrated. Since the first time he lifted up the staff and took on the responsibility of the four elements, he felt proud when he accepted his fate as wizard. But now he felt ashamed and bitter. His hand tightened around his staff.

If he could replace one thing about himself it would be his tongue. His mind was blazing fast. But his tongue was as slow and inept as a turtle.

Naveen scowled and turned toward his companions. They each stared into the fire, dwelling on their own private thoughts. Naveen bit his lower lips and knew he craved more power and the ability to smash any vampire to the ground like a bug.

A wheel inside a wheel.

Jared stared into the fire and pondered Champion's words. It was obvious that Champion had followed him for some time. How else would he know Jared's name?

If Jared had to compare his speed and skills against that of the vampire, especially at night, he knew the vampire had the edge. Supernatural speed was hard to go up against and win, unless you had something to counter it. Jared pushed that thought aside.

Did somebody want them to come and get the children? Was it that easy? Or was this a trap of some kind?

He shook his head. He had more questions than he had answers for.

Death, Jared realized, could have come to all of them tonight. The simple truth was they weren't ready.

This quest was dangerous and it showed Jared just how much they had to improve if they were going to come out of this.

Alive.

A tired grin spread across his face.

They were already dead. Everybody had a death curse upon them. Everybody except Rowena and the other two, Bruce and Rygil.

They didn't need friction on this trip.

They had a mission: find the children and return them.

He owed it to Naveen and Nix to push himself as hard as possible, for their sake. They didn't ask for the death spell to be placed on them, and Jared felt responsible for them.

Had Champion seen him before? Had he seen Champion before?

Jared searched his memory and nowhere could he pull up a memory of ever seeing Champion, either as a vampire or as a man. How old was Champion? How long had he been turned?

They needed a good night's rest, and then they all needed to train harder, and act as a unit. Individually, they would be destroyed, but if they stayed together and acted as one, they would have a chance. Bruce and Rygil were the odd people out.

He turned to search for them. Jared looked around and frowned. "Has anybody seen Bruce and Rygil?"

Naveen spoke as if from a faraway place. "They took off. Somewhere between Nix and Rowena they got on their horses and rode away."

Jared nodded. It made sense they'd save their own hide. At least, those two were gone. He breathed in deeply and nodded. It was better this way. The excitement suddenly left him and he felt extremely tired.

Champion told him they needed to practice, but as he looked at the others staring into the fire, it was something that would wait till tomorrow.

Jared wanted nothing more than to shut his eyes and sleep.

"No need for a watch tonight," Jared said. He stretched and yawned. "We're safe tonight. Everybody get some sleep."

Jared unrolled his blanket and lay out on top of it. He closed his eyes and quickly remembered nothing more.

Chapter Fifteen

THE PREVIOUS NIGHT'S defeat hung over them all day and even the weather mirrored their disposition. The sunlight never broke through; rather, the grey overcast dogged them. They rode in silence until they rounded a corner in the road and discovered a village.

They stopped their horses and considered the village from a safe distance.

"We can stop there and see what supplies we can use," Rowena said.

"Is that wise?" Nix asked, scratching his head. "Won't the spell know I'm not going forward?"

All eyes looked over at Naveen.

Naveen coughed and then answered. "I don't think we'll be in danger. We've already traveled many hours today. We've made good progress. And frankly, what Rowena said makes sense. If we need to stock up on supplies, now would be a good time."

Jared leaned forward and pushed off the stirrups, standing him in the saddle. His backside was sore from riding all day. "Then it's settled." He leaned forward and patted his horse's neck. "Find whatever tools and tricks to use against the vampires. But remember nobody is to know our business. We travel in secret."

Rowena said, "But if they knew what we were doing they could help us."

"No. They won't," Jared said.

"What proof do you have?" She gave him a fierce look and it reminded Jared of the fury she displayed when fighting him dressed as a woodsman.

"Think about it. We go to Vampire Nation to take back children that don't belong to them. Yes they would care, but they would care more that nothing bad comes down around their heads. We tell nobody our business."

"Don't they have generous natures here?"

"Even generosity has limits."

"I think you're wrong."

"I don't care," Jared said. "Just don't tell anybody our plans."

"I still don't get it."

Nix scratched his head and said, "It's simple. You live next to your neighbor on one side and on the other side of your neighbor is a hornet's nest. The hornet's nest is obviously closer to your neighbor than you. Would you want someone disturbing that nest if it was right next to your house?"

Rowena opened her mouth to respond, then closed it. She squinted at Nix.

"She gets it," Jared said.

Naveen dismounted and stretched. "Quiet is the word."

Rowena frowned. "What's our story then?"

Jared said, "We travel to find herbs to heal our sick companions. Let's find some lodging and then we can go our separate ways."

Jared handed his reins to the small boy. His forthright smile and dark eyes paid careful attention. "Take our horses," Jared pointed to all four of the horses they had, "and give them food and shelter."

"Yes, sir."

"Who is your master, boy?"

"His name is Eric, sir."

"Good. When the horses are taken care of, we'll need two rooms for lodging tonight."

"Aye, sir."

The boy gathered up the reins of Jared's and Nix's horse and led the animals into the small stable.

Shortly afterwards, Jared met with Eric the tavern owner. The large man greeted him with a welcoming smile and earnest brown eyes. He brushed the red hair off his forehead and showed them their lodgings for the night and accepted their money. After the arrangements were made, the travelers went outside.

Naveen and Nix looked across the street. One had an expectant look and the other had a thoughtful look to him. Naveen strode across the street and disappeared quickly into the crowd. Nix took a different direction and walked down a dirt road moving past the marketplace vendors and soon he was swallowed up by the distance and the people in the marketplace.

Jared watched as the wizard and thief went in separate directions. He turned to Rowena and said, "Don't you want to be on your own? I've never known a woman who didn't delight in looking in at the different shops for something she can have."

"I'm still," she hesitated. "It lingers. I'd rather have company right now."

Jared remembered her curled up on the ground after her encounter with Champion. He wanted to know what happened; he could only guess. Something broke inside her last night. When he woke up this morning he found her quiet and keeping to herself, with a hardness built up around her, and he noticed a steely resolution in her eyes as if she was still fighting the vampire right now, in her mind.

"It'll pass."

"How can you be so sure?"

"Because it does. What's the most important thing to you?"

"Getting my son back, safe and unharmed," Rowena said.

"Focus on that. Fear only paralyzes people."

"What's the antidote to that?"

Jared glanced across the street and noticed the careful glances of the villagers toward them; to them they were nothing but strangers. And strangers usually brought trouble with them.

"The antidote to fear is hope and a tough hide."

"I don't follow."

Jared picked up a stick from the ground and moved to a side alley away from the main foot traffic. Rowena followed.

He kneeled and drew a circle in the dirt with the stick. "This is the whole world," Jared said.

"Okay."

He made a smaller circle inside the larger one. "This is you. It represents everything you know."

Rowena stared at the circle within the larger circle and said, "So?"

Jared folded his hands. "Everything that happens to you has two outcomes. You can either control it, whatever it is, or you let it control you. There is no middle ground. The more you control yourself, the more you control your mind. And with your mind under control, the better able you'll be to overcome obstacles that get in your way."

"And the vam ..." Rowena glanced around and changed her choice of words so as to not frighten any who might overhear them. "The problems are obstacles?"

"Exactly. They're just obstacles. Deadly, but they can be killed. Just like us." With a flick of his wrist Jared tossed the stick away. He rose and they continued walking. "Fire can kill them. A well placed sword thrust can kill them. Don't lose hope."

"How?"

"Don't think how hard they are to kill, rather think about what you can do and build on that."

Her green eyes seemed lost. "I don't follow."

"Actually, you followed us pretty well that first day."

"I had to be with you and your party."

"Why?"

"Because my child needs me."

"Why?"

"Because I won't give up until my child is back home safe with me."

They crossed the street.

"Feel the passion you have for your child. Nothing can stop you, right?"

"Nothing will get in my way."

"Keep that thought and feeling inside you. Now, for the hard part." Jared looked into her green eyes and he saw desperation flicker in them. "What scared you last night?"

Rowena swallowed. "The fangs. I thought I'd be swallowed alive by them, and if I was gone then my baby would be lost forever."

"Face that fear."

"How?"

Jared leaned Rowena against the side of a nearby building.

She started to object but stopped as she brushed up against the wall and Jared looked intently at her.

"Close your eyes."

"Why?"

"Do it!"

She searched his face and frowned. She exhaled and closed her eyes.

Jared watched as she breathed deeply and kept her arms to her sides. "See the fangs?"

"Yes."

"Feel it?"

"Yes."

"How does it make you feel?"

"Small and scared."

"Now change the picture. I want you to feel the passion you have for your son and for his safety. Feel your strength as you protect him from harm."

"Ohh," Rowena shifted her weight. "I feel stronger."

"How do you feel now?"

"I feel invincible."

"Open your eyes." Jared saw a brief smile play across Rowena's face. "That is how you build hope and courage in yourself. Think of the good things in your life."

"Thank you," Rowena said. With an anxious look in her eyes, she bit her lower lip. "But feeling good isn't enough."

"I agree. We have a difficult journey in front of us. But would you rather have a determined attitude inside yourself or would you rather have doubt and fear circle you like jackals, nipping at your heels and drawing your attention away from what is important."

"And what's that?"

"The only important thing on this mission, above all other concerns, is getting the children back. I don't care how many obstacles we have, or what we have to go through, go around, or go under or over, we will get those children back and nothing will stop us."

"You speak like a warrior," Rowena said.

"Do I?"

"Well, not exactly. You seem to have a deeper mind than most."

Jared looked at Rowena and said, "We will get those children back, and we will get your child back."

"How do you know that?"

"Because I feel that we are just pawns in a game that I do not fully understand; but we are pawns nonetheless. Another hand is moving us across the game board."

"Who? Grinbell the wizard?"

"He may be a part of it. But I don't know for sure. Last night's encounter with Champion tipped me off that something wasn't on the up and up."

"Really? What was that?"

Jared ignored her question and said, "Let's go search for supplies."

"You're not going to tell me are you?"

"Not until I know something for sure."

She frowned.

"Let's go get some supplies."

Chapter Sixteen

NAVEEN WORKED HIS way through the streets and soon found himself standing in front of an herb store. The oval window, covered with grime and dirt, revealed a distorted, blurred image of a man inside the store. He saw movement at the counter.

It wouldn't hurt to look inside. Maybe he would find something useful. Naveen pushed open the heavy oak door and entered the store.

He walked past the dusty shelves and heard two voices talking. One spoke heatedly in urgent, measured tones; the other pleading, almost whimpering in submission. At the counter, Naveen discovered the shopkeeper and a broad shouldered man in a heated discussion.

The broad shouldered man reached across the counter and grabbed the tall, thin shop keeper. The old man, tried to pull back, but the other man held him in place, his fist wrapped in the man's tunic.

"I'll take what I want from you, old man, and you'll like it or else."

Naveen bristled. The broad shouldered man wore a black cloak over a gray tunic and black pants. A sword was strapped to his waist. With the cloak pushed back, the sword could be drawn easily against any challenger.

But the really troubling detail, especially to Naveen, was the staff in the left hand of the cloaked figure.

It had markings and sigils across the staff, similar to Naveen's own matrix of magic.

What was a wizard doing threatening an old man?

Naveen felt his anger rise. This was too much.

Magic gave one power to serve others, not to threaten and beat people into submission. It was unethical and immoral what was happening to the old man. Every bone in his body cried out for justice. But maybe he was hasty. Maybe the old man did something. Surely, however bad it looked now, the old man did something egregious to deserve this treatment. No wizard would act as base as this broad shouldered man, no wizard was this cruel.

"Is this the right place for herbs?" Naveen asked.

The tension in the air cooled between the two men as the cloaked wizard turned, facing Naveen, revealing an ugly scar across the wizard's left cheek. The scar was thick and stretched from the left cheekbone down to the corner of the wizard's mouth. "We're having a private conversation and we don't wish to be dis ..."

Naveen straightened up and planted his feet on the floor, facing both of them. He looked at them both, his own staff held in his right hand—the wizard's staff that he had worked on for six months. The sigils glowed with power and energy.

"Ah, a fellow wizard," the broad shouldered wizard said. "I was just teaching this fellow it is not right to mess with our kind. We are quick to anger, and we punish those we see fit to punish."

"Is this true?" Naveen asked the shopkeeper, never taking his eyes off the wizard. "Was he teaching you a lesson?"

"I know nothing of the dealings of powerful men like yourself. A wizard is beyond my humble calling. I am just a meager shopkeeper. Herbs and potions, I have. Earth lore and plant magic, I know; but that is all I know."

"Leave us," the broad shouldered wizard said, pushing the shopkeeper back with his hand as he freed himself from the tunic.

The shopkeeper stumbled and caught himself. Then he bowed his bald head, and with nervous eyes glanced between the two wizards. He stepped back, turned and disappeared into the back end of his shop.

"My name is Roloth; I am a wizard in these parts."

"I am Naveen."

"Why are you here? My cousins and I don't need any help."

"Cousins?"

"We are the staff here and we run it the way we see fit. There is no sword and shield in these parts, the area is too poor, but we protect it and keep the people safe."

"I saw how you handled the situation."

Roloth's dark eyes bore into him. It felt like Roloth was measuring his face, remembering it for all eternity. Roloth appraised him for a second longer and then allowed a small, wary smile to cross his lips. The smile died just at the cheekbones, never making it to the eyes. In a low, conversational tone, Roloth said, "They obey us because they fear us."

"You misuse your power and station, Roloth."

Roloth said, "And you can stop me?"

Naveen faced Roloth. "Stop you? Remind you of your calling. We are brothers of the same order. We should work together. Can't you see that what you did was wrong? Treating that shopkeeper in that way was no better than ordering around a poor animal."

"What is going on here?" a new voice said from behind Naveen.

Naveen turned and two more wizards stood behind him. One of the wizards, the tall, slender one watched Naveen carefully while the other wizard moved until he was in front of Naveen.

Naveen saw the move for what it was. He was out numbered. To his right was Roloth. In front of him was a stocky wizard, with two missing fingers on his right hand. And to his left was a tall slender wizard with a scruffy beard.

"Mmm." Naveen said, lost in thought.

"Very impolite. Do you know who we are?" asked the stocky wizard; his right hand, minus two fingers, gripped the staff firmly.

Naveen climbed out of his crowded thoughts and blurted, "Three weird brothers?"

The tall wizard shook his head. "That is an insult. We are wizards in this part. People respect us."

"Good for you," Naveen said, searching for a way out. Everywhere he moved, they countered him, blocking his progress. "Excuse me."

The tall one said, "I think not."

The stocky wizard said, "What should we do?"

"A lesson learned is a sorrow saved," Roloth said.

Naveen turned, the hairs on the back of his neck stood up, and a spell pummeled him, stunning him to the ground. His mind reeled from the unexpected attack. The last thing Naveen heard was a chorus of brutal laughter following him into the dark as he went unconscious.

Naveen opened his eyes and saw three pairs of boots on the ground next to his face. What was he doing down here? His thoughts were sluggish and he felt the cold from the ground press into his face. He shivered and raised his head.

"He is awake," said a voice.

"Then let's show him what kind of example we can make of him. A lesson learned is a sorrow saved I always say."

Naveen blinked and then rolled onto his back. He pushed up from the ground and fought against the motion of the world seesawing from one side to the other. When the world stopped turning so much, he squinted and made out the three wizards standing before him. Acting as one, they moved away from him and drew out their wands.

They pointed their wands at his chest and a force grabbed him. Naveen felt invisible tendrils slide over and under his body, wrapping themselves around him. His body lifted off the ground and rose in the air. He fought to stay on the ground, squirming and raging against invisible bonds to break free.

His staff was on the ground, but it was painfully out of reach. He stretched his arm out for it, but he was too far away.

"You can't do this. It isn't right."

Roloth stepped forward, placing his wand inside his coat pocket. He leaned against a nearby tree. "Right has nothing to do with it. Power and obedience is what people understand. As will you."

Roloth nodded to the other two wizards.

They pointed their wands at him.

Naveen kept rising off the ground and now he moved toward the nearby tree. He rose past the trunk to where the branches split off. He thought he was going the crash into the branches when suddenly he felt the invisible tendrils spin his body around until he was turned upside down.

With his feet in the air, his head closest to the ground, and blood rushing to his head, Naveen concentrated on getting out of this mess. He kept rising, his feet closer to the branches.

He had to do something, but what?

Something slithered out from the tree. Naveen gulped. It looked like a snake. He looked closer and saw vines from the tree wrap themselves around his ankle.

In the span of seconds, Naveen found himself hanging upside down and tethered to a tree by very strong, magically induced, vines.

A young boy turned the corner and Naveen saw him out of the corner of his vision. The boy, who looked familiar, glanced at him and then over to the other three wizards. The tall wizard shouted at the boy and said, "Go on now. No business of yours."

The boy turned and ran.

Nix came out of a bakery, carrying a loaf of bread. He bit into the fresh loaf, still warm in his hand, and chewed heartily. The taste was sweet and the bread, with fresh butter on it, made Nix feel a sense of contentment and satisfaction that he never got from any other source.

Nix wondered about that but then shrugged. Others liked their grog and spirits, but he preferred meat and bread.

He took another bite out of the bread when a boy turned the corner and headed toward the tavern. The boy had a serious expression on his face. Nix wondered about it for the span of a whole second and then bit into the loaf again. The bread tasted good.

Then the boy saw him and stopped. Nix wondered about that and then the boy made a straight line for him, at first, walking fast and then breaking into a run to Nix.

Nix realized it was the tavern boy, the one who sheltered their horses in the barn. The boy moved excitedly from side to side. He was a bundle of energy, with his cheeks rosy from exertion. "Sir, excuse me. He needs your help."

"Who needs my help?"

"Your wizard friend."

Nix shook his head. "He's no friend of mine." And he bit into the bread and chewed more.

"Sorry sir. I thought you could help. He needs it."

The boy turned away and the perfect moment for Nix to enjoy himself was gone. Here he was enjoying his brief time alone walking among the people, eating a loaf of delicious bread, and enjoying the quiet time he had to himself, when obviously Naveen had run into some sort of trouble. It certainly wasn't any trouble with vampires. Couldn't Naveen handle himself?

"Hey, boy."

The lad turned. "Yes sir."

"Have some bread." He handed the boy the rest of his loaf.

"Thank you, sir."

"Show me."

The situation was terrible. Naveen was upside down, hanging from the tree by his ankle. And beside Naveen, guarding the wizard, were three other men. They all had staffs like Naveen's. Again, the situation was terrible.

It was clear to Nix that Naveen had done something to incur the wrath of the three wizards. Of course, he looked down the length of the back alley, taking time to remember vividly the upside down hanging that caused Naveen's hair to stand on end.

One should savor such moments as these.

But it didn't matter. Naveen, even if he did interrupt Nix's couple of hours of pleasure, needed help. And there was no one else to help Naveen but Nix.

Nix couldn't just walk up there. The wizards would be suspicious. He would be. So what kind of story could he make up?

And then he knew. He would tell the same story that got Naveen thrown into jail in the first place. Foretelling is an art and that wizard had no skill in the matter. Confident of his cover story, Nix walked briskly into the alley and walked straight up to the tree and Naveen and the three wizards.

"Well greetings, good sir," said Nix. "It looks like you chased a cat up the tree."

"Go away, sir. This is no concern of yours."

"Oh, of course. I never trouble others in their affairs. It's too rude. But still, he does look familiar. I once had a wizard I paid great sums of money to foretell my future. But the man was a complete mess."

"Great sums of money?"

"Well, not to me, you understand. But when the foretelling turned false, I had him thrown in jail. He was a tall man, with a long nose and narrow face. Dark, beady eyes that made him look like a bird." Nix turned and studied the upside down form dangling in front of him. "I don't believe it. That's him. That's the wizard who couldn't foretell my future. How did he get here?"

Two other men quickly appeared. The one with the scar across his face said, "He slipped and fell up a tree."

"That's very good."

They all chuckled.

"Can I take him off your hands?"

The bearded wizard said, "What price?"

Nix considered it. "If I wait till you're done with him, I may lose all interest in the matter. But if I could have him right now, I have gold coins ready for his release."

"Show us?" the tall wizard said.

"Before I do that are you three agreeable to this arrangement? It is a pleasant day, and as much as I would want to take this wizard and show him justice, it rolls off my back like water off a duck."

"What would you do to him?" the bearded wizard asked.

"I would show him my displeasure at being taken as a fool."

"Exactly how?" asked the scarred face wizard.

"That is my concern."

"But it is ours as well," said the tall wizard. "We are all of a class here. We are all wizards. This is wizards business. What we do, we do among ourselves, and we need no outsiders to help or participate in what we do. So, we will not turn over a brother wizard to you, but since you want to pay us for delivering him to you to be roughed up, you can instead, be roughed up by us."

"Sir, you take me for the wrong reason." Nix stepped back, hands held up.

"No. We take you for the right reason. We can deal with our own, but we won't allow outsiders to push us around. We are wizards: we command the four elements. Show us your money or it'll go so much worse for you."

Nix brought out his coin purse and it was snatched out of his hand. The contents of the purse were poured into a flat coarse hand. "He had only four pieces of gold in here."

"Do you think?" asked the tall one.

"I do," the three fingered wizard said.

"It'll be my pleasure," the scarred face wizard said.

Before Nix could do anything he was lifted by invisible hands into the air, spun around until he was looking at the whole world upside down, and then he was attached to the tree by a vine around his ankle, next to Naveen.

"Hello," Naveen said. "Thank you so much for your expert help."

Nix felt the blood rush to his head. "You're so very welcome," he said sharply and watched, upside down, as the three wizards laughed and walked away.

Chapter Seventeen

THE TAVERN BOY pointed down the back alley. "There they are!"

It was night and Jared glanced down the alley. Hanging from under a tree he saw two figures.

The moon hung low in the night sky as Jared and the tavern boy moved closer. Jared could hear two voices, the closer he came to the tree.

"I came here to help you," Nix said.

"I didn't ask for your help."

"Whether you asked for help or not, I came here and when I get free of this I'm going to kick you and your friends up and down the street. I have never met such hard headed people in all my life."

"I would think that if any kicking were to be done, it would be done on you. You don't go up against a superior force unless you have a plan," Naveen hissed. "Any fool knows that."

"And any fool," Jared said, standing in front of them, with his arms folded across his chest, "would know his surroundings better." Jared withdrew his knife and cut through the vine that held Naveen upside down.

Naveen crashed to the ground.

Jared moved toward Nix. "And what's your excuse?"

He cut through Nix's vine and the thief dropped to the ground like a sack of rocks. "I was helping *him*."

Naveen raised himself up on one elbow. "Remind me not to use your help next time."

Naveen got to his feet, brushing off his robes. "I am so angry."

"Angry at them?" Jared stepped closer to Naveen. "I heard it was three to one."

"I was angry at myself."

"Why?"

"My tongue should be cut from my mouth."

"Why? I don't understand."

"Never mind," the wizard said, brushing off his clothes.

"No. I'm not going to *never mind*. We are going into dangerous country to rescue children from vampires. If something is wrong then I need to know about it now."

Naveen closed his eyes and squeezed tight his fists. "I c-command forces of nature. I know the magic purpose of fire; I know the h-hallowed edicts of air; I know the magic combinations and h-hidden designs in nature, but I c-cannot control my tongue when I am faced with an onslaught of decisions."

"You get tongue-tied. You're still a wizard, right?"

"I am. But I am a wizard who trips over his tongue."

"Again, so what? You still control magic. What's the problem?"

"If I c-cannot speak it effectively, then my magic c-cannot work effectively."

"Then don't talk."

"That'll be the day," Nix said.

"Be quiet, thief," Jared said, staring at Nix, who was brushing himself off.

The thief avoided Jared's scolding look.

"How am I supposed to work magic then?" Naveen asked.

"You command the forces of nature, correct?"

"Yes."

"How?"

"With my words, my feeling, my intention."

"Do all wizards do that?"

"Yes, why?"

"Do you have to speak your intention?"

"No."

"Do you have to speak your feelings?"

"No."

"Do you need to speak your words?"

Naveen rocked back and forth in silence; his face a blank expression.

Jared repeated the question: "Naveen, do you need to *speak* your words?"

"Words can be spoken." Naveen had a distant look in his eyes.

"Or they can be silent," Jared said.

"Yes!" Naveen looked up at him, his eyes alight with fire.

"What is faster than thought?" Jared asked.

"Nothing."

Naveen glanced at Jared and then over to Nix. A grin spread across his face. "Nothing is faster than thought!"

Naveen started laughing and, turning to Nix he lifted up the thief and gave him a hug. "I need *your* help."

Nix stared back at the wizard. "You called me a fool. That hurt. I am no fool. I may be a lot of things, but not that."

"That was my poor choice of words, Nix. I am sorry. But you don't go into situations like that without a plan."

"What do you want my help with? I'd bet it's almost midnight right now."

Jared said, "Aye, it is late. We move on tomorrow."

Naveen released Nix and faced Jared. "If I am right, this will be a good night for everyone." Naveen turned to Nix. "Come with me. I need your help. You said earlier you came to my aid. Thank you for that. But this will be even more important, and I promise, less painful."

Nix shook his head. "In for a penny, in for a pound."

Naveen glanced around about and saw in the grass by the tree his discarded wizard's staff. Naveen held it in his hands, the familiar weight and instant sense of humming power he felt seep through the staff comforted him greatly. He was surprised by how much he came to rely on it.

"Everything seems to be in order," Naveen said, inspecting the staff carefully. "Nix, we have exciting work to do."

"Where are you two going?" Jared asked.

"It's a beautiful night. We go," Naveen said triumphantly, "to practice." Naveen started laughing as he and Nix walked away, their path taking them past the tree and out toward the nearby fields.

As they turned down the alley way and disappeared from sight, Jared glanced down at the tavern boy. "You did good."

The tavern boy looked down the empty alley way. "Will they be all right?"

The grassy field was empty, except for Naveen and Nix. Under the low hanging moon, Naveen stood with his arms outstretched and his eyes closed.

Nix felt the heft of the stone in his hand. He glanced down at his feet and noticed the small mountain of rocks stacked in a neat pile. He turned to his left and noticed the dark shapes of cows in the field, and with the cattle were two dogs, keeping an eye on the herd.

Thirty feet away stood Naveen. With his arms outstretched, he said, "Throw it!" commanded Naveen.

Nix extended his arm behind him, took aim at Naveen, and threw the rock straight at his target, aiming low because he didn't think Naveen was one hundred percent right in the head, and he let the rock fly.

Nix remembered the concern in Jared's voice and didn't want to be responsible for being the person who injured their only wizard.

The rock sailed across the distance.

Nix heard muttering sounds from Naveen and the rock, as if it struck an invisible shield, changed its course and turned downwards sharply.

Nix couldn't believe his eyes. Of course, he had aimed low, but he saw a definite change of course for the rock.

The rock landed with a thud against Naveen's boot.

Naveen opened his eyes wide in pain and yelped. He hopped on his other foot while letting out a string of curses. The wizard tried to balance himself on one foot, but he couldn't and fell crashing to the ground.

Nix ran to him. "I tried to aim low," he explained. "But I'm a terrible shot, I suspect."

Naveen rubbed his sore foot. "What's the use?"

Nix shook his head. "You blocked it. Don't you get it?"

"I did?"

"Yes. I saw it. It was marvelous."

"My eyes were closed."

"Why don't you open them?"

"I need to concentrate. It's all new to me. Later, I could probably do it with my eyes open."

"You didn't use words, right?"

"No, but what's the use? My shield didn't work."

"An hour ago you were all fired up. You can't let a little thing upset you."

"I'm no good at this."

"No," Nix said, looking down at the wizard. "You have magic. We need you. We need something to equalize us against the vampires."

"But I'm not good with combat magic. It's no use."

Nix lowered himself and was inches from Naveen's face. "No it isn't. Just focus on one thing; focus really fast on it; then let go."

Naveen stared back at the thief, his mouth opened in shock. "How does a thief know about mind control?"

Nix settled down next to Naveen, who sat on the grass rubbing his sore foot. "When I enter a target's place, ready to steal something, I have to control my reactions and keep my mind sharp. Being focused helps with that."

"Okay," Naveen said, nodding. "That makes sense. Let's try again."

Nix helped the wizard to his feet and handed him his staff. "Do it all in your mind; use your thoughts. I know you can do it."

"Go back to your pile of rocks. I'll be ready in a minute," Naveen said, walking tenderly on his sore foot.

Nix ran to the pile of rocks and glanced back at the wizard. "Ready?"

There was no answer from the wizard and suddenly Nix got an intense urge to aim the rock at Naveen's head and wake him up. Was the wizard paying attention?

Nix wanted more than anything right now to sleep and he had nobody to blame but the stupid wizard. If he wasn't going to pay attention then at least Nix could give him a pay back for not treating this with the proper respect it deserved. He exhaled, and without thinking, he threw the rock as hard as he could.

It was almost over before it started.

Nix watched as the rock shot across the space and then there was a brief flash of golden light, a vivid bluish spark of light, revealing a domed surface in front of the wizard. The rock sailed for the wizard's head and it bounced off the domed surface of the shield and into the field by the cows.

The dogs, excited by something landing near them, started barking and went off to sniff out the intruder.

Nix jumped up and down excited. He ran toward Naveen, who finally opened his eyes. Nix was the first to speak. "That was marvelous. That was great."

"What do you mean?"

"Didn't you see?"

"What?"

"The rock went straight for you, but then there was a dome around you, not all the way, and then it struck it and bluish sparks lit up the area. The rock fell that way into the field. Did you hear the dogs barking?"

"I did that?"

"The rock didn't alter course by itself."

"Let's practice some more," Naveen said, a surge of pride filling his voice.

"Hey, why sleep?" Nix said, "In another hour or so the rooster will be up and a new day begins."

Morning arrived and Nix and Naveen walked back from the field toward the tavern. The streets were still empty, and the tavern was down the road seven structures away. Nix yawned and stumbled, caught himself and said, "I'm depressed."

"Why? This was the best night of my life. Magic wise. I made a breakthrough."

"For you, that's good. But I'm still just a thief against vampires. They're quicker than me."

Nix shook his head. "Rowena has great passion for her child. Jared has a great sense of planning and tactics about him, and no doubt, abilities we haven't seen yet. You have your wizard skills. But where's my edge?"

Naveen's face lit up. "You, my friend, go to sleep. A couple of extra hours will do you good."

"What about you?"

"I have work to do."

They were outside the tavern when the tavern boy stepped out into the street. "There you are. You're back."

"Yes, lad," Naveen said. "And my friend here is very tired."

"Friend?" The tavern boy looked from Naveen to Nix and Nix remembered what he said the other day about Naveen not being his friend.

"Friendships take time to develop," Nix said quickly.

The tavern boy nodded and said, "I tried to help you."

Naveen said, "It was a great and mighty help you provided us, a kindness that cannot be repaid, except with more kindness and consideration back for you."

The boy looked at them both and said, "There is something to you both."

Nix suddenly stopped and caution was clearly seen on his face. "What do you mean?"

"Yes," Naveen said. "What do your eyes see?"

The tavern boy considered them and said, "You, all of you, are on a mission."

"We are," Nix said quickly.

Naveen added, "We seek herbs that can heal our fallen comrades and brothers."

"If that is what you say," the tavern boy said.

"What do you say?" Nix asked, his eyes blurry and they felt like sand, making it hard and scratchy for him to move his eyes.

"There is more to all of you than meets the eye," the tavern boy said.

"Well," Naveen said, "if there is would you keep quiet about it?"

"Of course."

"Thank you." Naveen searched in his robes and pulled out a coin. He handed it to the tavern boy.

The tavern boy looked at the coin, felt the weight of it in his hand, and gave it back. "I don't need money to keep my mouth shut. But if you need an herb store, see the third store on the other side, one street over."

"Then this," Naveen said, handing the coin back to the tavern boy, "is for your help in locating for me an herb store."

Nix shook his head and he gained insight into the wizard. Naveen had discovered an herb store the other day, so it was obvious to Nix that Naveen was being nice to the kid. Never before had he seen a wizard treat a kid with special attention and kindness. The wizards he had seen, including Grinbell, were always filled up with their own self-importance.

Nix patted the boy on the head and moved toward the tavern door. He stopped and yawned. "Good night or, should I say, good day to you all." He opened the front door and disappeared.

"What's wrong with him?" asked the tavern boy.

"He was up all night."

"Oh, I don't like going out at night, not when everybody is sleeping anyway."

Naveen tilted his head to one side. "Why's that?"

"Too many strange things go on at night around here. It's safer inside."

Chapter Eighteen

HE ENTERED THE same shop as before but this time Naveen didn't see any evidence of Roloth and his wizard friends about. Instead of the old man standing behind the counter, like what he had witnessed yesterday, there was an old woman. He doubted she could help; but it never hurt to try.

He had come here looking for herbs that maybe could help Nix "have an edge" against the vampires while on their journey.

"Good morning, sir," the woman said. Her tone was pleasant and to the point. Her gray eyes, alert and aware, took him in and her eyes widened just a fraction and then a mask came over her face.

"I was hoping to see if you have any quicksilver available."

The old woman brought her hand to her chin and frowned. "Let me see," she said.

She turned and walked back from the counter into the stacks of shelves behind her. "We don't get much call for quicksilver. You know quicksilver is really the combination of two plants. It's the off-spring between Malora and Venaris."

Naveen raised his voice because he couldn't be sure if she would hear him from within the depths of the stacks. "Yes, I know my herbs, but was hoping for quicksilver itself."

The woman walked out of the stacks, a box in her hand. She beamed at him. "Yes, you are a lucky man today. I have a bottle of quicksilver for you. Mind you, not many people ask for it. It is rare."

Naveen raised an eyebrow at her.

"How much?"

The old woman named her price and Naveen considered it for a moment and then said, "You're a robber, you know that."

"If that's how you feel about it, I'll take it back and put it on my shelf." She leaned forward to grab the box, but Naveen reached forward and pushed her arms to one side with his hand.

"I've heard, from very reliable sources, that merchants like to haggle over prices."

"I've one question," said the old woman. "Tell me the answer, truthfully—and I'll now if you don't—and we can come to a mutually agreeable price."

Naveen found a smile broaden across his face. "Oh, Nix would like this."

"Who's Nix?" asked the old woman.

"Oh, this is for him."

The old woman nodded and asked, "Why do you want this rare herb?"

Naveen leaned closer. "Can you keep a secret?"

He paid the old woman for the quicksilver potion and when the old woman partially turned her back to him, Naveen dropped an emerald gemstone into the bottle and stopped up the potion again.

The woman bowed to him and gave him back change. "It's not often we get wizards that walk into my shop. Are you here long?"

"Yesterday another man was behind the counter. He and a wizard were in the middle of a discussion. And when I turned around two more of his friends showed up. Also very demanding."

"That's Roloth and his cousins, Jaen is the one missing fingers, and Haryek is the tall one. All three are wizards and all three are worthless." She spat on the floor on her side of the counter.

"Do they do that sort of thing often?"

"When don't they?"

Naveen leaned against the counter, closer to the old woman. "You don't seem frightened of them. Why?"

The old woman stepped back and folded her arms. "I was doing things before you were born and I know things that your kind scoff at. Wizards don't frighten me. Besides, I'm an old woman. What can they do to me? Break my bones, stab me with a knife? They won't."

"How come?"

"Because if you want any herbs, magical or otherwise, you see me."

"Magical or otherwise?"

"Yes."

"What is your training?"

"I cannot divulge that. I made a promise to an ancient and wise friend."

"Surely, you can make an exception in my case."

The old woman eyed him. Then she leaned close to him, almost nose to nose and whispered, "If you told me a secret and you wanted me to keep it because it was important to you, you'd want that, right."

"Yes, especially if it was important."

"Well I gave Nightwing my promise."

"Nightwing?" Naveen asked. "What is that?"

"It's a name I gave to the one who taught me how to make herbal potions."

"Magical or otherwise."

"My lips are sealed."

Naveen wondered how long the three wizards had been terrorizing the people in these parts and wondered at the old woman's strength. He swept the thought from his mind, and said, "What is the name of the old man who was here the other day?"

The old woman cracked a smile against her wrinkled face. "That is Heon."

"Any relation to you?"

"Yes, he's my brother. He works for me when I'm not here."

"Where is he now?"

"He is at home resting. He doesn't do too well when wizards confront him and tell him how things are going to be. Of course, I don't blame him. Nobody likes to be told what to do."

"My name is Naveen. I'm a wizard too."

"I gathered that. Not from around here, are you?"

"No. I am passing through with my companions. We go to search for herbs to help our fallen ones."

"What herbs do you need?"

"Good lady, you have a great store of herbs, but none that will help my companions. But this," he tapped the small bottle on the counter top, "will definitely help us."

"I saw you slip something into the potion. What did you do?"

Naveen grew alarmed for a moment and realized that the herbalist must have seen him. He thought he had made an easy movement of slipping the gemstone into the potion, but he was too hasty for his own good. "I added concentrated power to your potion. And I will adjust it as needed over the next day or so."

"For what purpose?"

"For mine," Naveen said, smiling at the clerk and keeping his lips closed.

"The only reason to add the power of the earth to a potion is to enhance it with a certain aspect and gems can do that, certainly. Gems can help one reach the spires of heaven or the crevices of hell. Not too many wizards or others know to do that." She bowed to him.

Naveen nodded.

"If, in your travels you come back this way, please visit. It would be a good comfort to learn from other masters what they can do with herbs."

"And who should I call upon when I visit again?" Naveen asked.

The old woman nodded. "My name is Lily."

Naveen left the shop before he started telling her his whole plan for the potion. There was an impulse to share with her, from one practitioner to another, what he hoped the bottle could achieve. He doubted whether she'd put a spell on him. His wizard senses didn't feel anything foul from the woman. On the contrary, she was uplifting and remarkably frank. He wanted to share with someone what he was doing. But for the safety of himself and his companions, it was best for now if nobody was privy to what was going on.

Secrecy was the goal for now.

He stepped into the street and moved toward the tavern where he lodged when a voice shouted out to him.

"Naveen!" Jared and Rowena crossed the street and came to him.

"There you are," Jared said.

"Coming here was put to good use." Naveen slid the bottle inside his cloak.

Jared pointed at the small bottle. "What's that?"

"A gift."

"For whom?"

"A friend."

Jared raised an eyebrow. "Be ready to go within the hour."

"I am ready to go right now. A wizard with his staff and hat is always ready."

"Hopefully Nix will feel the same way."

Naveen beamed. "I'll get him ready if we need to."

"Good. See you then."

Naveen walked away, ready to face whichever vampire wanted to leap out and end his life. With his new skill, and with the potion, he felt better than he had in a long time. It was the start of a great day.

Naveen sat in the saddle, with the reins lightly resting in his hands, looking expectantly forward because of the breakthroughs he had just experienced, when suddenly he felt tired all over. The energy that surrounded him disappeared. His body was drained and he wished to stay awake.

A sudden thought occurred to him: another wizard or practitioner of magical constructs must have hit him with a devious spell.

It was so sudden.

He turned around in his saddle and scanned the village for any signs of Roloth and his cousins. Maybe they were behind this. His eyes couldn't see anybody except for the normal crowd of people hunting from stall to stall in the marketplace looking for deals and good opportunities.

He panicked for a moment and then calmed himself down. His senses would have picked up magic being used against him. What did he do that made him so tired?

He shook his head; it was obvious. He was tired because he had stayed up all night. He stayed up, practicing his spell weaving skills. Excited by his breakthrough, he later stayed up so he could help Nix find something that wouldn't make him as vulnerable to the vampires as he was now.

Nix leaned forward in the saddle, his hand resting on the pommel. "You okay?"

"Oh I should have slept some," Naveen said.

"I second that," Nix said, forcing himself awake.

"Okay," Jared said, "let's move on."

They rode on their horses, moving slowly out of the village. Naveen was sorry to leave the village. He would love to sit down and talk shop with Lily and learn more about what she learned from this character called Nightwing.

But time pressed against them and moving forward was the only way they could all live again, that is if they survived any of the vampires they encountered while on their quest.

The question nagged him: How did Champion know him? For the last three months, a desperate time in his life, he never told anybody his name, except for this company.

A part of him wanted to run away from the mistakes he made, and another part just wanted to die because of those same mistakes. Jared had made a vow and failed his brother and sister in the process. He was sorry for that and daily he wished for a different outcome.

Maybe even in death the failure would haunt him.

When he arrived in Grinbell's village and was framed for murder, something deeper died inside. He had punished himself long enough, the guilt and shame reducing him, until all he thought about was killing vampires—at least he could do that.

If he had to die he wanted to do it on his own terms.

Perversely, he felt alive.

With each passing second of the day, with each step down the road, they came closer to their destination of Vampire Nation. When he had something to fight against, it gave him more spring to his step, more power passion flowed through him.

He hated vampires.

It was extremely easy for him to do so.

He had two good reasons for it.

Jared leaned forward on his horse, feeling the sturdy animal underneath him, and noticed Naveen and Nix stopping on the road. They were pointing at something but he couldn't see what it was they were pointing at until he turned the corner.

"What do you think they're looking at?" Rowena asked.

"Dandelions probably," Jared said.

Rowena beamed. "Or maybe pansies."

They both chuckled and turned the corner in the road and stopped next to their companions.

Jared looked past Naveen and Nix and heard a sharp intake of air. They were all staring at the massive structure. It seemed to have stepped out of a myth. He was sure Rowena was staring at the structure, overwhelmed by the massive size of the fortress.

Across the valley and a sea of trees, was the castle. They were days away from it and still the castle was large and visible. From this distance, the castle was old, majestic, and ruined.

"That's a big castle," Jared said, scanning the structure with his eyes, dividing it and taking it in sections. He noticed the protective outer wall crumbling away at the western corner of the castle.

"That's Castle Harkin," Naveen said.

"What's Castle Harkin?" Nix asked.

"The beginning of Vampire Nation."

"Our destination then," Jared said.

His heart beat loudly in his chest and Jared thought the others could hear it. He wondered how others couldn't hear it.

"Is that where my son is?" Rowena asked.

"Probably," Jared said. "But we won't know until we get closer."

"Is that all there is to Vampire Nation?" Nix asked. "One castle? You would think they'd have more places than just one castle."

"Maybe," Jared said. "Naveen, what do the wizards know?"

"Not much, I am afraid to say."

Rowena said, with a hardness in her voice, "They are creatures of the night and have different needs than we do."

"What kind of needs?" Nix asked.

"They avoid sunlight and they drink blood to stay alive."

"Animal blood?"

"And human blood."

"If you're going that way," a voice said from behind them, "then you're as good as dead. And if you're dead then we'll take your money as money is only good for the living. Because if you go forward, you won't be needing it."

Jared turned and found a motley crew of men armed with staves and pikes, and pouches filled with small rocks, surrounding them. "We'll keep our money," he said.

"Really?" said a stout man with a weather-exposed face and dark eyes. "I think if you're going in that direction we'll take your money and spend it wisely upon the living. Many men have died in that foul country. If you want to join them, be our guest. But your money stays here. With us. Now hand it over!"

"What if we say no thank you?"

"Then we kill you!"

Chapter Nineteen

JARED TOOK NOTICE of the men again. Their pikes and staves and pitchforks were no match against Rowena's bow and arrow, against his own sword, and against the wizard's magical staff.

The highwaymen were clearly outmatched.

"So, why rob us?" asked Jared, not moving from his horse and looking at the man who first spoke to them.

"You go to your death if you go in that direction. And from your conversation, that is exactly what you plan to do."

"I do."

"My name is Sol, and I am the leader of these men. I will know why you go there, into that foul country."

"Our business doesn't concern you."

"It might. We live on the border of this foulness. If something bad happens over there it might sweep upon us in the middle of the night and that we cannot endure. Again."

Jared said, "My party and I are looking for herbs."

"Herbs?"

"Aye. Our village was struck down with illness not long ago. We have been tasked with a mission. We are to bring back the herbs our village needs."

"Then it must be a very great need."

"It is."

Sol said, "And yet, I don't see any herbalist among you. I see a bunch of warriors, male and female, armed. I see a wizard, but I don't see any herbalist. I think you lie, stranger."

"We need to defend ourselves."

"Your money first. Then you can go in the direction you desire. If you resist then your people will get hurt. I promise you one thing, stranger."

"What's that?" asked Jared.

"Go into that land and you'll never come back again."

Naveen leaned on his staff and said, "What specifically is in that direction, besides Castle Harkin?"

Sol paused and then said, "I never heard it called that before. All we know is that it is a foul castle and a blight lies upon the land around it. Once the castle was fair, but not now. It is cursed and we are cursed with it."

Rowena said, "Why? What happened?"

Sol hardened his eyes and looked past them with a vacant stare reliving some memory that was beyond them. "Take them."

In unison, the motley crew aimed their staves and pikes and readied their rock pouches and faced Jared and his company.

Jared weighed the possible outcome in his mind. Today they had traveled long and far to get here and it would be the height of stupidity to create a ruckus and get somebody killed when it could be avoided. "You can have our money," he said, holding up his hands toward the sky.

Rowena said, "How can we help?"

With a distant stare, Sol said, "You can't."

Just then an old woman stepped out of the nearby forest, from a path that Jared hadn't noticed before. She wore a purple shawl over her shoulders and a withered hand, with the veins and bones and knuckles readily visible, gripped her oak cane. She turned and faced the crew of men. She stared at each of them in turn and, man by man, they lowered their eyes to the ground. At last, she laid eyes on Sol and said, "Stop this. These people do not share our grief."

Sol said, "Go away, old woman."

"Enough! Let these people and their property go."

Sol said very softly, "But we have *need*."

"Not like this."

The old woman and Sol faced one another. The old woman, bent forward and leaning on her gnarled walking staff, kept a steady focus on Sol. The broad shouldered man razed her with his angry blue eyes. He kept staring back at her—it was a battle of wills, passionate and powerful, until his shoulders started to slump and he took a breath and looked away.

The old woman, tired from the contest, smiled at Sol, and whispered to him. Sol stood rock still, not moving. And then his head turned and he let out a painful sob. "Let them go."

Rowena looked between the old woman and Sol and said to Jared in a whisper, "What happened?"

"She won," Jared said.

The old woman took Sol by the hand and addressed Jared and the others, "Come with us."

"We have to go in that direction," Nix said, pointing toward the castle.

The old woman shrugged. "Come."

After several seconds, Jared nodded. "Let's follow. Maybe we'll find something useful here."

The pathway tramped through the forest for a couple of miles, the trees blocking out most of the sunlight from overhead. Walking through the dim forest reminded Jared of a dream—half awake, half asleep, and it was a perfect place for an ambush. He had gotten off his horse and helped the old woman into the saddle. He walked ahead of his horse, pulling him along the now narrow pathway.

Something told him that it was important to go to this village, but he was careful. The highwaymen seemed angry and hopelessly mired in some deep seated pain of their own.

He glanced over at Naveen and the wizard walked next to him, shoulder to shoulder.

In a whisper Jared said, "I don't trust everyone here. Watch out for us."

The wizard started coughing as the others continued forward. The wizard stopped and bent over, hands on knees, and coughed.

"Is everything okay?" Sol asked.

"I'm fine," Naveen said, pressing a hand against his throat. "Go on I'll catch up."

"Suit yourself," Sol said.

Jared glanced over his shoulder and saw the wizard step away from them. If they were walking into a trap, at least with Naveen behind them, the wizard would be able to help them and out flank whoever might attack them.

The trees at first were large and tall as they journeyed through the forest. But later Jared saw evidence of recent cuts as the trees started to thin out. They must be reaching the village soon, thought Jared.

Their path sloped up. Jared tugged on the reins and guided the horse forward, step by step. At the top of the crest Jared rested and said, "Are we almost there?" The old woman, seated in his saddle, said, "It is not far now. Just over the next small hill."

They continued and when they reached the next hill Jared saw the village nestled between a valley on one side and mountains jutting out of the ground on the other. The only way people could arrive here was either by traveling through the fields, climb down the sheer mountain walls, or coming through the forest path.

The old woman held her head high and announced in a husky voice, "Go straight ahead."

They passed the animals in the fields and entered the village. Trades people stopped and stared out their shops at them. The children were oblivious to them, running and squealing and playing in a world of their own.

"This looks peaceful, maybe not so quiet, but children are children," Nix said.

Sol said, "It was better a year ago."

Naveen frowned. "What happened a year ago?"

Sol said, "Our animals, one by one, started disappearing. Then later, even more. We couldn't figure it out. Until we found one."

"What happened?" Rowena asked.

"The poor creature had its hide torn off. The blood was drained from its body. We saw several bite marks."

"Vampires?"

"They were breaking the treaty."

Jared moved past several low buildings to his right and the old woman pointed toward a lone building with smoke rising out of the chimney. "There."

Jared nodded and came to rest in front of a small rectangular building. Empty fields surrounded the building. Jared helped the old woman off his horse. Sol stood next to them, offering a hand as the old woman touched the ground.

The old woman patted Jared on the arm and, tapping her cane twice against the ground, moved across the grassy fields. "Follow me."

Jared looked to the others and shrugged. They'd come this far; what was a couple of more steps? He wrapped the reins around a post and followed her. The others got off their horses and joined as well.

Jared covered the distance across the brown fields, keeping his eyes on the old woman in front of him. She walked to the top of a crest and then walked down, her head disappearing below the horizon.

At first Jared thought she fell, but when he got there he saw the large depression and how the land slopped downward and ended at a grove of trees.

The slope had disappeared as Jared stepped closer to the old woman and walked through an open archway covered with vines and flowers.

Tall trees, fifty feet away, formed a half-circle. Within the concave half circle of trees, Jared could see the freshly turned earth, neatly arranged in three rows with six grave sites in each row.

Rowena said, "What is this?"

"Our lost hope," the old woman said.

Jared wondered what happened here. He counted the grave sites.

One, two, three.

"How terrible," Rowena said.

Four, five, six.

Naveen said, "Your lost hope?"

Sol shuffled forward. "It happened so quickly. We were unprepared."

The woman raised her arms, encompassing the whole burial grounds ...

Seven, eight, nine.

"These are our heroes," the old woman said.

Ten, eleven, twelve.

"Our village suffered an attack from vampires."

Thirteen, fourteen, fifteen.

The old woman continued. "They came at us without provocation. We were attacked."

Sixteen, seventeen.

"We fought, we killed, some died here, the lucky ones; the rest of us died here as well."

The old woman glanced at Sol and then faced Jared.

Eighteen.

"I am sorry," Jared said.

"All hell crumbled down around us," the old woman said.

Eighteen fresh grave sites stood before them all. Eighteen deaths. Lives that were cut short, with people fighting for what they believe in, the ability to live life with freedom and peace.

Jared closed his eyes and imagined the hard working farmers grabbing their tools and turning them against the vampires. It was the right thing to do, but in the wrong way. It was like going up against a beast without a sword or weapon in hand. Survival wasn't even on the agenda.

He imagined the war screams and the death screams at night.

Rowena said, "We mourn your loss."

Sol looked ashen as he stood before a grave site. He knelt before it and reached out and grabbed a fist full of dirt. He looked down into his hand, at the dirt, and his dark eyes swam in pain.

Jared bowed his head. Sol pushed away from the grave and turned around.

Jared said nothing but locked eyes with the troubled man and felt for him. Wife or child, it didn't matter who was buried. The pain it caused was evident and Jared wished there was something he could do to take away the pain, but there wasn't.

The old woman brushed her white hair out of her face, the wind gently blowing past them. "As we will mourn your loss if you continue moving toward that cursed land."

Rowena said, "The children, are they alright?"

The old woman studied her.

"The children are all we have."

"I don't understand. Why take our children and not yours?"

The old woman shook her head. "We don't know."

"So they attacked you without cause, without reason."

"Maybe it was the blood lust on them."

"What are you going to do?" Nix asked.

"Do? We hold on. We have scant supplies and harvest is weeks away. There is talk of moving. There is also talk of driving cold steel into their black hearts."

Jared felt suddenly small and old as he looked over the grave yard with raised dirt over each of the eighteen grave sites.

He loosened his coin bag and held it out for the old woman. Sol, standing behind the woman, watched.

"This is for you. It is a small measure of the loss you and everyone here has endured. Nothing can bring them back."

"I can't take this," the old woman said.

"What was tried by force is better given up by our shared pain."

The old woman bowed her head and accepted the decision. "You are generous."

"We must go now."

The old woman grabbed Jared's hand. "If you go there, I see death coming your way."

Nix stepped forward. "Are you a seer?"

The old woman smiled at him. "No. I have no talents in that regard. My only talent is surviving what has befallen our village. If you go toward that cursed castle and the land around it, you will die. All of you will die."

They rode silently away from the village and stood again in the same spot where they had first seen Castle Harkin. Sol and the old woman, with three of the villagers journeyed back with them.

Sol warned Jared, "You sign your death warrant going in that direction."

They said their goodbyes and descended down into the valley, disappearing into the line of trees. Very quickly they were gone from sight.

The band of men turned and headed back toward their village when the old woman stopped. She stared out over the ledge with a commanding view of the valley below. She gazed down and a grin came to her resolute lips.

For the best part of the afternoon, they pushed on while they still had light. Jared held up his hand. "We have a clearing up there. We'll rest here for the night."

"But we can still make more distance," Nix said.

"We are in the enemy's land now. They travel at night. We need rest. Sleep would do us good."

The wizard pulled up next to Jared. "What do you think lays ahead?"

"The unknown."

The wizard's eyes widened in surprise and fear.

Jared said, "But met with our courage and strength and resource-fulness, we can overcome the unknown. It is all that any man or woman has to offer."

Naveen sat straighter in the saddle. "Of course."

Naveen turned to Nix. "I have something for you."

"What is it?"

Naveen held the small bottle in his hand.

Nix took the bottle from Naveen and started to unstop it.

Naveen placed a hand over Nix's. "Easy! Treat it special and take it with caution! One drop, maybe two is all you need."

Nix gave the wizard a puzzled look.

"It will last an hour. It, I trust, will increase your speed and reflexes."

Nix grinned. "Magic in a bottle. Now I won't feel naked going into the unknown." Nix bowed his head. "Thank you, Naveen."

"Let's set up camp and then I'll show you how it works. I owe you."

Camp was set up quietly and quickly and Jared lay out on his blanket holding a brooch in his hands. Nix and Naveen were talking as Jared heard the sound of approaching footsteps.

Rowena smiled down at him. She sat down next to him; her arms wrapped around her legs and studied his face. "What's wrong?"

"I don't have children, so I don't know the pain you're going through. But I understand the pain of a village when they lose almost twenty people, men and women, without reason. What kind of mon-sters would do that?"

"Maybe they have a different kind of reason, but I don't care," Rowena said. "They're monsters and they took from that village, just like they took from me."

"There's a difference."

"What?"

"Your son isn't dead."

Rowena said with a hardness in her voice, "No, he isn't. And I want him back safe."

Jared noticed her trembling hands. "Courage, strength and resourcefulness will see you to the end."

Rowena frowned. "I may not make it."

"This from the woman who stalked us for a day, who stood up to us with bow and arrow, and then held a knife to my throat. You have strength and stamina."

"But if I die, what about my child?"

"I can't promise the outcome of a fight. But I can tell you that when we get to the castle we'll know what lays in front of us better and be prepared for it."

"Are you always this upbeat?"

Jared exhaled. "People defeat themselves with their own thoughts. They quit before they try. In our case, we have to be prepared. Physically we are. Mentally we are. Soon, we will be in the thick of it and we will need all of our wits about us. No nay-sayers."

"Only yes then."

"Yes is a powerful word."

"You really are strange," Rowena said softly.

Jared shrugged. "I seek the advantage where ever it may be. If that is strange then so be it."

Rowena shook her head. "I didn't mean to ... you're just so resolute. You have an iron will that surrounds you."

Jared chuckled. "Really? A week ago I would have killed myself." Jared held the brooch close.

Rowena pointed to the brooch. "She must be pretty."

"She was."

"Past tense?"

"She's dead."

"I'm sorry," Rowena said. "Was she an old girl friend?"

"Nothing like that," Jared said.

Rowena watched him stand up, brush himself off and pocket the brooch. He walked to another part of the camp busying himself. She touched a nerve in him and he wondered what was it that made him so hard on himself?

Off by himself in the woods, it didn't take Nix long to discover that what Naveen had said was true. The elixir made him faster, stronger, and even more confident than usual. Two of the additions were welcomed, but confidence could lead somebody to a quick death if they weren't careful, especially if it was false confidence. Even so, it was difficult to rein in the emotions he was feeling.

Freedom, unbounded joy, and the sense of limitless possibilities lay open before him. And all of that because of what he did; his thoughts, his actions were speeded up. He was as fast as a falcon in a headlong dive chasing a rabbit.

When Naveen placed one drop on his tongue an explosion of fire and openness spread throughout him; Nix knew he was experiencing something he never experienced or dreamt of before.

He could do more with this than he could without it.

Naveen warned him about its uses; and then, like taking candy from a blind man, Nix snatched the bottle out of the wizard's hands and was gone before the wizard's sentence left his mouth.

He could say that he wanted to figure out the elixir by himself, which was true, but equally important, if he was to fail, he didn't want any eyes to be on him. With his satchel, he ran to the tallest tree he could find and climbed it. He broke free of the lower branches that surrounded him and felt the wind in his face.

He suddenly felt like a kid ready to explore all the gifts bestowed upon him for his birthday. He braced himself between branch and truck, his feet pressed against branch, his back secured against trunk; he searched in his satchel and found it.

The runes on the golden spyglass looked ancient and were written in a language he didn't understand. The spyglass was his target when he invaded the wizard's workshop. He almost didn't make it out alive, but he did and with not one thing but two. He stared down at the stone and touched it. The stone warmed him immediately, and he felt no cold at all even with the wind blowing and adding a chill to the air. It was a fire-stone, he mused. Whatever that was.

Well, it was good for when the weather was cold, but it didn't help during the hotter parts of the year. How the stone worked, he didn't know. He had never seen a stone like this before. But since it was in a wizard's workshop, it must have been important. It was no ordinary stone; that was evident.

Nix cradled the satchel in front of him and with it open, he touched the fire-stone again and the warmth traveled through him, making it feel like summer. The wind didn't bother him at all.

Nix pushed the fire-stone deeper into his satchel and withdrew the spyglass.

Nix extended the beat up, scratched up, bronze colored tube. There were nicks and dents in the spyglass. It had been through a lot, and Nix wondered what it was exactly. He brought the small end to his eye and searched through the trees, from the direction he had come, until he saw the clearing where they camped.

He grew frustrated by the small size of the image and said, "I wish I could see closer."

Suddenly the image magnified and the camp was almost within reach. Nix pulled the spyglass away. "What magic is this?"

He eyed the spyglass carefully noting the runes and unknown language symbols written on the metal. "Magic tech. Good. And what else can you do?"

He brought the spyglass up to his eye and looked through the lens. Far off, a long distance away, he saw a tiny shape and recognized it as the castle and their next destination. "Okay. Let me see the castle up close."

The image suddenly changed and the castle filled the lens. Nix grew still and let his eye scan the image in front of him. It was marvelous. He knew what he had.

The spyglass was a tool that would be invaluable in war and for spying upon the enemy. This spyglass was worth anything Nix owed. It was worth a king's fortune. In fact, that was too small. It was the equal worth of several kingdoms.

Should he give it up? What were the things he could do with this device? He couldn't go around and boast because that would draw attention. The spyglass was a powerful weapon that needed to be used in strict secrecy.

He looked through the spyglass and carefully moved over the ruined aspects of the castle wall. He frowned. He couldn't see the space around the castle. "Too close," he said. "I need to see some land around the castle."

Instantly, the view changed and he saw the castle from a greater distance back. The spyglass showed him a different angle; it showed him the back of the castle. Something caught his attention.

Surrounded by bushes was the entrance to a tunnel that led up to the castle. Nix sat there dumbfounded.

He found a secret entrance and exit to and from the castle. It was probably locked up, maybe even rusted. But that shouldn't stop him. He had his tools with him. He beamed and pulled the beat up spyglass away from his face and looked at it.

It wasn't flashy or showy. Rather it looked old, with some dents on the body. The runes and symbols were anybody's guess and it just added to an old world feel of the device long before Nix's time. He collapsed the stock and placed it securely in his satchel next to the fire-stone. He secured the satchel cover and climbed down the tree, twisting and turning his body searching for hand holds and support for his feet as he went down.

With or without a magic potion, climbing up a tree is one hundred times faster than climbing down, Nix decided.

Chapter Twenty

NAVEEN EXTENDED HIS wizard senses, trying to better prepare himself for the coming fight. It would be stupid to neglect his duties, and his duties now included gaining proficiency in wordless combat. It was so strange to him. He loved words—he loved how words sounded and rolled off his tongue when they did it so effortlessly. When the words didn't flow from him, when they jumbled up on his tongue, it was pure frustration.

Learning wordless combat was the hardest thing for him to do. It wasn't the action that was hard for him to do, rather it was getting through to himself that a wizard, a proper wizard, would resort to such tactics. It was the equivalent of coming up to a person and hitting them in the head without warning.

He always believed words of magic—words with power and authority—needed to be spoken. The energy behind the word, the sound of its vibration, was enough to cause the magic to chain react and happen. At least, he always thought that. The better wizards he looked up to always spoke their spells for others to hear, making them know that a master of magic was present and anybody would be foolish to go up against such a wizard.

The mistake was his. He saw that now. He did so love the power and authority of words when he spoke, especially when directing a spell. But if he could win a fight while keeping silent, then that would be what he would do.

He clenched his jaw. He stepped away from Jared and Rowena and pushed his senses out deeper into the forest.

There.

Something was coming toward them. It weaved in and out of the trees. Fast.

"Something's coming our way." Naveen tried to keep the urgency out of his voice, but he failed. He could hear Jared and Rowena getting to their feet.

He shut out their voices and concentrated.

It was coming straight toward them. Whatever was coming was approaching fast.

He gripped his staff and the sigils lit up with his power. He mentally worked out a barrier spell and placed it immediately around the camp. The barrier was firmly set, between them and whatever was approaching them.

"It's coming fast," Naveen said.

"What is it?" Jared asked.

"Don't know." Naveen grunted. "Stand by me," he commanded. Jared and Rowena flanked him on each side, their weapons drawn and ready.

The barrier was up when something slammed into it, strands of green light flickered around the camp and centered closest to the source of disturbance. Green light flickered and arced twenty feet to their right, just on the other side of the massive rocks.

Naveen grabbed his staff and moved carefully toward the rocks; Jared and Rowena flanked him.

Something groaned behind the rock.

"What was that?" asked Rowena.

"I don't know," Naveen said.

"Swords ready," Jared said. "Lower the spell."

Naveen released the spell, letting the energy dissipate. The green wall lowered and dissolved around them and revealed Nix, lying on his back, one hand against his bleeding nose.

"You?" Naveen said.

"Uh?" Nix tried to get up and collapsed to the ground, his arms and legs rubbery.

"I had no idea," Naveen said, shaken. "If I knew it was you I wouldn't have made this barrier."

Rowena aimed her bow at Nix. "Are you sure that's Nix?"

Naveen nodded.

"But can't somebody fool us and look like him?"

Naveen said, "What did Nix call me in our jail cell?"

Nix looked up at him bleary eyed, holding his nose tenderly with one hand and said in a nasal quality: "You're not a wizard. You're a fat whore."

Naveen broke into a broad smile. "It's him. I sensed something out there but I didn't know it was him. It was coming straight toward our camp. I couldn't allow something to overrun us!"

"So how can Nix elude your wizard senses?" Rowena asked, taking the tension off the bowstring and lowering her weapon.

"Only if he took more of the elixir than what I suggested." Naveen kneeled to Nix.

Jared said, "Nix, how many drops?"

Nix groaned. He held up four fingers.

Naveen shook his head. "Is that all?"

Nix closed his eyes. "I've got a headache."

"That explains it, I think," Naveen said. "The excess drops must have changed his energy signature. I didn't know it was Nix. Rather it was Nix plus additional elements."

Jared and Rowena stepped forward and lifted Nix, a hand under each arm. They dragged Nix in front of the small camp fire. "What were you doing out there?" Jared asked.

Nix squinted. "Some scouting."

"Did anybody see you?" Jared asked.

"I doubt it. I'm very fast now, when I want to be."

"The elixir?"

"Yeah. Naveen, thanks. A couple of drops and I'm a new man."

Rowena handed Nix some cloth to press against his bleeding nose.

"What did you see?" Jared asked.

Nix said, "There's a back door to the castle. A secret tunnel."

Rowena said, "That's impossible. It's several hours away. How did you discover that?"

Nix reached into his satchel and pulled out the spyglass. "With this." He then filled them in on the spyglass and its secrets.

"What other surprises do you have?" Rowena demanded.

"None."

Jared took the spyglass and held it up close for inspection. "It must have a very powerful lens."

"Magical lens anyway," Nix replied. "I figure we're half a day's march from the castle."

Jared nodded. "Draw us a map of the castle. We can use it to our advantage."

"May I see the spyglass?" Rowena asked.

Nix handed it to her while rubbing his head with his other hand.

Rowena extended the stock of the spyglass and, bringing it to her eye, said, "Show me my son."

Rowena watched as the lens in the spyglass changed what she was seeing. The images of the nearby trees faded away and then another image came in front of her. The spyglass, incredibly light in her hands, showed her a dark place.

Light crept in little by little. It was a dark place. Rowena saw many children hunkering down, dejected, on cold stone floors in a dungeon cell. Large hollow eyes looked out of the cell.

The image shifted a second time and a boy was sitting in the corner with his back to the cold wall. His arms circled his knees.

Short dark hair fell forward over the boy's forehead. The right ear was larger than the left ear. The dirty face was stained with tears. The boy looked around the dark cell and then rested his chin on his knee.

"It's Steen. He's alive! My son is alive!"

Rowena pulled the spyglass away from her face and stared at the device. It was a miracle. What magic made this glass see her son many miles away? She didn't care. All she knew, to the very core of her soul, he was alive.

A hand reached toward the spyglass and snatched it from her. "What is this?" Naveen's face was red with fury.

"A spyglass," Nix said.

"Give it back," Rowena demanded.

"It is not a normal spyglass. That is one thing we know for sure. Another thing we know for sure; this can jump over distances and that isn't a normal thing, is it?" Naveen collapsed the lens and whirled toward Nix.

"Tell me the complete story and leave nothing out. The details may be important. How did this came to be in your hands."

Rowena pressed against Naveen, her hands trying to yank the spyglass free from him. "Give it back. I want to see my son."

Naveen lifted the spyglass out of her reach. "No. It could be dangerous. It's one thing when it changes images from near to far, Rowena. But this magic is more powerful than I anticipated. More powerful could mean more deadly."

"So we can't use it?" Rowena asked.

"This device has powerful magic in it. Whether fair magic or foul, I don't know yet. But ignorance will not save us if this spyglass can somehow be used against us."

Nix looked up at the wizard. "Why?"

"Magic has many layers to it. It requires energy, skill, and a certain amount of passion for it to work. To have this enchanted device show us lands from far away could corrupt our senses, and lead us to a wrong conclusion."

Jared said, "You mean it may only show us what we want to see."

"Yes. It could cloud our minds; that is my worst fear."

"But I just saw my son."

"I believe you saw him. But was it really him or was it what you wanted to see?"

"He was in a cell, with other children."

"Then let that be a sign to us that we are on the right course of action, for now."

Naveen leaned close to Nix. "How did you come upon this?" Rowena pressed closer and hoped that the magic in the spyglass was harmless. Nix looked at them all with a guilty expression.

The intelligence was specific, of that Nix was confident. Collect the spyglass and leave. That was all that the client wanted. All expenses had been paid, but Nix didn't take any of the money. Whatever he stole was his until he was done with it; so he never took money as a retainer. Never.

It gave him the option to keep what he stole, or to sell it to another buyer more eager to meet its agreed upon purchase price.

Nix crouched at the top of the stairs. He used magic to get past the defenses. Just a slight hex, to gently ease past the protective layer around the workshop. He turned the door handle to the workshop and held his breath. The door swung inward easily; the hinges remained silent as the heavy door opened.

He was in the wizard's workshop and Nix quickly closed the door behind him. It wouldn't do to leave something suspicious like a door left open in a secure area to draw unwanted attention.

With his heart hammering in his chest, Nix paused and took in some deep breaths, calming his heart down. He walked softly into the cluttered workshop. On the narrow table in the middle of the room was the spyglass. It was banged up and dented, and etched on its sides were runes and symbols that Nix didn't understand. He placed the spyglass in his satchel.

His brain was yelling at him to go.

Go.

Go now.

Don't stay around.

Go.

On the table, next to where the spyglass had been, was a stone, rough surface, slightly oval, with elaborate designs seemingly carved into the rock. The stone was warm to the touch.

His body suddenly felt warm all over.

In fact, his mind stopped racing and he turned momentarily to bask in the warmth and glow that came from the stone.

Nix placed the stone into his satchel, next to the spyglass. He was feeling satisfied, when suddenly the door to the workshop burst open and Grinbell rushed in. Grinbell raised his staff and Nix turned and raced toward the open window.

Nix leaped out the window and tucked his legs into his body, going into a roll. He somersaulted on the roof below and ran to the edge of that roof and leaped again.

The open air enveloped him.

Nix held his breath and landed on the roof and got to his feet. He turned and glanced back. Two roofs up was the open workshop window. Grinbell raised his staff and spells rocketed toward him.

Nix dodged the spells. He wanted to catch his breath but a sharp whistle cut through the air.

The guards were after him!

He quickly checked his satchel: the spyglass and the rock were both unharmed. Satisfied that his targets were safe, Nix turned and ran to the edge of the second roof. He searched wildly for the down spout and edging himself down over the lip of the roof, he slipped his fingers behind the down spout and climbed down.

Ten feet down he found a balcony just to his side. If he could make it.

Nix pushed away from the wall, angling himself to land on the small balcony. He felt his heart racing.

He pushed away from the wall, falling in the air and moving sideways at the same time. He gripped the iron railing and felt his arm being almost pulled out of its socket. He grabbed hold of the railing with his other hand and pulled himself up.

He tried to open the door window to the house.

But it was locked.

He looked below.

Nobody spotted him. The guards would be swarming around him soon. He turned his attention to the door again when a passing hay wagon drove below him.

Nix saw his new escape route. He abandoned trying to get into the house from the door window. He climbed onto the railing and balanced himself.

He looked to the street below.

The flatbed wagon moved closer. An older man was driving the hay wagon through town, with a team of oxen that obeyed his angry, shouting instructions.

The man was even with him.

Nix pushed off the railing and aimed for the wagon. He ducked his legs into his body and then rolled forward a half rotation and then opened his arms and legs, his back driving straight down into the haystack.

He landed in the soft texture of freshly cut down hay and rolled to the end of the wagon.

Nix slid off the wagon and smiled. Cat and mouse.

He turned and there was the market place. He was in the middle of the market and saw a small girl playing with her toy pony.

"Why did you steal from him?" Jared asked.

"I had clients who were interested in magic tech and they told me where I could find it."

Naveen frowned. "Magic tech?"

"Yes. For years there have been no new magic improvements. In fact, notwithstanding the wizard in our company, the magic of today isn't equal to the magic of yesteryear."

"And they wanted you …?"

"I am a thief," Nix said. "I am the best, but I also choose my opportunities."

"Why go up against a wizard?" Naveen stood there perplexed.

"If you think you're the top dog of the pack, then you won't have the security you should have to protect your secrets. He was over confident. It was easy to steal from him."

Naveen stepped away, his head bowed in thought. "I have heard stories of old magic coming back. But it was only whispered, never spoken out loud. I suggest we all keep this knowledge to ourselves."

"The one you stole from is the one who selected us for this assignment," Jared said.

"Yes," Nix said.

"What else did you steal from him, that you're not telling us?" Jared reached down and grabbed the satchel away from Nix.

He opened it up and there was a stone laid deep in the satchel.

"What's this?" Jared pulled the rough hewn stone from the satchel.

"I found it on his workbench. All I can tell you is its always warm to the touch."

"A piece of hell where ever you go," Rowena said.

"I suppose." Nix worried eyes scanned them all. "If you want to keep warm just touch it; your whole body will feel warm."

Naveen stretched forth his hand and almost touched the stone and stopped. "I cannot touch it. Not until I know exactly want it is." Naveen turned to Nix. "And you cannot keep it."

Naveen glanced to Jared. "But you could keep it."

"Okay," Jared said. "I'll keep it and the spyglass too." Jared grabbed the spyglass out of Naveen's hands and said, "But who wants a rock?"

Chapter Twenty-one

JARED LEANED BACK on his bed roll and felt the warmth of the stone next to him. The sun was almost down and the shadows lengthened around them, but he felt warm and pleasantly sleepy, balanced between sleep and wakefulness. His thoughts, the way they always did, carried him back to his regret.

He wished he could scrub clean the screaming sounds in his head.

The massive cave was a slaughter house, with sword and shield against claws and fangs.

At the end of it, he made himself an outcast.

What lay behind the murky intrigue of magic tech? How was Grinbell supplied with the old tech?

When he started playing chess, he felt helpless against better players. He was always driven into corners, or being forced to castle. The feeling of being manipulated hovered over him again. What unseen hand was moving events around?

"Circles within circles," he said and laid his head down, exhaled and went to sleep.

The small fire crackled as the wood split open and ashes fell to the ground. The moon was rising above the mountaintops.

"How are you doing, Naveen?" Jared asked. The wizard, cloak wrapped around him, looked into the fire without blinking. Nix and Rowena were on the other side of the fire keeping warm.

The wizard leaned forward. "I've been thinking. There are one or more unseen hands at work in this."

"I agree," Jared said.

"You do?" Surprise was evident in his tone. He broke away from the fire and locked eyes with Jared.

"Yes," Jared said. "It's the magic tech. Who would benefit from it? Just about anybody. But where would it come from?"

"That is a good question, and it is something that I will have to bring up to my fellow wizards."

Jared nodded. "You're not as inept as you seem."

"What?"

"Circles within circles," Jared said. "It looks like you have a story you haven't told us …"

"I don't …"

"Don't interrupt, wizard. You're here for some purpose as well, but keep your secrets. I just want to know one thing: can I trust you? My life and the life of others may hang in the balance."

"You can trust me."

"Good." Jared walked to the other side of the fire and set his eyes on Nix.

"Nix, I have a question for you?"

Nix stirred and looked up at Jared. "What?"

"You were working for unknown customers. But what I want to know: can I trust you?"

"What makes you say that?"

"Too many coincidences. You are dealing in magic tech, so we have to be careful. Can I trust you with our lives?"

Nix looked back at him, clear eyed and said solemnly, "Yes, you can trust me with your lives."

"Rowena?" Jared asked. "What about you?"

Rowena said, "I am in this for my son, as you are in this for the children. But to answer your question, you can trust me as well."

Naveen quickly said, "And you, Jared, also have an untold story about you. Can we trust you?"

Jared nodded. "Regardless of the Death Collars we wear, I give you my word that you can trust me. We will find the children and bring them back home safely. That is our goal nothing more and nothing less."

Nix glanced over at Naveen and said, "Naveen, have you looked into the death collars around our necks?"

The wizard nodded. "I have."

"Any chance to get free of them?"

Naveen shook his head and stared back at the fire.

Jared looked away from the fire. Night was deepening around them and they were in enemy territory.

The smoke rose from the camp fire and drifted up. A hand grabbed Jared's shoulder.

Jared opened his eyes.

"Something is out there," Naveen said. "I put warning alarms out there and now they're going off."

"Magic sentries?"

"Something like that," Naveen said standing back and turning to face the darkness.

Jared turned from the fire and the sound of leathery, flapping wings cut through the night. The flapping wing sound changed to heavy footfalls as if people were running toward them.

"The enemy is upon us," Jared said. "Rise."

Suddenly he wished he had used the spyglass to see what else was out there, but it was too late. Panic, only momentarily, rose up in him. He grunted and shoved it back down. He grabbed his sword and stood ready.

Three shapes came out of the blackness.

Naveen gripped his staff, the runes glowing with feverish light.

Nix fingered his knife with slender strong fingers.

Rowena notched an arrow and made ready for combat in one easy motion.

They were steel and guts facing the vampires. Would they survive?

The three vampires came within the circle of light and the middle one, with a scar across his forehead said, "This is really a surprise. It truly is. We heard about your last encounter from Champion. Our king has sent us here. He welcomes you to his land. He bids you welcome and health."

The vampire laughed and the other two joined in. Soon the laughter carried far into the night.

A shiver went down Jared's spine and he grew uneasy.

"What is so funny?"

"You are. This is going to be so easy for us. But our king made us come."

Jared faced them, feeling the comforting grasp of his sword in hand.

Laughing and holding his side, the middle vampire said, "This is really quite simple. Defeat us and you can go forward as guests."

As quick as lightning, an arrow sliced through the night air and went through the left eye of the middle vampire. The arrow was half way embedded into the brain when the legs gave out and the body crumbled to the ground. The vampire dusted away.

The vampire on the left raged, but before he could do anything an orange and green colored lance of light glommed onto him, covering him from head to toe. The vampire couldn't move anymore. He tried to scream but the words got jumbled in his throat as he fell down dead. He dusted away as Naveen grunted in satisfaction.

The last vampire, a berserker, moved forward and reached for Rowena; but Jared slammed into the berserker from the side, knocking him off balance.

The berserker got to his feet, but Jared was ready for him. Jared leaped closer and shoved the point of his sword into the stomach and ripped a vertical gash from groin to chest.

The berserker grabbed the sword, bellowing in pain.

Jared shoved his foot into the vampire's chest and pushed him away. The vampire staggered, all the while looking at his exposed organs.

Jared, holding the sword with two hands, stepped closer, planted his feet, and swung at the vampire's neck.

The blade went clean through the neck, the head moving a couple of inches, toppling to the ground. The headless body stood still for an instant and then it collapsed in a heap to the ground. The body dusted away.

All four stood ready, breathing heavy, looking at where the attackers had come from.

"All clear," Nix said. He sheathed his sword. "It looks like I'm better at thieving than fighting, but I was here for you, for us."

Naveen stepped forward and clasped Nix on the shoulder. "You did well. You didn't run."

"I said I wouldn't," Nix said, in a hurt tone.

Jared accessed the situation. Wizard, mother, thief, and a warrior, had defeated in the span of a minute, three vampires. "Were as ready as we're going to be."

"Won't there be more of them?"

"Probably, but they won't harm us."

Rowena lifted an eyebrow. "How do you know that?"

Jared shrugged. "We defeated them, we can go forward. Simple." He picked up his cloak and wrapped it around his shoulders. "Let's pack light and move closer to the castle. Maybe we can make it by sunrise and turn this to our advantage."

With the others packing, Jared moved toward Rowena.

"I need your help," Jared said.

Rowena looked up. "What?"

"I want you to look again." He held out the spyglass for her.

"For what?"

"Tell me if your son is still okay."

"But what about Naveen's warning?"

"I'll chance it. I don't think this will harm us. I think it's a tactical weapon, that's all. So, let's use it."

"Okay."

"After you check in on your son, I want to see if you can direct the spyglass to look at the outer walls of the castle."

"What for?"

"One thing at a time," Jared said, handing her the bronze object. "Will you?"

Rowena nodded and held the spyglass in her hands.

Jared stepped away and started gathering his supplies. Naveen and Nix also noticed Rowena with the spyglass, but they kept busy, gathering up their belongings.

Rowena closed her eyes and inhaled deeply and then she brought the spyglass to her face and looked through the lens with her right eye.

She said something softly that the others couldn't hear. Her right eye was magnified by the lens and looked straight ahead as if seeing something very dear to her from far away.

A fragile smile grew across her face and she said very softly, "Thank you, thank you, thank you."

Chapter Twenty-two

THEY RODE SLOWLY and steadily for many hours, on horseback, until daylight peaked over the mountain range. The castle laid before them in waste and glorious ruin. A large ditch, empty of water, circled the castle. The chains, Jared noticed, attached to the drawbridge had been broken many years ago, so now the drawbridge knew only one position, open.

The open drawbridge was a sign to anybody who came upon it: you can enter if you're either brave or foolish.

The castle was magnificent and larger than any castle he had ever seen. The castle walls, built of stone and mortar, were like rotted trees in the forest, with parts of the wall crumbling and falling away. Although the walls were no longer useful as a defense against outsiders, still they held a beauty and charm in their destruction. The crumbling walls and the individual stones seemed to make the castle more remote as if springing up from myth and legend.

They rode carefully over the drawbridge and Jared noted the skeletal remains of men and animals scattered about them. There were several piles of human and horse bones jumbled together across the drawbridge. There must have been quite a large battle here at one time. To their right, in the ditch, was a surprise for Jared. A large dragon skeleton with its wings spread out was laid on top of three horse skeletons. The large dragon skull and the rest of the dragon's body remained inert in the middle of the dry moat. The dragon's eyeless sockets seemed to follow them. Jared stopped and looked at the remains and wondered what battle was fought here. He had never seen a dragon before and had doubted their existence, but here was proof that at one time dragons existed.

"Let's go," he said. "There's nothing to see here."

They rode past the outer wall, going single file into a narrow channel under the keep. The clop-clop-clop of the horses' shoes echoed on the stone pavements. The quiet that surrounded the castle made even the slightest sound louder than Jared cared for.

Naveen scanned the castle. "It seems deserted."

Nix said, "I don't like the feel of the place. Did you see that dragon's head back there? That must've been one awesome fight."

"We're close." Rowena glanced around the castle walls.

"Let's move on," Jared said.

They rode on and moved through another narrow passageway, coming out into the courtyard of the inner castle. Jared dismounted. "We go on foot."

The others dismounted and Nix pointed at the western wall. "They had slaves here."

Against the wall, tethered by chains, skeletal remains of humans were evenly spaced out. Jared counted five stations; next to each station was a heap of skeletons.

Rowena dismounted from her horse. "We should use our time now."

"I agree," Jared said. "Naveen and Rowena, take the second floor. See what you find. You stumble upon something, you shout."

Naveen looked at Rowena. "Understood."

"Our enemies are asleep now but they may have guard dogs about."

Nix said, "What are we going to do?"

"You and I," Jared said, "are going to search the main floor and anything below that."

"Are you sure?"

"Frightened?"

"Well, I prefer sunshine and a fresh breeze."

Jared and Nix entered the main entrance hall. They could see scattered plates half-filled with rotten food, rats moving from plate to plate in search of something edible. Chairs had been knocked over as if a great fight had taken place here.

"I don't get it," Nix said.

"What?"

"What would vampires want with food? They drink blood."

"Maybe the staff needs food."

"Staff?"

Nix tightened his fingers around his short sword and loosened it.

"Where, do you suppose, is the passage way?"

Nix turned around and studied the room. "It would be, my best guess, in the back this way."

They walked quietly through the hallway and Nix led them to a spiral staircase. With sword drawn, Nix stepped onto the stairs and headed down. Jared followed, sword in hand, finger gripped tightly around the worn handle.

They made two complete circles going down until another floor presented itself to them. They stepped quietly onto the floor.

In front of them was a tight hallway, barely shoulder width. Beyond the hallway was another larger room.

A loud clash of sound erupted in front of them. Nix and he remained silent; both were ready to spring into action if needed. The sound came from the room opposite them from the tight hallway. But what made the sound?

Nix crept forward, quietly, both hands free. He looked back at Jared and motioned him to stay.

Jared let the thief venture forward alone. He would wait here ready to assist if needed.

"We need our sleep," a harsh voice said.

Nix slid into the shadows and waited until his eyes adjusted to the reduced light. A single candle against the far wall flickered, bringing out a small tendril of light.

Nix counted eight bodies in the soldier's room. The beds were laid against both walls and a small table was in the middle. Plates and dishes were scattered on the table and a goblet caught the light from the candle. A thrall picked up the goblet and set it back on the table.

"Sleep now. But we have to be up soon."

"You worry too much," said a voice.

"I worry but we keep our necks safe."

The thrall crawled onto a bed and lay still, deeply exhaling.

Nix crept back, padding softly to Jared.

"There's too many," Jared said. "If those are thralls, and I believe they are, then what do they guard?"

"Maybe the children, and if so, they must have keys nearby?"

"What are you suggesting?"

Nix developed a tight smile. "Stay here. I can do this."

Jared grabbed his arm. "Are you crazy?"

Nix faced Jared. "You couldn't do it. Naveen and Rowena couldn't do it, but I can."

"What makes you so special?"

"Because of my training. There's eight bodies in that room," Nix pointed to the room twenty feet away from them, careful to keep his voice down. "I can go in there and see if they have any keys about them."

"And if they do?"

"It's a good thing you have me here then."

"No. I won't let you."

Nix nodded. "I understand." He raised his face and his eyes went wide with fear. "Ohmygod."

Jared turned around, ready to face whatever Nix had seen. But when he saw nothing was there, he turned back around, but he was too late. Nix had slipped quietly back inside the guard room, moving in the shadows.

Jared gripped his sword, the palm of his hand suddenly wet with sweat, and waited. He hoped Nix would come out safely.

Nix felt bad about tricking Jared, but only a little. He hated people telling him what he could and couldn't do. He survived this long by relying upon himself, not on the will and whims of others. Just because Jared was the leader of this group didn't give him the right to tell Nix what to do. Besides they were here for the same thing, to rescue the children. And if the thralls are here, then chances are good they were guarding something. And if they were guarding something then they would have keys nearby. And if they had keys, then Nix would find them.

He crouched and listened intently to the breathing of each of the thralls. They made awful snoring sounds, some tossed on their beds, talking in an ugly almost incomprehensible language. One, next to the candle on the far side of the room, sneezed.

Loudly.

Nix froze.

The thrall sneezed again. Three times.

Then he turned and faced the wall, trying to get more sleep.

Nix searched the room, creeping closer to the middle. At each bed he turned and faced those behind him. None stirred.

He moved forward.

The small table was littered with food and spilled drink. He looked forward and his eyes caught sight of the burning candle. Next to it, hanging on the wall, was a set of keys dangling from a hook.

How easy can this be?

He padded quickly to the far side of the room, his object, in sight. He leaned against the table and, reaching across the space toward the wall with fingers outstretched, he lifted the ring off the wooden hook, careful not to make any noise.

The thrall that sneezed turned over on his back and said loudly, "Intruders. I smells them."

Like he did when Grinbell entered the workshop, Nix kept his eyes fixed on the means of escape. Fighting was never his favorite thing.

But here, in the room, he had to trust to his skills and now to his speed.

Nix heard motion behind him and the thralls shouted and rose from their beds.

He saw Jared rushing toward him and standing in the entrance to the guard room, with sword in hand.

Nix rushed past a thrall when a hand grabbed him by the sleeve. Nix tugged hard—to get away—when his sleeve ripped and Nix was suddenly free.

More thralls were on their feet now. Several had their swords drawn and were rushing toward them.

Nix rushed past Jared and stood outside the guard room.

"Come on," he shouted.

Jared followed him and together, they slammed shut the door to the guard room. Jared picked up chains and stretched them tight across the door, locking the thralls inside.

"Was it worth it?" Jared asked.

Nix held up the ring of keys. "Where to?"

"You're the thief. Your best guess to the dungeon."

Nix raced away from the door, going back over the ground they had traveled. Jared was right behind him; over their shoulders they heard the cursing and hollering of the thralls trapped in their sleep quarters.

Chapter Twenty-three

JARED MOVED WITH powerful strides, his sword ready in case any attackers appeared. His eyes scanned the walls and rooms ahead of them, with his senses on alert.

He wasn't taking any chances.

Coming upon those thralls brought home how much danger they were in. Just because they were close to their objective didn't make the danger any less real.

He could be killed right now if he wasn't careful. And he made a promise to bring the children safely back to the village.

This castle was filled with danger, and any careless step could be his last. The journey here was just preparation for whatever happened now.

His heart suddenly leaped into his throat. He shoved it down and ignored it.

The vampires were here and they knew that guests had arrived. He'd bet on it.

For now, he trusted the chain would hold the thralls back and with the sunlight overhead it gave them time to find the children and get out of the castle before night fall.

Jared had defeated vampires before but never in a one-sided fight where he was out numbered ten to one.

If they didn't find the children and get out of the castle by afternoon they were dead men, regardless of the promises from the vampire king.

The castle chilled him. He shivered even though it wasn't cold. He felt the oppressive evil of the castle descend and wrap itself around his shoulders, a living beast that was ready to devour him, but not before it had its fun at his expense.

Jared shook off the feeling of oppression and focused on Nix.

The thief moved like a prowling animal, carefully following a scent, leading them past the main hallway. Nix had his own way of scanning a room, spotting where hallways and secret passages were liable to be. Nix moved toward the corner, touched a panel and the wall pivoted open, revealing a stairwell that started on this floor and only went down below ground level.

Jared followed down the spiral staircase barely catching up to the dark shape of Nix in front of him. He marveled at how easily Nix could merge into the shadows and stay hidden if he wanted to. There was more to him than being a simple thief, of that Jared was sure. The thief had connections and intelligence that would be prized very highly in other courts across the land.

Jared wondered how the thief had come to be. Did he fall into that kind of life because it was a skill he enjoyed or was he forced to do it and never had any options in life? If the former, then Nix was truly a master thief, an extra sense about him, keeping him from trouble. If the later, did he ever consider doing something else with his life, and if he did, what would it be?

Nix stopped up ahead and turned back.

"Shhh. I hear voices."

"I can't hear a thing," Jared said.

"You don't practice listening," Nix said, a slight inflection traced with humor.

"What do you think?" Jared strained to listen beyond the hallway that led to the dungeon but all he could hear was his own heartbeat and the rushing of blood in his ears.

"Only one way to find out," Nix said. "Stay here. I'll see what I can discover and report back."

Once again Nix crept forward, quiet as a still lake, footpads falling silently on the ground. Jared turned and listened for anybody following them. He strained to pick up any sounds of somebody coming behind them; but he was confident they were alone.

He turned around and faced forward. He looked through the darkened hallway but couldn't find Nix if his life depended on it.

"Ohmygod," came the words, barely above a whisper, laced with horror and fear and a steely resolve.

Jared rushed forward, his sword in hand, ready for battle. He turned a corner and stopped.

A torch light was set in the wall and the flickering light revealed children huddled on the floor of the dungeon cell. Expectant eyes and sad faces glanced up at them.

The children looked back at them with faces caught between hope and fear on the other side of the cell bars.

Nix kneeled in front of the cell door with a faraway look on his face as he studied the lock.

"Can you get it open?" Jared said.

Nix inserted the first key from the key ring he had taken from the thralls. The key glided in easily. He turned the key; a dull "click" sounded and the cell doors swung open.

The children didn't move, hesitant to move forward.

That wasn't normal.

Nix put the key away and said, "We're here to take you back, but we need to be quick about it, and you all need to be quiet. Can you do that?"

A voice said, "How do we know we can trust you?"

Jared searched for the owner of the young boy's voice. The children parted and a small boy, with blond hair and a face smudged with dirt and tears looked at him.

"We're here for you, all of you," Jared said.

"I've never seen you before," the boy said.

"No, you haven't. But we opened the cell door for you and we're risking our lives to break you out. Please come."

The other children looked at the boy and his face was quiet for a moment. His face was alive with thought, his eyes scanning back and forth across the other children.

"Sarah needs help and so does Amy. They're frightened."

"What happened to them?"

"The vampires."

Something dark burned inside Jared and all he wanted to do was kill the vampires that hurt those children. He couldn't save his own but at least he could make up for it by protecting these children from any further harm. He held his sword in front of the children and said, "I pledge my sword and my life to getting all of you out of here. My name is Jared and I swear it, with all I hold dear."

The corners of the boy's mouth turned up slightly. His eyes twinkled with hope. "Maybe this is a sign."

Jared stood up.

"You lead us, Nix; up the way we came."

Nix started to go, but Jared stopped him. "Go carefully," he whispered. "We have children. Consider them battle wounded. Right?"

"It will make our progress slower."

"Slow and steady then. I don't want to lose a single one of them."

"Okay," Nix said, his dark eyes scanning the children as a stony resolve hardened in him.

"Children, follow Nix and be quiet."

"We have it, mister," the blond haired boy said helping the other children out of the cell.

They traveled out of the dungeon and as they passed the hallway they all heard several screams throughout the castle. The children's frightened faces told him everything. "Have hope children. We'll get you out of here."

"This castle is enchanted," Nix said.

The words struck Jared in the chest and the longer they settled there the more convinced he was of Nix's assessment.

"Keep moving forward, eyes straight ahead."

They climbed the stairs and Jared looked out the spy crevice. Daylight was gone. Night had fallen.

When did that happen? Just minutes ago it was daylight.

He stared out the crevice and shook his head. They weren't here all day. Maybe an hour or two at the most, but according to the weather outside, it was night and the vampires would come out.

"Nix, it's night outside."

"I'm going as fast as I can," Nix said. "A moment ago it was daylight. Now nighttime."

Nix stood by the entrance to the main hallway and ushered the children into the large cavernous room. The children huddled together, each of them touching the other, a slight smile crept across their faces. Jared brought up the rear and closed the door behind him when a voice said, "Steen!"

Jared turned and there was Naveen and Rowena. Rowena rushed toward the children and lifted the blond haired boy into her arms. They fell into a mad hug and they twirled around for a few moments.

Rowena kissed her son and then grabbed his wrists, one at a time, and pushed back his sleeves, examining his skin. She did it to the other arm. Then she started to pull the boy's shirt off of him and Steen said, "Stop mom. I'm okay. I haven't been bitten. But others have been."

"Who?"

"Amy and Sarah."

"We're getting out of here," Rowena said.

Steen nodded. "They said you'd be here."

Rowena stopped smiling. "Nobody knew we were coming."

Steen looked up at her. "They knew."

Rowena's face grew upset and then she raised her face and locked eyes with Jared. *Get us out of here.*

Jared gathered Naveen and Nix to him. Jared said to Nix, "Can you get us out of here? You mentioned a back door to this place."

"Yes. I saw it on our way in." Nix glanced across the main hallway toward a small alcove with stairs and moved toward it, lightly stepping across the stone floors.

"Follow him." Jared watched as Rowena and Naveen took the children and followed after Nix toward the stony stairwell.

"The children will make this difficult," Naveen said.

"That's why we're here," Jared said.

Naveen looked like he had been slapped.

"Sorry," Jared said. "We need to get out of here and I'll feel better when we're away from here."

"I can keep them back," Naveen said.

"How long?"

"Long enough."

"Hold off on that," Jared said, "until we need it."

Naveen and Jared raced across the main hallway, after the children, and descended into the stairwell.

Nix was leading them past one hallway, then another and he opened an old musty tunnel with a dirt floor. "Come on," Nix said. "This is the way."

The children grew wide-eyed and murmured in excitement as they rushed forward moving past Nix. They raced down the pathway and turned the corner.

The hairs on the back of his neck stood straight up. Jared turned and looked down the hallway they had come. He didn't see any vampires.

"Do you feel them?" Naveen asked.

"Yes. You?"

"Absolutely."

"They know."

"Yes."

"Let's get out of here," Jared said.

They raced down the hallway when the sounds of children's screaming filled the tunnel.

"What is it now?"

Jared ran as fast as he could and turned the corner and saw Rowena and Nix standing in front of the children, their heads buried, their eyes averted from the vampires that screeched at them from the other side of the closed bars that reached from ceiling to floor in the tunnel.

The path to freedom was closed.

Trapped here, they couldn't go forward.

Several of the children lost hope and started crying, collapsing to the ground.

Jared turned around and several shapes moved through the tunnel toward them. He gripped his sword handle, ready to use it. He had vowed he would. He would gladly lay down his life for the children. Of all the things he hated the most, vampires were at the top of his list.

From the tunnel came a voice, "We don't want to hurt them."

"Like you did two of them," Jared said.

"Accidents," the voice said, "they happen."

Jared lowered his voice and shuffled next to Nix. "Can you get that bar open?"

"Of course. But not now. I need time, which we don't have."

"Understood."

The voice said, "The children have safe passage. I promise you that."

Jared recognized the voice and said, "Is that you, Champion?"

"It is."

"How do I know your word is good?"

"Because I am not a weak human like you. I keep my word."

"Until you don't."

"You have my king's word. No harm to you or your companions. And the children are not to be harmed."

"But how do I know?"

"You speak of trust, human."

Jared frowned and tried to reply but Champion spoke again.

"Trust isn't easy to come by and must be earned. It can be earned through words and through actions. So listen and look at our actions: we could have rushed you by now, crushed you and taken you to our reception area. But the king demands you and your party to be treated with honor."

In a quiet voice Jared said, "We're damned no matter what."

"It is a difficult choice," Naveen said.

"The choice," said Champion, "is relatively easy." A torch was lit and light jumped out of the tunnel and spread toward them. Ten vampires stood at the end of the passage way and in front of them was Champion.

"Trust is the issue here. We offer you safe passage, but the king's patience is not infinite. Please decide. If you don't, then let me make it easy for you: I have ten berserkers with me. And more upstairs. We don't want to see any of the children hurt."

"Why did you take them?" Rowena shouted. "They're just children."

"Yes," Champion said. "My king would be glad to answer your question."

Jared faced Champion and ran through the avenues open to him. Surrender and die. Fight and die and have the children die as well. Or play along with him, stall for time and hide behind the rules of ancient custom. If they had to attack the horde, it would be better with only one lot at one time, pulverize them with sword and shield and some magic, and then sprint away during daylight with the children safely away from the monsters.

"You promise our safety?" Jared said.

A deep throated "No!" escaped from Rowena as she clutched her son tightly to her body.

"Yes." Champion stood still, imperious.

Nix grabbed Jared and snarled, "What are you doing?!"

"Can you go forward?" Jared asked.

"No."

"Can you get through them?" Jared pointed back at the vampires standing behind Champion.

"No."

Jared remained quiet.

Nix boiled over with anger. "Are you crazy?"

"Do you have any solution?"

"Fight."

"We're trapped."

Naveen said, "We were close to getting free."

He felt eyes upon him, especially the eyes of the children. He was the one who had given them hope and now they were stopped in their tracks. Surrender meant death. Fighting meant death. The only way out, the one way for all of them to survive laid plain before him and he hated it with all of his soul.

"Let's go see the king of vampires."

Chapter Twenty-four

"WE ARE GOING into a room full of vampires," Naveen said. "Doesn't that sound a little one sided to you?"

Jared leaned close to the wizard. "It does. But if you have any good alternatives, speak now."

"There has to be something we can do."

Jared heard the stress and tension in Naveen's voice. He was only stating what the others in the group felt.

"If we attack," Jared said, "they'll roll over us and the children are destroyed in the process. I won't have the children hurt."

"I'm saying ..."

"I know what you're trying to tell me, Naveen. Let's listen to what their king has to say."

"He'll probably say something original like 'off with their heads' or an approximation of that."

Champion held up his hand and the line stopped.

Jared excused himself from Naveen and headed toward the front of the line. He felt a sense of fear and bitter determination; both settled over his shoulders in equal amounts. He would see this to the end, no matter the cost.

He tried to keep the irritation out of his voice as he stepped up to Champion, "What is it?"

Champion said coolly, "You might want to pause before you step through this last door."

"Why? Don't think we can handle it?"

A curious smile played upon Champion's face. "If you have nightmares, this could be one of them."

Jared turned to Rowena, "Make sure the children keep their eyes to the ground."

Rowena nodded, "Understood."

The instructions were passed on and presently the children placed a hand over their foreheads, cupping their eyes, with bowed heads.

Jared held his head up high. "Let's meet your king."

Champion pushed open the door.

Jared stepped through the doorway after Champion; the first sensation he had was one of tingling fear shooting down his spine. The main hallway was filled with people; men, women, young, old, skinny, fat, poor, rich.

The tingling fear was still present, screaming for him to turn and run away.

He pushed back the fear that rose in his stomach and breathed deeply. In front of him in the midst of a party, holding glasses, laughing, and joking, was a room full of vampires.

His eyes scanned the room: in the center of the room on a raised platform a tall thin man, wearing dark pants and a red shirt, was seated in a large wooden chair with red cushions. The vampire's face had high cheek bones and a deep set pair of hollow eyes that locked on to Jared.

Jared faced the vampire, looking back at the creature without letting him sense any fear. Jared fought to keep the fear down. The vampire was reading him, taking measure of the kind of man he was.

Jared breathed deeply, calming himself when he heard the laughter of a woman's high voice. The voice, swinging with gaiety or so it seemed to him, rose above all the murmurs in the room and then everything crashed to a sudden stillness.

The laughter died away as all vampire eyes turned to Jared. The room full of hungry, angry eyes stripped him naked. Some of the eyes found him disgusting, while others assessed him with approval, and still others look at him as nothing more than a meal to be bitten and then discarded.

They were, Jared realized, in a room full of wild and hungry animals.

He shook off the fear that wrapped itself around him. A lone man in a room full of wild animals. This place wasn't safe for anyone, especially children.

The children.

Jared turned and said, "Keep your eyes down children. Keep your eyes down," he repeated for emphasis.

He turned and watched as Rowena and Nix stood behind him with the children. They had their heads bowed and their hands over their eyes.

"Hold hands children," Rowena said. "Step forward and keep looking down. Move slowly."

Naveen let out a gasp of surprise. The wizard quickly recovered and stood next to Jared. "We are outnumbered fifty to one, at least."

Jared gripped his sword hilt. It was a mistake to come here. He saw that now. The children were losing hope. Some started sniffling, while others started crying.

The king regarded the children's tears and Jared saw a cruel smile flicker across the creature's face.

Nix flanked Jared on the other side. "That's the obvious. Look for the weakness in them. Focus on that."

Naveen said, "What weakness?"

"The hidden kind. Everybody has it."

"What do we do?" Naveen said.

Jared said, "We see the king and go from there. He gave us safe passage all the way here, as long as we defeated his vampires along the way. Remember that."

"You're right." Naveen gripped his wizard's staff.

Jared turned to him. "How many fire spells to scatter them?"

"It depends, what do you want to do?"

"Keep thinking fire spells, Naveen."

Champion stepped in front of Jared. "Bring your whole party forward. The king would like to see you all, up close."

Jared nodded to Nix and Naveen. "Let's go."

Before they could move Champion said, "The woman and children too."

"I'd rather they stayed against the wall."

"The king would rather see them."

"Then we have an impasse."

"I would die for my king," Champion said. "Would you start a battle when it is easily avoidable by the simple act of courtesy?"

"I don't like being told what to do or how to do it?"

"And yet you have been given safe passage."

"I won't be the only one who doesn't make it out alive," Jared said.

"I can meet you anytime of your choosing and beat you. But the call for violence is unnecessary and my king grows impatient. Bring the children, and avoid the unforgivable."

Jared weighed his choices. He could fight right here and enjoy watching Champion's head sail through the air. But Champion was just a foot soldier.

If he wanted to do real damage, he had to get close to the king. If he fought and killed the king that would scatter all the vampires, and in their moment of fear it would give Jared time to get the children out of here.

Jared turned his back and said to Rowena and Nix, "Gather everyone close and tight. We go forward."

The children shuffled closer, clinging to each other. Nix led the children. Rowena was in the middle of them, her arms protectively draped over her son.

Jared glanced at the tight knot of arms and legs even as a ringing bell sounded in his head. This was a trap. It had to be. He looked around them, panic clutched at his throat. It was all a trap and he had walked straight into it. He had failed.

Now it was just a matter of when the trap would be sprung. He had tried to steal the king's victims away from them, even though they had been granted safe passage through the Old Ways of Conduct. It was a gambit and Jared knew they already failed. But if they did fail then to get within striking distance of the king was too good to give up.

Champion spoke out loud, his voice filling the hallway. "Your majesty. I present a foot soldier named Jared Whitestone, along with his companions, Nix, a thief, Naveen, a wizard, and mistress Rowena, a craftswoman and hunter."

Jared pushed down the fear that rose up inside of him. They knew his name. How was that possible?

Jared swallowed his surprise and stepped forward into the buzzing crowd. They parted before him and a dizziness swarmed around his head. He felt strangely disconnected as he walked through the crowd. It was as if he were suddenly drunk, not sloppy drunk, but with a certain sense of lag about him between his thoughts and actions.

He looked back. Nix and Rowena both seemed fine.

One of the vampire women walked in front of one of the children. When she passed by, a child was gone.

Jared blinked his eyes.

"Keep moving forward," Champion said. "The king needs to be addressed."

The words beguiled him into action. He kept walking forward and found himself pressed into a throng of other bodies, cooler to the touch, their laughter and hypnotic voices made it hard for him to walk straight.

A warning bell lethargically went off in his head, but he brushed it away. He felt good.

He turned around.

He caught sight of Naveen staring at the children and then stepped toward them. Everything was fine.

He frowned even as the alarm rang louder in his head, rising through a muffled cloth of contentment and feeling good. It had been a long time since he felt good. It was a narcotic to him. He forgot what it had felt like to feel like this.

A dark blur passed in front of him and a child disappeared.

Then two more.

Jared turned around and saw two more children taken in hidden snatches, out of sight. The children were bundled up, hands placed tightly over their mouths so there were no cries, no alarms, no calls for help. Only the worried and frightened looks he saw from the children's eyes.

For the life of him, he couldn't bring himself to respond. His only direction was to keep moving forward, and he was almost there. A couple of more steps and he now stood in front of the raised platform.

Seated on the high back chair was the king.

A scratchy tired voice sounded: "My son is gone! Where the hell is my son?"

Jared turned to the noise. And was surprised to hear Rowena's voice.

Rowena looked around her, her eyes scouted the room and then locked on to the figure seated before her. She looked up at the vampire king. "This was your doing."

The vampire king steepled his fingers together. "The children are well looked after."

Rowena's emotional outbreak cracked the spell that clouded his mind. Clarity and sharpness flooded into him. Jared shoved the last bit of the spell away and said, "Why take them?"

The king looked down at him with his hollow eyes. "Since you met the challenge and killed three of our finest warriors, be our guests. Feel free to mingle."

"Where is my son?" Rowena asked.

"Accept our hospitality, please," the king said, with a finality that closed the door to the conversation.

An attendant bowed low and whispered something into the king's ear, drawing his attention away.

Rowena turned around and took a few steps backwards, moving toward where they had just traveled from. "Where."

Her movement had been blocked.

She turned left. "Is."

Rowena pushed through two women in white party dresses and saw their curious smiles and the sharp pointy tips of their fangs. They smiled at her in passing. "My."

Rowena tried to go forward and was blocked.

She turned to the left and was blocked again.

She turned to the right and was blocked again.

Exhausted, she pulled out her knife; the steel blade flickered in the light of the room. She raised it high to strike at the nearest vampire when a hand reached out and grabbed her.

"This is impossible," Rowena said.

"That's the idea," Jared said. "Put the knife away."

"But my son was right next to me. My arms were around him."

"I know Rowena. I know." He felt the softness of her skin and found himself thrilled by her touch and by her passion. Jared realized, she was a strong woman and she loved deeply and passionately. How many women would brave the wilds and a castle full of vampires to save her son?

She was one of a kind and Jared marveled at her strength and tenacity to go on in the seemingly one sided conflict they were engaged in.

It was foolish to keep going on. The vampires had them out-numbered.

Jared shook his head and realized the effects of the mind cloud still lingered in him. He had to watch that or there wouldn't be any hope left for any of them.

He pulled Rowena close. "Let's get Nix and Naveen."

"Here we are," Nix said, parting the crowd of vampires before them. The four of them stood together and Nix turned and faced the nearest vampire. "Give us some space!"

A murmur rose through the crowd and suddenly a protective area of six feet lay on all sides of them. But something else changed.

Maybe it was the way Nix had spoken to them, but now the vampires stopped talking to each other and their red eerie eyes and blanched mouths and sharp fangs stared at them, taking the measure of them and found them all ready to snack on, ready to drain blood, and kill them, and scatter their bones around the castle ground like so much detritus.

"We have to do something," Jared said.

"I want my son back, and pity any man or beast who gets in the way."

"That's why we're here," Jared said. "I thought we could trust to the code of conduct, but I was wrong."

"We have the potion ready. We can fight right here and now." Nix patted his vest pocket.

Jared stared at the crowd before them. They were surrounded by vampires on all sides. If a fight was to break out they would be over-run. Fighting against an enemy on all sides was suicide. Tonight he didn't feel like dying.

"Not here." He scanned the room and found a wall. It provided protection and nobody would be able to come up from behind. Of course, they didn't have any place to retreat to either. "Move over there," he pointed.

They started to move when laughter suddenly cut through the air.

The laughter had a lilt to it and memories rushed into Jared's head with amazing speed. He remembered summers in his father's house and playing with his sister and brother. The summers were the best time of his life, the sun was warm and the days lasted seemingly forever.

The laughter continued. It was calling to him, talking to him in a private language that only he could understand. Whether it was some dark magic being used on him or not, he couldn't tell.

Jared broke away from his companions and headed toward the far doorway. The laughter came from there.

The vampires parted before him.

He leaned against the doorway as if just crossing the room full of vampires made him out of breath. He peered into the smaller room. A woman dressed in a white gown stood by the castle window looking out. The moonlight from outside shone down on her through the window.

The woman laughed again, pressing her hand against the cold stone.

"Christina," Jared said. He stood there and couldn't believe he had spoken her name.

She had died.

But she was standing right here. He must be dreaming.

"Christina," he said softly, doubting what his eyes plainly told him.

Turning from the window, the woman faced him. The strong resemblance in her face was still present. "Brother, you've come at last. Family blood called you to me. I missed you so."

"Christina, is it really you?"

She edged closer to him, almost shy; her eyes searched the floor, hesitant. "Yes, it is."

He lifted her chin and, after searching her face, opened his arms and held her in a tight embrace. "Christina."

A torrent of emotions flowed through him, each tumbling hard against him.

She was alive.

She died.

She's here.

In the cave he heard her voice. The flames had engulfed her, flesh sizzling and popping until the skin was gone and muscle and ligaments were exposed underneath. At least, he thought it happened that way.

She couldn't be here.

Yet, she was here.

She was alive in his arms.

Her voice, her words, her laughter.

She was real, she was in his arms, she was back from the dead. He'd been wrong. His sister never died.

And the tilt of his world suddenly changed. The vow, the promise he had made would have to be re-assessed later.

Standing before him was his sister. The key to his happiness was alive.

The words tumbled past his tongue in a rush to get out into the air, to be the first to be spoken.

"The last … I thought you dead! I thought the flames had consumed you."

She looked directly into his eyes, her gray eyes held him. "Did you miss me?"

He pressed his forehead against hers and whispered, "Every day and night. I missed you." He touched her face with his fingertips. "Now I can rescue you."

"It's important for family to be together," Christina said. "I missed you so. But what's this about rescuing me? Why?"

"I lost everything when I failed to rescue you. But now I can take you with us."

"Would you?"

"Yes. In a heartbeat, and I would rescue the children like I promised."

"Not the way you failed to rescue me?"

"Be kind, sister. I thought you died. I was wrong, obviously. Now you're here, and that's all that matters."

"What is your plan?"

"To spirit us out of here."

"Can you trust them?"

"We are their guests, they gave their word. But that is as far as I can trust them."

"You should be wary of them."

"Why? You are standing before me; this is a dream. I was a fool and would have come sooner if I'd have known about you, regardless of the death collars on us."

"Death collars? I don't see any collars."

"A wizard placed them on us before we went on this quest, to make sure we searched and found the children. We faced hardship and uncertainty every step of the way while walking straight into death's large mouth."

Her gray eyes smoldered with anger. "I'll rip him apart."

The anger behind her words shoved away the comforting thoughts that swirled through Jared about his sister. But he brushed that thought to a tiny corner of his mind, set it in a box on a table, closed the lid and turned his back on it. No matter how much he wanted to open the box and look at it, he steeled himself from it. Why explore it? It was such a small mystery. How could that compare to actually having his sister here now. Seeing her now, before him, made him the happiest person alive.

And because she was alive, he could live again.

"Forget that, my sister. Let me take you away from here. For I fear we won't last the night."

She touched his face with her cool hands. "My dear brother."

"What?"

"I am changed," she said softly. "I wish you had rescued me, but that is past. All that is important is that family is together. Family is everything and now that you are here, I feel happy."

"Sister, speak plainly."

He looked down into her eyes and saw the softness being replaced by stony resolution and crackling power and strength.

"I am the night wind," she said. "I am the cold moon. I am the lonely cry at midnight."

"You are ..."

The words rushed out of both of their lips at the same time, dancing and merging together and then breaking apart.

"Vampire," she said.

"My sister," he said.

"No!" the words ripped out of his chest and laid there broken. Jared staggered back and looked at her with fresh eyes.

"Frightened?" she asked.

"Who did this to you?"

"Would you still fight for my honor?" Her eyes widened in excitement.

"I would show you the honor, bravery and love I could not show you last time. You are not like the other vampires, surely."

Christina rocked back on her feet; the power that coursed through her eyes softened at the mention of the word she heard. She looped her arm through his and led him to the doorway. "See the king?"

"Yes."

"He took my life. He's tried to keep my family from me. And family is the only important thing we all have."

Jared felt his heart beating wildly in his chest; it banged and strained to escape the tiny confines of his body. Tears flowed down his face as he stormed away from his sister and found his hand on his sword. He moved through the sea of vampires and pointed at the king sitting on his red cushioned throne.

"You killed my sister, you ugly fanged bastard. I challenge you to a duel."

The king turned and looked down at him from the platform. "You do not know what you speak of."

"I do, you foul thing. You took my sister's life. Now I will take yours."

Jared swung the sword in a mighty circle around him, pushing back the crowd of vampires pressing in on him and then he stared up at the vampire king.

"I would not fight you." The king looked across the room and locked eyes with somebody. He paused for a second and then continued speaking. "But I'll make an exception."

Runes and words of power, what was going on? First Rowena broke the spell that encapsulated them all, then Jared wandered away and then Nix took off because he saw something bright and shiny like a magpie. Now Jared, in a sea of vampires, pointed his sword up at the vampire king. He was going to get them all killed. What happened to the cool headed man he knew these many days? Some kind of mind control was evident.

Naveen scanned the room. Jared, a sword in hand, his words stirred up the vampires around him. The vampire king answered Jared's challenge. But then the king paused. He looked out across the sea of night creatures and there was a woman by the doorway dressed in white. She nodded her head and then the vampire king continued talking.

That's the chain of command, Naveen thought. The king wasn't the one in charge. He was the proxy for her. But who was she? This was a new twist. All the reports the wizard council had received about Vampire Nation were never this concise and detailed, but here it was laid out plain for anyone with eyes to see.

He looked around the room for Nix and thought he saw the thief head at an angle toward a vampire who wore a shiny key attached to a red ribbon around his neck.

Naveen pressed his lips together. They were all going to die.

The vampire king stared down from the edge of the platform and leapt toward Jared.

Jared swung his sword and waited for the impact. He would cut the flesh away from the vampire, peeling back layer after layer of skin, until the vampire howled in pain.

Then he would add salt to the wounds and, near the end of his torture, he would sever the head and take a pike and plant the head in the heart of the Vampire Nation for all to see.

He'd let all the blood suckers know that there was one man not afraid of them.

The vampire king howled and, showing his fangs, disappeared into a cloud of inky blackness.

Jared swung his sword, but hit nothing. He staggered to the floor, caught off guard by what happened. He got up quickly and pivoted. He turned left, then right. He was alone.

He swung the sword several times, making defensive strikes both high and low, in front and to the sides where he stood.

Each time he connected with nothing but air.

Jared stopped swinging the sword. If his eyes couldn't help him, maybe his ears could. Where was the vampire king?

He turned and watched as Christina walked forward. The crowd of vampires parted before her and Jared thought that was strange. Why would they part before her?

Before he could muse on that, he was knocked to the ground, his left shoulder taking the main brunt from a heavy force. He slammed into the ground and tried to turn around, but the vampire king was on his back!

Jared struggled and grabbed at the vampire king, but nothing would work to his advantage. Then he grabbed a finger and pulled it back until the bone snapped. The vampire king howled in pain, releasing Jared at the same time.

Jared turned and brought his feet up between him and the vampire king. "You killed my sister and took her life."

Suddenly the crowd was quiet and eyes looked back and forth between the king of the vampires and the lady in white. "You do not know of what you speak," the vampire king said.

The vampire king looked across the room as Jared leaped up and stabbed him in the torso, on the left side, below the heart. He stabbed again and again, twisting and turning the blade of steel until blood poured out of the wound.

The vampire king hissed and struck Jared down with the back of his hand, sending Jared to the cold stone floor. With sadness and tenderness in his eyes, the vampire king glanced at Christina.

Blood rushed out of his wound, and the vampire king staggered.

Jared watched as the vampire slipped.

He crashed to the ground and lifted up his head. His body started dissolving away. "I tried my best," escaped his mouth as he dissolved away into nothingness.

The vampires murmured and looked angrily at Jared. Jared braced himself for an attack. He would tear down this room and take them on.

"Christina, come on," Jared said. He held out his hand for her.

Christina shook her head. "Family is important."

"Christina, come on. We don't have any time."

Christina said, "Take him and his friends to the dungeon. No harm is to befall any of them."

Jared glanced at her, puzzled.

Her dark eyes pierced him and her mouth opened even more, revealing her true heritage. Twin fangs protruded from her mouth.

She hissed at him and issued more commands, but he wasn't listening. Something went out from him and Jared felt himself suddenly lifted into the air, his body supported horizontally as he was carried out of the room, never touching the floor, struggling against the powerful hands that held him tight.

He turned and saw Naveen and Nix and Rowena being herded together as well.

"No, Christina. No!"

Christina laughed, and Jared heard a spiraling madness growing in her voice. The other vampires joined in with her laughter as well. It might as well have been the sound of a rancorous death sentence, as far as Jared was concerned.

It was simple.

He had doomed them all.

Chapter Twenty-five

THE DUNGEON CELL door clattered open as the others were shoved into the tiny cell. Powerful hands lowered Jared from above and, grabbing him by his shoulders, threw him, as easily as a rag doll, head first toward the stone wall.

Jared put up his hands to shield himself, but it was too late. He slammed against the dungeon wall and slid down, the air knocked out of him, pain throbbing in his head.

The vampires gave them all a vicious, hungry look, turned, and slammed the cell door behind them and left.

After a moment, Jared glanced over at Nix and Naveen and Rowena.

"I made a mess of this," Jared said.

Nix shook his head, "Didn't we start out like this?"

Jared sat up, with great difficulty, and said, "Everybody alright?"

Naveen said, "That depends on your definition. We were fine until you went berserker out there. What happened?"

"I lost my mind."

"Why?" Rowena asked, a frown across her face. "What was different?"

"Two things: I found out my sister is alive, and that she's a vampire. The king turned her into one of them."

"You mean—that must hurt if she's one of them," Nix said.

"Yeah. It does. Now my sister's a vampire."

"I'm sorry," Rowena said.

"I didn't know. I thought she was dead. She was the reason why."

"Your sister," Naveen said quietly, "is now a vampire. She is the enemy."

Anger rose in him as he looked across the cell to Naveen. Next to Naveen, sitting on the ground, one leg pulled up in front of him was Nix. He stared into space. Rowena was next to the thief, looking back at him, with fire in her eyes.

"Whether your sister is dead or alive, a vampire or not, we still have a job to do, right?"

Jared nodded. "Yes. You're right." He climbed to his feet. Of course, his sister was a vampire, but that didn't mean she was the enemy. He couldn't just kill her outright. No matter what she had become, she was still his sister. His family. His blood. To hell with Naveen. She was family.

Naveen said, "If we go up against them, she may be hurt."

Jared shot him a look. "Why do you say that? She is my sister."

Rowena answered instead, "We have a duty to fulfill. Find the children and bring them back to the village. If we forget that, if we let family blood get in the way, none of us may make it out alive."

Naveen dropped his voice and said, "She is right. Were you under some kind of influence back there?"

"What do you mean?"

"One moment you're talking to a woman and the next you issue a challenge to the vampire king. What was that all about?"

"I told you, the vampire king turned my sister into one of them."

"No," Naveen said. "You have it all wrong. She played you for a fool."

Jared rose to his feet and felt the floor sway under him. He leaned against the wall until the floor was solid and unmovable again. He felt his heart beating strongly; the pain faded from his body. "Be careful."

Naveen said, "She was the one in control of the whole situation. You didn't see it. I did. She controlled the whole thing. The king looked to her for guidance. And while you were fighting the king, she came forward. You didn't see that part because you were busy protecting her honor. But the crowd of vampires parted before her. *They parted before her.* Why would vampires do that? Why would the king of vampires look to her when he was talking? Why?"

Jared staggered back against the wall. All the fight suddenly went out of him; he shook his head and doubt multiplied in his mind.

The doubt grew thicker and more incessant inside him. In his mind, he was back in that tiny room with a box on a table. He crept closer to the box and stared down at it.

He opened the box and, with a critical mind and attitude, he reached inside. One. The children were taken away from them, and although he saw it, he didn't react properly to it. Two. They boxed them all in. Three. Christina was alive, but he saw her in flames. Her body was never discovered. He thought the ashes were all that was left of her. That assumption was wrong. What else was he wrong about?

Four. *Rescue me? Why?* she had said. Nobody in their right mind wanted to be near vampires, except other vampires. Five. *You should be afraid of them.* They were a food source surrounded by creatures that drained people of their blood. Six. *I'll rip him apart.* That wasn't like the Christina he remembered and loved.

Seven. *I am the night wind. I am the lonely cry at midnight. I am vampire.* Her own words marked her and the change she went through since the last time he saw her. Her body was cold to the touch, unnaturally so.

Eight. *Take him and his friends to the dungeon.* Whatever motivation moved his sister, she was no longer family or blood of his blood. Or was she?

Jared pushed away from the wall, his legs unsteady but growing stronger with each step. "We have to get out of here. Our job isn't my sister. Naveen's right. We came here to rescue the children."

Rowena pushed against the cell door and pointed at the hinges. "Both of these had stress fractures. If we can apply more stress to them, we might be able to break out of here."

"Is that all?"

"It should do it."

"What about the tunnel, can we get through it?"

Nix turned around and showed a golden key in his hand—the one he had taken from the vampire. With his other hand he fished out the key ring he had taken from the guard room. With the key ring in his hand, Nix smiled. "We can."

Naveen blurted out, "You used the potion!?"

Nix said, "Of course."

"I should have known," the wizard said.

Nix said, "If we can get the children, we can make it out through the tunnel, and we won't be stopped."

"We were last time, thief," Rowena said, arching an eyebrow at him.

Nix held up the golden key and his brown eyes sparkled with mischief. "We open the gate and continue on through the tunnel."

Rowena said, "What if there is another gate at the end?"

"There may be," Nix shrugged, "but so what? I have keys. And if these don't work, we have magic and brute strength," he said, pointing at Naveen and Jared.

"I hate it when he's right," Naveen said.

"Let's get out of here. I don't want to be a guest here any longer than we have to be," Jared said.

Nix inserted an old rusty key into the lock, turned it, and click! The door swung open and they walked out of the dungeon cell.

Rowena said, "Which way?"

Nix looked left and the hallway dead ended twelve feet away. He headed down the opposite direction and stopped at the intersection. He tilted his head to one side, and closed his eyes. He put up his hand.

"What is it?" Rowena asked.

"I hear them," Nix said, his eyes closed tight.

"Where?" There was tension in Rowena's voice.

Nix opened his eyes and pointed, "This way."

"How can you hear so well?"

"I'm a thief."

They moved down the hallway, past the torches set in the walls, and pushed open another doorway that led down another hallway. Across the way was a cell, and huddled on the floor were children.

Rowena rushed to the cell door. She clapped her hands. "Children, get to one side now."

The children were startled by this sudden appearance and moved away from the cell door.

Naveen stood next to the cell door. He pushed back his sleeves and held out his staff.

Something out of the corner of his eye caught Jared's attention. Before he could say a word to the others, a guard moved from the corner behind them. The look of surprise on the vampire's face told Jared everything he needed to know.

Jared raised his sword and rushed toward the vampire.

The guard stepped back and grabbed a rough hewed stone with both hands. The stone was similar in size and shape to what Nix had and that Jared now carried next to the spyglass.

Jared braced for the impact as he swung his sword down upon the vampire's head. But the vampire gripped the stone and vanished. One moment he was here, and then he was gone.

Jared sliced the air with his sword, making sure nothing invisible was standing next to him. When he was satisfied he retraced his steps and an explosion rocked the dungeon.

Jared fell against the nearest wall, the blast ringing in his ears; he coughed the dust away. When he stood up, he heard shouts from down the hallway.

He raced toward the dungeon cell and found Naveen, Rowena and Nix helping the children out of the cell.

"They've heard that. They know we've escaped."

Naveen shook his head and coughed. "I—I'm not very good with combat magic, like I said."

"It's lucky the children weren't hurt in the explosion," Rowena said, giving him a frosty look.

Naveen nodded. "I took care of that. I placed a shield around them."

"Nix, get us out of here. I ran into a guard and he vanished in front of me. And with the sound of this explosion, they'll know what happened."

Nix smiled weakly. "Right. Let's go." Nix took the lead, followed by Rowena and then children.

Jared and Naveen traveled in back, but after they had moved through several short hallways and climbed a flight of stairs, Jared moved up the line until he was step by step with the thief.

They came before the entrance to the main hallway, the same room where the vampire king and his horde had been. The only thing that protected them from the vampires was the massive door that stood closed between them and the horde of vampires inside.

"Nix, you go to the side door and get the children there."

"We have fifty feet or so to cross."

"Rowena you go with him. Naveen and I will draw the vampires' attention to us."

"How are you going to do that?" Rowena asked.

"Fireballs?" Naveen said.

"Exactly. The bigger and brighter and hotter, the better."

"Everybody ready?"

Rowena suddenly moved away from the children and, standing on her tiptoes, kissed Jared on the cheek. "Don't be a hero. Come back in one piece. You're better to us alive." Rowena turned and, before Jared could say a word, she had the children bunched close together, giving them instructions.

Jared pushed against the door and it opened easily on its hinges.

The room was in pandemonium. The vampires were busy listening to Christina issuing orders. Their backs were turned to them. No eyes were on them. All Nix and Rowena had to do was move slowly with the children in tow; was it thirteen or fifteen children, Jared didn't know. Just move them to the other side of the room, travel along the back wall and slide into the other connecting passageway. That was the easy part. The hard part was protecting the children while they moved. Naveen was itching to let loose some fireballs, but Jared made him wait. They had to be in position to protect Nix and Rowena and the children as they made their run across the room. If they could keep all the eyes on them, then the children would have a chance of escape.

Nix and Rowena hurried the children quietly across the space, hugging the back wall until Nix opened the passageway door and slipped inside. Rowena stood at the door and guided the children into it, one at a time, until the last one came up to her.

"Look," a voice said. "The humans are fleeing!"

The vampires stopped what they were doing and, in mass, turned and stared at Rowena and the child. They were caught frozen at the door by one hundred or more hungry eyes aimed at them.

Rowena, Jared noticed, glanced over his way, nodded her head, and then closed the door.

One of the vampires moved toward the passageway when a bright green-yellow spell glommed onto him. All the vampires stopped, as if spell-bound, and watched.

The vampire, encased in gelatinous substance, turned slowly back toward his comrades. He lifted his arms away from his body when suddenly a spark erupted, turning him into a fire stick.

The smell of burning flesh, vampire roasted, filled the hallway.

"Hey, uglies! Over here," Jared said, above the din of scared voices.

Christina turned and Jared saw her take stock of the situation. Her eyes narrowed and she strutted across the platform, pointing her hand at them like a sword. "Get them. Bring them to me."

Jared quickly lost count of the vampires as he stared back at the sea of fangs and red eyes and animalistic cruelty before him. He was amazed by the number of vampires in this room. He had never seen so many in one place before.

And he knew, without a doubt, that both Naveen and he were easily outnumbered. He guessed there were one hundred or more fighting machines facing him.

His sister strutted across the platform as Jared noted the vampire standing next to her. It was the same vampire who disappeared from the dungeon. The vampire held the stone in his arms, cradling it carefully. He leaned forward and whispered something into his sister's ear.

His emotions galloped away from him at the sight of his sister. He was furious with her. She was the cause of all of this. She had maneuvered everything to this point. He pointed at the platform with his sword and said, "You caused all of this."

Every pair of red eyes turned toward him. His sister whirled around at his voice and placed her hands on her hips. "What do you mean, brother?"

"You planned this. You had me under your watchful eye."

"Join me," she said. "Families are better when they're together, not apart."

"Was that your plan? Did you want me to join your family?"

"Maybe," she said, a slow smile stretching across her face.

Out of the corner of his vision, Jared saw Naveen whirl his staff and send out a spell to their right flank, pushing back a wall of vampires.

"You had me followed. You had one of your people kill an innocent man and framed me for it."

"I want our family back, the way it was."

"You framed me for murder. The old Christina would never do that."

"Family belongs together."

"Never."

"Get them!"

Jared raised his sword and watched as Naveen raised his staff and three of the closest vampires on the left were slammed against the nearby wall, flattened against it. Jared leaped forward and sliced the head off a nearby vampire. The headless body dissolved by his feet. Jared grabbed the head and tossed it toward his sister.

The head rolled across the platform and came to a stop by her side. The vampire's head, Jared could see it even from where he stood, had a surprised look on his face.

She shouted orders and the vampires grew angry and converged upon them, swearing oaths, hissing and growling.

"Fireballs would be good now." Jared stuck his sword through a torso and then placed his boot against the vampire and kicked him back, freeing his sword.

Naveen raised his staff, the runes glowed with brilliant light like daylight, and suddenly a ball of green fire leapt over the vampires in the front and smashed against the vampires in the rear part of the room. The vampires jumped and shrieked and a stampede occurred.

From the middle of the platform, Christina shouted orders. Another fireball leapt from the top of the staff and landed on the opposite side of the room. It caused a stampede over there as the vampires dived and climbed away from the fire.

The smell of burning flesh filled the hallway and mingled with the shrieking cries of vampires.

Two more fireballs landed in the crowd, driving back the vampires, causing them to huddle in the middle of the room.

"Now what?" Jared asked.

Naveen didn't answer. Jared saw that he was too busy concentrating and had failed to see a vampire crouching slowly up on Naveen's blind side.

Jared rushed to Naveen's aid, sword raised, and drove the other vampire back, the blade slicing through the creature's wrist and severed the hand clean through at the wrist.

Blood flowed from the wound and the vampire screamed in torment and then charged forward, eager to kill Jared for what he had done. Jared braced himself between Naveen and the oncoming vampire.

Jared swung high, causing the vampire to duck low. Jared pivoted, waited an instant, then turned and made two downward slices like an X mark in front of him with the sword. The blade sliced into the right side of the neck and dug deep into the flesh.

The vampire howled in agony.

Jared yanked the blade out of the vampire's flesh and watched as blood erupted like a geyser from the wound. He stabbed the vampire two more times and kicked him back.

"There," Naveen said. "I've done it."

Jared turned to watch.

It was a beauty to behold. It was as if an invisible wall had swept across the room, pushing back the vampires, squeezing them together in the middle of the room. In the center of it was Christina, who raged and pushed her troops on to battle. Next to her was the vampire with the stone.

"We've outstayed—" Jared said.

"Our welcome," Naveen added.

"Exactly. Time to go. Can you do one more fire thing?"

"It will be my last until I can recover."

"Do it."

Naveen was quicker this time, whether it was because he was tired or he was getting better, Jared didn't know. But the fire-spell left his staff and the green flame traveled straight toward the platform and Christina. Before it approached her, he saw her instinctually grab the stone from the guard.

A green explosion roared through the room from the platform. Jared averted his eyes and felt the blast knock him down. He got to his feet and helped Naveen to his feet. They stumbled across the room to the passageway Rowena and the child had escaped through.

Naveen had trouble walking; he was limping on his right leg. Jared inspected the leg and saw a small knife embedded in his calf muscle.

"You have a blade in your leg. I'll help you once we're out of here."

"I understand. Let's move," Naveen grunted.

He helped Naveen to the door. Naveen might have to push himself if they were going to win this fight. If Naveen was out of it, then Jared faced a losing battle.

Jared hoped the wizard was strong enough to endure.

They paused at the door; the sound of screams caught their attention. Three vampires were running sticks of fire, careening frantically back and forth, wounded animals screaming in pain. The sound of cries filled the hallway as the magical flames leapt from one to another whenever the vampires were within arm's reach of each other.

Jared glanced back at the raised platform. He saw no sign of his sister Christina.

He grabbed Naveen and pushed on through the door, careful to close it behind them. They raced, as best they could, through the tunnel. In seconds, they were at the same spot where earlier Champion had stopped them. The gate was swung open and the lock had been thrown to the ground.

"He opened it?" Naveen said.

"He's a thief. Now let's catch up to the others."

Christina clutched the stone and willed herself back into the main hallway. Her people needed her. She was the queen and would not abandon them. They were family and family would survive. She would see to that. Family, she knew all too well, was the most important thing in the world. She learned that from before and she carried that with her.

She stood there and watched as her people twirled in pain and shrieked because of the green flame from the wizard's damn staff. He would have to die. She couldn't stand him hurting her people like that, especially when they had been given safe passage.

She watched as her people swarmed in confusion in the hallway. She reached out and grabbed one of them. "We are the night," she said.

The vampire looked back at her and shrieked.

"We are the night," she said again.

The vampire gained some self control and said, "We are the night."

"We are the moon," she said.

"We are the moon," he said, after her.

She repeated the refrain, going from one hurt vampire to another, letting the words focus them, give them hope, give them peace and succor.

Give them promise.

The vampires pulled together, one mass closing tight around Christina. The other vampires had either stomped out the fire or had been consumed by it. She saw the fearful looks in their eyes. The fire frightened them. She repeated the refrain and they chanted in unison with her.

"We are the night."

We are the night.

"*We are the moon.*"

We are the moon.

"They dare to defy us."

They dare to defy us.

"After them, my people. Show them blood and fangs."

Show them blood and fangs.

Chapter Twenty-six

RUNNING THROUGH THE tunnel, Jared heard sounds ahead of them. With every other step, Naveen grunted. Even with Jared offering assistance to Naveen, the wizard stumbled a few times. If the wizard was unable to fight, they would be at the mercy of the vampires.

The sounds became clear as Jared turned a corner and heard several of the children coughing, clearing their lungs of the fine dust in the air. Several children, bent at the waist, spit and cleared their throats.

With the children out of the dungeon, they had taken baby steps toward freedom. Now they had to bring the children home safely.

What was his sister's part in all of this?

He thought back to his father's court. All the children knew how to handle themselves in a court situation to maneuver and gain the advantage. It was one of the first lessons they learned. Christina had executed flawlessly what she had observed her whole life. She had learned how to move the levers of government. What promises she had made and to whom, he didn't know, but she was deadly and feral.

And vampire.

He sighed, and leaned against the cave wall.

Naveen stepped past him and leaned against the wall, too.

"Nix," Jared said, pointing at Naveen's leg, "Can you bind him? He needs help."

Nix saw the blade sticking out of the wizard's leg. "It'll be temporary, at best."

"Do what you can and fast."

The thief was capable and sure-handed as he leaned against the wizard and pulled out the knife and blade. He quickly applied a powder to the wound and tied a piece of cloth around the leg, staunching the blood flow. Then he applied another piece of cloth to the wound itself.

Naveen grunted and a mask of pain held his face tight. It lasted for seconds and then his face relaxed and Naveen exhaled. He nodded to the thief.

A hand brushed him on the shoulder. Jared turned and there was Rowena. She placed a hand absently on his shoulder. "You did good back there. I'm glad." She breathed in deeply. "Glad you didn't get hurt."

"Why's that?"

"Because we aren't out of here yet." She grabbed his hand. "Come."

He followed her lead, leaving Nix and Naveen in the last part of the tunnel, and strode past the huddle of children and through the open gate. They stood in a plain grassy field. Jared noted the grass under his feet. It felt good.

The moon, overhead, shined down brightly, illuminating the tree line a hundred yards out from them. Behind the tree line lay the forest.

"We are in a terrible position," Rowena said.

A spark of irritation flared in his voice. "Yes. Well, we can always go back, if you want."

"No, that's not what I want. I want to get us all out of here, hopefully in one piece and alive."

Jared surveyed their position, looking at it as a soldier and battlefield tactician. Directly behind them, one hundred years away, stood the imposing castle. Nobody would come at them from that part of the castle.

He turned and knew the attack, when it came, would come from two directions: either from inside the tunnel or from the tree line, and later, if they were pushed back into the tunnel then the opening would be circled by angry, hissing vampires.

Jared felt his face go white.

This could be their last stand.

He felt the back of his throat suddenly go dry.

They were defenseless if they fought on the grassy plain, three hundred and sixty degrees of defenselessness.

And if they were forced to defend themselves from the tunnel then it would be a war of attrition. Who could stay alive until daylight? The four of them and the children against the vampires was one-sided, weighed heavily in the vampires favor.

They had to survive until daylight. Then they could hurry back to the village and show the Captain of the Guard and Grinbell what they had done and demand their freedom.

Nix came toward them.

Jared said, "How bad is her?"

"Not that bad. No major blood vessels. Muscles will be sore and the wound needs time to heal."

"But not tonight," Jared said. He leaned forward and clapped Nix on the back. "By the way, good job with the gate."

"Thanks."

Jared said, "Rowena was showing me our position. We're exposed here. We have two sides against us."

"What two sides?" Nix raised his voice, irritable at being told he made a mistake.

"We can be attacked from out there," Jared said, pointing to the tree line. "And we can be attacked from behind." He pointed down the tunnel they had come from. "Can you lock it back up?"

"I can't."

"Why?"

"The lock was rusty and the key broke in it."

"Great."

"Nobody told me beforehand."

"Battle is never static, thief. Battles can change in a heartbeat."

Nix swallowed and lowered his head in shame. "What do you expect me to do?"

Jared wanted to scream at himself. He was being too hard on the thief. Nix didn't know anything but stealing and his own craft. He couldn't hold Nix accountable. Besides, it took a lot of bravery to lead a group of children and Rowena into the unknown with only a key to open a closed tunnel gate.

Nix showed bravery and courage, and Jared couldn't diminish that by calling attention to something Nix wasn't responsible for. It wasn't right.

Jared laid a hand on Nix's shoulder.

"You took a group of children and led them here under battle conditions. You did a brave and courageous thing. I want you to know that, no matter how this night ends, you did good, thief. You did good."

Nix stood taller and swallowed and then he excused himself.

Jared surveyed the group. Rowena was back with the children, closing them together around her. Naveen leaned against the earthen wall, his hand resting on his bandaged wound, his fingers playing lightly across the wound.

Maybe he was giving himself a healing spell, thought Jared.

They didn't have long before they would be under attack.

Rowena looked down the tunnel and then up ahead of them and got to her feet. She stepped close to Jared. "We're exposed here."

"I know that," Jared said.

She stared up at him, her back straight, her neck stiff. "Do something."

"I have a wizard who is wounded and tired after fighting a room full of vampires. I have a thief who has admitted to not being very helpful in battle, that he'd rather steal, and I have a woman who was dead on with getting her kid away from vampires and now she tells me the obvious. And I am out of my mind. My sister, whom I thought dead, is a vampire, and she was the mastermind behind all of this. So tell me, what am I supposed to do?" he said heatedly.

Rowena remained silent, her eyes slightly tearing.

"Because frankly," Jared said, "I don't know what else to do. Wait here and fight them the best way we can."

Rowena felt the anger rush up from her and explode in a torrent of words. "We have to secure the tunnel from a sneak attack. I heard you say that. Do it. Grab the wizard and kick him until he can bring down the roof, if need be. Then get some fire sticks going, because last I heard vampires don't like fire."

Jared took in the sight of her and started laughing. He laughed so hard he held his sides. After a moment of laughter, he stood up and bowed. "Thank you. I needed to laugh. It felt good. And you are right. I should push them harder."

Jared walked to Nix, with Rowena behind him. "Nix, you and Rowena get some wood and make fire. We'll need a lot of fire sticks."

"Where am I going to find them?"

"I don't know. Look."

Jared turned and moved toward Naveen, leaving Rowena with Nix. He approached the wizard and leaned against the wall. He started to speak, but the wizard turned.

"I heard. She's right. I can put some fireballs down the tunnel; that should make then wary to come down this tunnel."

"That's a start. But can you pull the roof down? Maybe aim at some of the support beams and create a cave-in?"

A hard glint of resolution flickered in Naveen's dark eyes and the wizard pushed off the wall and walked down the tunnel, staff in hand.

Jared accompanied Naveen, his sword in hand. A scattering of sound echoed through the tunnel toward them. "Wizard, stop. They're coming. Do something now."

"I didn't hear anything," Naveen said.

"You're tired. They're coming. Throw a fireball down the tunnel. Quick!"

Naveen braced himself, held the staff in both hands and the runes glowed with eerie brightness and a green fireball jetted away from him. Down the passageway, the fireball traveled until it burst against the side of the tunnel walls. The flames exploded upon impact and traveled further down the tunnel, plastering the roof, the walls and the floor with mystical flames.

A cacophony of screams echoed toward them.

Naveen exhaled deeply and shouted in a language Jared didn't understand. Maybe it was a string of oaths or maybe it was a complex spell he was working out. But either way, Naveen picked up his feet and raced deeper into the tunnel, shouting as he went.

"Wait!" Jared shouted. But it was too late.

Jared was torn between staying here with Rowena and Nix because he was certain an attack was coming from that end, (it was what he would do) or race after the fool wizard and pull him back from certain suicide.

All he wanted was for the roof to cave in.

He couldn't afford to lose his wizard. Not now.

They had barely escaped the dungeon and they certainly hadn't reached any relative safety, so the power of a wizard was paramount to their survival.

Jared swore under his breath and raced after Naveen.

He turned the corner and saw Naveen, arms raised, concentrating on a spell. He had seen that look many times now and was familiar with it. A vampire raced through the now dying green flames and was headed for a collision into the wizard.

Jared raced faster and drew his sword. The vampire saw him and changed course. The vampire leapt to the wall of the tunnel and clung to the dirt walls. He hissed.

Blood pounding in his brain, Jared raised the sword in both hands and charged at the blood- sucker. He swung at the creature but he was too slow.

The vampire darted to the tunnel ceiling, just out of reach.

"Hurry, Naveen. Not much time."

The vampire hissed and dropped straight to the ground, crouching low.

Jared moved toward the vampire, keeping himself between the wizard and this night creature.

Hisses from the tunnel echoed up to them. More creatures were coming. It was only a matter of time when they would be overrun. Not for the last time would he give everything for two more wizards, battle hardened, to be here in the tunnels with them. Wizards that were cunning, filled with the power of the sun and the earth at their commands, and all the knowledge of great and terrible wizards. But he had only Naveen, and that, he figured was as good as he'd ever have.

He pointed his sword at the crouching vampire and said, "Prepare to die!"

The vampire hissed and rushed forward with the speed of the wind.

An arrow caught the vampire in the head, the tip entering the ear on one side and exiting through the jaw on the other side.

The vampire skidded to a stop, shrieking in pain.

Jared glanced over his shoulder at Rowena standing tall with her bow in hand. She fitted another arrow to the string and pulled it back.

"Hurry," Jared said.

A humming sound emanated from the staff and Jared turned away and pressed his hands over his ears; the sound hurt so much. He and Rowena moved behind Naveen and watched. The sound grew in pitch and loudness and then the spell cut loose and moved across the tunnel, vibrating the walls as it went. Down the tunnel vampires shrieked and howled in pain. The earth rocked and shook as if it was a tiny toy in the hands of an angry and petulant boy being rattled and then discarded.

A low rumbling sound erupted from the bowels of the earth and then the sides of the walls cracked and the fissure spread away from them toward the castle. The floor shifted and cracked open. There was another shift of the earth and Jared fell to the ground; the walls were shaking so badly.

And then everything went silent.

Jared looked at Naveen and glanced back at the tunnel. It was still passable. Cracks and fissures appeared in the wall and across the floor, but it wasn't anything to stop vampires from coming after them.

They were doomed.

Hope seeped out of him. His wizard had tried his best, gave it his best shot and still the tunnel held. Now they would have to fight on both sides.

They weren't going to make it. He had gambled and thought they would actually make it, but he was a fool.

Of course they wouldn't make it. It was stacked against them from the start. His sister had seen to that. She had rigged the game from the beginning. His only regret was for the children.

He did this for the children and now he had failed them.

He stood up and yelled. "Come on you bastards! Come here. I'm not afraid of you."

The vampires crouched on the floor, dancing around the last of the green flames, looking at the ceiling above them. The earth groaned and made rumbling noises. The vampires moved slowly down the tunnel, glancing nervously at the walls.

Suddenly the earth shook again and the pressure caused the roof to fall in; dirt piled on top of the vampires until they were buried. Rock and granite fell into the tunnel and dust kicked up everywhere.

Dying screams were heard, then muffled by rock and earth.

Jared brushed away the dirt and dust and tried to breathe, but all he could do was cough. He doubled over and sucked in small amounts of air. When he looked up the roof had fallen down and the tunnel was effectively blocked off from any attack.

Jared grinned, got up and slapped Naveen on the back.

"That was a great job. Great job."

"I am a wizard, after all."

Jared found himself laughing and between him and Rowena, they helped the wizard back to the mouth of the tunnel where Nix and the children were waiting for them.

"You did more than good, wizard," Rowena said. "You were marvelous back there."

Nix cried out, "I heard and felt a rumbling. Is everything okay?"

Jared smiled.

Rowena said, "Don't mess with the wizard."

Naveen leaned back against the wall, and rested his hands on his thighs. "Just a cave in. Nothing to worry about."

"He shook the earth till it collapsed," Jared said, staring with admiration at the exhausted wizard. He walked past Naveen and said to Nix. "Do you have some more of that potion?"

"Yes."

"Make sure everyone gets some of that potion now."

"Now? Why?"

Jared stared up at the tree line. On the ridge, under the full moon, was an army of vampires staring down at them.

"Get the children out of the way. Rowena take care of them."

Nix pushed the contents of the dropper into Naveen's mouth. He took some drops for himself and then he pushed some drops into Jared's mouth. Rowena took a sip from her stopper and put the bottle away.

The elixir coursed through him, strengthening him and making him more alert than before. Jared felt refreshed and strong. Moments ago he was ready to give up but now with the potion inside him, he felt confidence rush through his blood.

A row of vampires, three deep at least, looked down at them from the ridge line. He raised his chin to them, defying them with this small gesture. He allowed a memory to brush his mind: it was something he had been taught. A battle can change in a heartbeat. Battle was a living thing with its own ebb and flow. If the battle was with you, you would survive. But if it wasn't, you'd better make plans.

He made it his business to always seek the best advantage in any situation, and now, on the eve of this battle, it was no different.

He counted the vampires and after thirty he stopped. The number didn't matter. The odds against them didn't matter. Naveen brought down the tunnel and closed it down. He was humbly thankful for that. It was one less thing to worry about. Now they needed fire and they needed archers.

Luck would be appreciated too.

"Naveen. I need some fireballs. Light up the trees around them."

Naveen limped forward and stood next to him. He lifted his staff and wordlessly fireballs appeared in a mass, swarming like insects around light.

Naveen released the balls of energy, one, two, three, the fireballs sped up the hill toward the ridge line.

Brilliant light exploded against the trees as the flames started growing and consuming the dry bark. The vampires, discovering that the flames had missed, stood on the ridge and stared down at them. They were an army, now enraged, ready to descend upon them.

But then smaller pieces of the fireballs leaped away from the trees and glommed onto nearby vampires—attaching to arms and legs, or torsos and necks.

The vampires stopped laughing.

One vampire, a gob of fire attached to the side of his head, screamed in rage and frenzy, moving in an erratic circle trying to snuff out the flames on his head. No matter how much he patted his head, the flames wouldn't die.

Another vampire, surprised at the gob of flame on his right thigh, tried to put it out, but the flame traveled up to his torso and soon he was engulfed in flames.

A third vampire, eyes wide in horror, swung his arm away from himself while full of fire. His burning arm brushed some of his comrades and they scattered, the line on the ridge breaking apart. The fire spread quickly to other vampires and half the ridge was lit up in flame.

The smell of burning flesh was strong in the air as vampires shrieked in madness and pain.

"Rowena, I need some archers. Aim for those who try to outflank us."

Rowena stepped away from the children, and fitted an arrow. She brought the bow up and pulled back on the string. She sighted a target, tracked it, and let the arrow fly. Fooomp!

The tip of the arrow went through the soft tender eye of the vampire and broke free of the skull on the opposite side. The vampire screamed and turned to dust, its death cry cut off.

A scout vampire ran down the hill toward their tunnel opening. Jared charged at the vampire, coming at it from an oblique angle. With sword gripped tightly in hand, he leapt forward and lobbed off its head.

There was a pause: Jared watched the head roll across the ground; the vampires that weren't on fire looked down in a cold fury.

Jared felt the silent fury from the angry, hungry looks and raced back to the tunnel entrance. He braced himself for the attack.

Suddenly the tide broke and a mass of vampires ran toward them, screaming, hissing, angry.

Nix said, "I wish I had hope. I feel all hope has left me."

There was something Jared was forgetting, but what was it?

Rowena said, "We tried our best, but it wasn't …"

Naveen said, "I have some tricks in my bag, but not as many or as big as my earlier ones."

A light went on in Jared's eyes and he grew bright as he searched inside his tunic and found the gift that had been given to him. *Use this when you have need of hope.*

The children screamed and out of nowhere two vampires rushed toward Naveen and Rowena. How was that possible? The tunnel had been sealed shut from behind. Where was the breach?

Rowena shoved the questions aside and gripped her short knife, rushing forward. A large vampire stood in front of her and raised back his arm, exposing his massive chest and ribs, and swiped his arm and claws across her. She ducked under the swiping claws of the creature and, moving inside with blinding speed, she struck the vampire in the heart, twisted the blade with great exertion, and then pulled it out. The knife made a small sucking sound as fluids dribbled out of the hole.

The vampire dissolved into nothing.

Rowena turned and saw as Naveen lifted his staff and a fire spell swarmed over the vampire's head, lighting him on fire. The vampire shrieked and ran out of the tunnel, into the night, toward its comrades.

Now the children screamed and looked at the spot between the two of them.

Rowena rushed toward the children. The ground above them had been lifted up and a hole had been made for the vampires to slip in behind them. Her fear grew as she searched for the other vampire. She wouldn't let anybody hurt her son. He was the reason she had come. But as she went past the kids, she couldn't find any vampires. Obviously, it was a sneak attack.

She looked for her son. "Steen?"

A shriek erupted behind them. Rowena stood transfixed, her hands made into fists. "Where is my son? He's gone. MY SON IS GONE!"

Jared felt helpless and didn't know what the small bag could do. He looked around at the vampires: some were running about with flames licking their flesh, others were fearful and holding back, and still others were ready to charge again. They were grossly outnumbered and it would only be a matter of time before they were knocked down and defeated.

They needed hope right now. He opened the bag and a mote of light, small and shining, sparkled before him with a dull transparency. It was a ghost light, barely visible except within arm's reach.

It bobbed back and forth on the air currents.

Jared swallowed and in a small, quiet voice said, "Help us. It's for the children. It's for Steen. It's for his mother Rowena. It's also for Naveen and Nix. We're surrounded by vampires. We need hope, a lot of hope."

The faded light made a slow circle in front of him and then zigzagged up into the night sky; quickly it was out of sight.

"What was that?" Naveen asked, his head whipped around and he narrowed his eyes at Jared.

"It was nothing."

"No it wasn't. I thought I saw something there. And you were talking quietly."

Rowena stepped forward. "What?"

Jared slumped and all hope left him. "The Lady failed us."

Naveen shook his head in disbelief. "No." His eyes searched Jared's face, noting the downcast eyes, the look of hopelessness in them. "She did," he said quietly. He lowered his head, "I'm sorry. I should never have brought you there. It was all my fault."

"Your fault?" Nix asked. "How do you figure?"

"If I hadn't brought him to her, he would've died and that would have been the end of it. I gave everybody a false sense of hope."

Nix shook his head. "If you didn't do that, you'd never have met those wizards and after being humiliated, you'd never learn wordless commands."

"But it's not enough," Naveen said.

A voice distant and hard spoke. "Whether it's enough or not doesn't matter. We came here for the children and we'll give them the best we have to offer. We came to rescue them and I won't leave them behind, not a single one of them. Are you with me?"

Nix and Naveen and Rowena stared back at him with surprise. Jared had stood and spoken those words with a quiet passion that surprised even him.

"Are you?" he asked again.

"Yes," they said in unison.

"For Steen and the children," Jared said.

"For Steen and the children," they repeated after him.

"Let's go and face them, and teach them that they can't take our kids away."

Jared moved up to the ridge, his sword out and ready when he was suddenly surprised at the brightness of the moon. He looked at the ground and his shadow was definitely there. But it was night? Where was the light coming from?

He stopped. "Naveen, the light."

The wizard glanced around and Rowena said, "Look!"

The moon was small and bright and low in the sky. Not enough light to cast a strong shadow, but Jared turned and felt a wave of heat bounce against him. He looked over his shoulder, straight up into the sky, and in the middle of the night, the darkness shrank as the mote grew larger in pulsing waves, sending wave after wave of heat and light.

Jared felt a rush of hope fill him.

He lowered his head; the light was blinding.

The vampires stopped, except those on fire, still thrashing about, gesturing for help from their comrades, and screaming from the tendrils of flame that burned them alive, and said, "Where is the night?"

All fighting stopped as the vampires looked up into the brightness above them. Some of them ran, instinctively fearing the light. Others stayed there and gazed into the sublime warmth, faint memories of what they once had.

The vampires who continued to watch the light screamed.

Smoke rose from their eyes, searing the eyeballs until the vampires were made blind. They hissed and groaned and cursed their luck. Several of them cried out to their queen.

But there was no answer as a great ruckus sounded about them and several figures charged forward from the surrounding forest, screaming and crying as they attacked the blinded vampires, chopping off their heads.

Jared stepped forward and couldn't believe it.

Sol and his men and others from the village scrambled over the ridge and, descending into the shallow valley like madmen with swords and axes, savagely engaged the vampires. Three men ganged up on one vampire and, with many sword thrusts, the vampire laid on the ground bleeding and dying. The men went from one creature to another.

As the massacre continued, Jared stepped back and grabbed Rowena by the arm. "What happened?"

"My son is missing. He's gone."

"We'll find him. Show me where," Jared said.

She took him to the back of the tunnel entrance where the children were. The gate behind them was locked and before that laid the cave-in, with slabs of rock and earth resting in the tunnel, effectively blocking anyone or anything from coming that way for a sneak attack from behind. Jared quickly moved away from the tunnel entrance and climbed around the entrance, standing on the earth-covered roof.

He stood above the tunnel entrance and gazed out in front of himself. The fighting was almost over. He could see the villagers beating the vampires back with flame and swords. Naveen was out there giving them a hand. Even Nix, with his small dagger, added to the fight.

He turned and inspected the area. The castle wall was behind them, but there were no paths to lead one around the castle. It was a dead end.

He remained tight-lipped as an answer suddenly came to him.

"Maybe the answer lies in the castle," Jared said, wanting to give Rowena hope, but he felt it the height of foolishness to offer something that he wasn't sure of one hundred percent. Had they saved the children only to have Rowena's son sacrificed?

No. He shoved that thought away.

A voice behind him said, "What good is being afraid?"

Jared turned and the old woman from the village walked toward him.

"It isn't."

"Exactly. Sometimes you have to remind yourself that life is to be lived and not feared. And I figured rightly that you weren't looking for herbs either."

"Yeah, well maybe you're right," Jared said.

"How can we help you?" She raised her old gnarled handled cane and swept it around them.

"The children. Can you shelter them? We must go back inside the castle."

"Why? The children are here, aren't they?" She pointed toward the cluster of children huddled in the tunnel entrance.

"One was taken."

"My son," Rowena said, her voice still and quiet.

"We have to find him," Jared said.

"You're a good man," the old woman said. "We'll shelter the children; treat them as our own until you come back."

Jared bowed his head in thanks. "Nix, stay with them. I don't think we'll need your services."

Nix shook his head no. "In for a penny, in for a pound."

"Then let's go. We head back to the castle."

Jared turned and headed toward the castle wall. Rowena followed after him, laboring over the slopes and controlling her emotions. Nix and Naveen brought up the rear guard. The runes glowed with a savage light from the staff.

Sol glanced at the old woman and said, "He looks driven."

The old woman nodded her head slowly. "Some men are driven by impulses buried deep in their minds."

"Tortured?"

"It takes a tortured one to see a kindred brother. Aye," she said softly. "He's tortured all right."

Chapter Twenty-seven

JARED GLANCED SIDEWAYS and saw the remains of a large dragon sprawled out on the dry moat. Several arrows and lances stuck out of the skull. The tail had been broken in several places.

Jared walked across the drawbridge, with the orb above them, following them, lighting the area. The orb of hope provided comfort, and Jared knew that others found refuge in it, too. With the orb above them, it was certainly better than stumbling around at night, tripping over stone, dragon skull, or dead body.

"What are we looking for?" Rowena raised her voice, the tension clearly evident. "My son was taken back there."

"Leads," Jared said.

"Where would we look for them?"

They stepped into the great hall, the platform was still there but all was silent now. The stink of death lingered in the room. It was only hours ago that they stood there surrounded by vampires.

Nix stepped forward and stopped. "Can we leave?"

Jared said, "Something is here ..."

Rowena folded her arms. "You're following the wrong lead. My child is missing. A monster has my child."

Jared placed the satchel on the platform and pulled back the flap. "I know Rowena. Trust me."

"What are we doing here? My child is missing."

Jared pulled the stone out of the satchel and cupped it in his hands.

Rowena pointed at the stone. "That's not going to do us any good; it certainly won't do anything for my son."

Jared held up his hand for silence. "When we left this room Naveen had filled it with fire spells, giant green balls of fire exploded everywhere. I looked at the platform and saw Christina in the middle of the fire spells, but then she disappeared."

"Are you certain?" Naveen stepped forward, his eyes scanning the rock with new interest.

"And in the dungeon, a vampire saw us escape and he was standing in front of me one moment, but the next moment he was gone. Both my sister and that guard had one thing in common. They both held in their hands a stone like this."

"It can't be," Naveen said.

"What?"

"It sounds like you're talking about dragon stones."

"Dragon stones?"

"But that's impossible," Naveen said.

"If these stones can transport people between places then that would make a lot of sense."

Nix snapped his fingers. "It would make communication between distances a lot easier."

"And alliances can be made and no one would know about it," Naveen said.

Jared frowned and tapped his finger against the warm stone. "If Christina had these stones."

Nix said, "Grinbell would benefit. He had the stone in his workshop."

Naveen said excitedly, "That would be where the magic tech appeared. New magic was popping up but we could never locate the source of it."

All eyes turned to Naveen.

Naveen sighed. "I was assigned to find out where the magic tech was coming from. I thought it was Grinbell, but I could never prove it."

Jared stared at him. "So this was all a ruse for you?"

"No. I stutter. I was guilty of foretelling without a license, and I did spend time in jail. But beneath all of that I was to watch and listen for any signs of magic tech popping up in the area. That was the extent of my mission."

Jared turned to Nix. "And you. Do you know who hired you?"

"My contact with my client was through a third party—I never knew who exactly commissioned me to break into Grinbell's workshop and steal the spyglass."

Jared frowned. "All roads lead to Grinbell and they tie here to the vampires. But to what purpose?"

Jared reached down and placed both hands on the stone and felt the warmth of summer flood into him, filling him up and leaving with him a contented feeling.

A loud click sounded from the passageway and an agent stepped into the main hallway. He wore a wide brimmed hat and carried two dragon stones, one under each arm. He looked up and turned to run.

An invisible force pulled him violently backwards as the stones fell out of his grip and landed on the floor. The agent fell backwards. The hat fell off him and the agent, a thrall, with green skin, stared up at Jared and Nix and Rowena, who quickly surrounded him.

"I know you," Jared said. "You framed me for murder. You were the one who got the guards on me, and you were at our trial."

"I was."

"Why?"

"She wanted you."

Nix frowned. "To kill him?"

"Maybe," Jared said.

The thrall got to his feet.

"Tell me all about the stone. How does it work?"

The thrall pointed at the stones on the floor. "Those are dragon stones."

Naveen leaned forward, his staff close to the agent's face. "I believe that you think they're dragon stones. They are the stuff of legends, but how can that be when there are no more dragons?"

The thrall gulped. "I don't know about legends, but I have seen a dragon. There is one."

Naveen stepped back as if hit in the face with a mace.

"So these are dragon stones?" Jared asked.

"It would seem so," Naveen said.

Jared stepped in front of the thrall. "Tell me about the stone."

"It takes me from one place to another. I lay my hands on it and think where I want to go and it takes me there."

Naveen murmured, "Like flying in the sky on a dragon."

The thrall said, "Crude but accurate. Faster than any dragon alive."

"Who did you plan on meeting here?"

"The queen."

"And if she's not here where would you meet up with her?"

"At her beginning. Where the dragon stones are."

Jared shook his head in anger and pressed the flat of his sword blade against the man's green colored neck. "Speak plainly or my blade might slip even deeper into your neck."

Wide eyes looked back at him and Jared had the man's complete attention. "The cave where she was born. She talked of that night often. She called it the beginning of her new life."

Jared remembered the burning flames and the smell of burned flesh. He watched as the flames ate up his sister and he thought she had died. He pushed himself away from the agent and tried to collect his thoughts and make sense of everything that was happening.

Nix stepped closer to the agent, his own knife held tightly in his hand. He pressed the tip of the knife, with steady and firm pressure, against the agent's throat.

Jared spoke quietly. "Any more dragon stones here at the castle?"

"No."

Jared shrugged. "Naveen."

Naveen brought the tip of his staff to the man's head and instantly the man was asleep and he fell to the floor in a jumble.

Nix said, "What's our next move?"

Jared looked up at the shining light above them. The orb danced in the air and then shrank as it came down and drifted in front of his face. Jared held open the small pouch, a gift from the Lady of the Lake, and the mote of light disappeared inside.

Jared said, "I'll go to the cave where my sister died. Hopefully that is where she went and maybe the child is there, as well. If he's there, I'll bring him back."

Rowena said, "I want to go."

"It's too dangerous."

Jared felt a heaviness descend upon his shoulders. "Naveen, take the other dragon stone and return to our village. Be careful with Grinbell, if he's in league with the vampires," and he left the rest of his sentence alone.

"Understood. But you shouldn't go alone."

"There's no time. Everybody stand back."

Jared placed both hands on the dragon stone, feeling the heat fill him and warm him up, filling up all the dark places inside him with fire and energy and vitality.

He closed his eyes and remembered the cave where he set out to rescue his sister. He thought of the cave and felt two arms wrap around his waist and he felt the pressure of Rowena's body against his.

Before he could do anything, the castle room disappeared and he felt like he was flying through the air on the back of a fire breathing dragon.

Chapter Twenty-eight

TRAVELING WITH THE dragon stone held tight in his hands, and with Rowena's arms wrapped around him, Jared couldn't believe what was happening. He found himself surrounded by white everywhere, with the wind whipping past him, making him close his eyes. The wind buffeted him, and made hearing nearly impossible. He had to shout to be heard. He could hear sounds from Rowena, but the words were hard to decipher.

One moment, he had been in the main hallway with Naveen and Nix looking at the bloodied battlefield that was the castle hallway. Next, he was in some other place, surrounded by white, neither light or dark, but a land of twilight, where the only thing he could feel was the wind whipping past him, Rowena's arms around his waist, and the rough stone between his hands.

The wind stopped just as he caught his breath. The ride was over and they landed heavily against the ground; both the sound and pressure of the wind against him died away.

He blinked several times, waiting for his body to stop spinning. When he opened his eyes for the final time, he discovered that even the ground had stopped moving on its own. He inhaled, deeply relieved that they had survived, and felt the pressure of Rowena's body next to him.

Jared looked up at the massive rock wall in front of them and it struck a distant memory. He had been here before. They stood outside the cave.

The rescue party, with him as its chief member, had come to this cave once upon a time to claim back Christina; and it was here where the attack against the vampires had ended.

The memory of that night stared back at him. He shook off the memory and reached out and grabbed Rowena's hand, tugging on it until she faced him. He leaned into her until she was mere inches from him.

"You tricked me. Don't ever do that, Rowena. Are you clear on that? I told you this was a dangerous mission and what do you do? You go ahead and take the risk anyway. I can take care of myself, but now I have to take care of you too."

"I can take care of myself, Mister High and Mighty."

"Maybe you can and maybe you can't. But I know one thing that you seemed to have forgotten in all of this."

"What?" Rowena's eyes were filled with contempt. Her voice mocked him. "A woman's place is in front of the fire preparing a meal for her lord and master."

"No, because you don't have a man, do you? Your number one job, in case you've forgotten it, is to be there for your son and to raise him up to be strong and proud of his parents."

Rowena stepped back.

"But how can he do that if you put yourself in danger and—God I hope this never happens—you die. Then what will the boy do?"

The words knocked the steam out of her.

In a softer voice, Jared said, "You've already proven your courage, Rowena. You don't have to prove it anymore. Stop risking your life; it isn't right."

Jared continued, "A mother who loses her son is a terrible thing. But a son who loses his mother is even worse. You promise me that you'll not rush in if he's here."

"I won't promise anything where my son is concerned!"

"I need you to. I know how to talk to my sister, you don't. If she has him here then maybe I can get him free. Without harm. You have to trust me. Can you trust me?"

Rowena pulled out her knife and held the blade in front of her. "I've drawn a knife many a time, to kill an animal or to skin it. What you're asking is a very hard thing to do. I love my son with all my heart and if he were to be hurt then I would pull at the edges of the world until everything came tumbling down."

Tears appeared in her brown eyes and Jared placed a hand on her shoulder. "I make you this promise, Rowena. We'll get your son back."

Rowena looked at the blade and then sheathed it. "Where do we go?"

Jared stuffed the stone back into the satchel, and turned and faced the massive opening of the cave. "In here."

Rowena craned her neck. "It's so tall." She glanced up to the top of the cave's opening.

"Afterwards, we had men lined up. It's twenty large men floor to ceiling, and forty seven men across touching fingertip to fingertip." Jared found them standing in the middle of the opening and felt small. "It's where we found some of the victims and where I found Christina. I thought I was here in time, but I wasn't."

"Maybe you'll make up for it today."

"That is my hope."

"Maybe we'll find my son before it's too late for him."

"We will," Jared nodded. "Let's go."

They moved their way through the battle ruins, walking past shattered swords, dented pikes, and cleaved shields. Jared walked to the end of the cave and stood before a small tunnel.

Rowena said, "Did you ever go through this tunnel?"

"No. Our fight took place out there. We never inspected the caves. Not beyond this anyway. We were too busy with our dead and our grief."

Jared felt a tightening in his chest and moved forward, walking down the sloping floor. They moved on like that for fifty steps and then the floor leveled out and they emerged into an even larger cave. It was as if a giant had scooped out large chunks of the earth and planted plateaus and mountains in the distance.

"I hope we find him."

Rowena's voice broke with emotion and she lowered her eyes away from him.

Jared wanted to protect her. She had been so brave and so strong during all of this, but who helped her? He put an arm around her, his hand on her shoulder.

"We'll find him. Let's go search."

Christina's plan was working.

It had all fallen into place, more or less, and now she was standing tall, ready to reap her rewards. She threw her head back and laughed. Her laughter mingled with the sulfur scents in the air.

This was the place where she would resurrect her long dead brother. Blood for blood. That was why she needed the children. The blood had to be fresh. It had to come from pure vessels.

The blood had to come from innocence.

The leathery strap was wrapped tight around his wrist. The other end was looped and knotted through the stake pounded deep into the red earth. The boy could struggle and squirm all he wanted, but he wasn't going anywhere, Christina knew, because the stake was secured deep into the ground.

Christina stepped back from the edge of the abyss, the fire sea below her bubbling and churning. The heat bounced off the high plateau walls and hit her in wave after wave of intense, almost overpowering heat. It was hot and the sulfur lay thick in the air, but this was the place for her kind of magic: a magic that would make her new life like her old life. And, once again, she would be surrounded by family.

She pulled away from the edge and faced the boy. She pulled her knife from its sheath, holding the blade in front of her, and she spoke slowly and without emotion. "Do you know what I use this for, boy?"

The boy stopped squirming against the stake and looked up at her defiantly. "You're just a girl. You don't frighten me."

Christina chuckled and admired the boy's spunk. She twisted the blade until the razor sharp edge of the steel was in position. She stepped closer and kneeled. She held the boy's cheek firmly between thumb and fingers, pinching the skin until a small roll of flesh appeared.

"Be still, boy. If you move this could be worse."

The boy's eyes widened in alarm. His voice squeaked. "What are you doing? Don't do that."

She pressed the flat of the blade against the boy's cheek. For a second, the blade rested on top of the skin. Then she turned the tip of the blade downward, digging into the boy's cheek. She drew a small line across the boy's face, just below the cheekbone with the razor sharpness of the blade.

"Oww," the boy said, pressing a hand against his face. "I'm bleeding. You cut me."

She pulled the knife away, inspecting her work. Christina laughed and bowed to the child. "Your blood will be put to good use."

She lowered herself and moved the child's free hand away from his face. Then she pressed the blade gently against the open wound. "Be still and this will be over."

"I want my mother," the boy said defiantly.

"Well, so do I. We have that in common. I want my mother, too."

"Really? What happened to your mother?" asked the boy tentatively.

"I left her. But soon, she and my whole family will be reunited with me. And then we can all be happy together."

"Are you a vampire?"

"I am."

"You're not like the men who took me. You're beautiful for a vampire."

"Maybe when I'm done, I could make you one, too."

"My mother wouldn't like that. Neither would I. I'd really miss her."

"We all miss our parents at some time. It's natural." She held the blade against the cheek until blood, red and brightly colored on the blade, covered the metal and dripped slowly over the edge. "That'll be enough, I think. Thank you, brave master. Your blood was the missing ingredient."

The boy tugged at the stake, but it wouldn't budge. "Missing ingredient for what?" He put his hand up to his face to staunch the bleeding and looked at her.

Her laughter drifted back to him as she walked to the fiery ledge and started chanting in an unknown language.

She stood before the abyss, the heat filling her up, her nostrils flared. She was at the moment of birth. She had the ingredients, she had the magic, she knew what to do to bring back her brother and that was so important to her. What is a family without brothers? She would have Honor first and then Jared. And then their parents would join them and she would be the ruler of their kingdom.

She looked down into the bubbling fire river below. The fumes wafted up to her and she breathed it in deeply, her eyes closed now as she went through the steps one more time, a last preparation before calling her brother forth.

She held the knife over the fire river and twisted her wrist until the blood slid off the steel blade and, drop by drop, fell into the fiery river below.

Words ancient and deep came out of her, words that caressed and cajoled and then became insistent and demanding. She surged forward in her words, passion flowing through her, her arms waving streams of magic between air and earth and blood and fire.

A shape rose out of the river bed, indistinct. A spiral mass of iridescent colored energies of green and purple quickly formed around the shape, turning it into flesh and bone, all the while held vertical in mid-air. The shape moved toward Christina and her eager eyes devoured the changeling, noting the rapid change from a mound of energies to flesh and blood.

It was happening. Faster than even she thought was possible.

A thrill raced through her. She breathed deeply and expanded her chest, filling her lungs with air and sulfur fumes. She wanted her youngest brother, Honor, with her for the longest time, and now it was coming true.

She clapped her hands in joy and turned halfway and faced the boy. "Your gift has been beyond price, boy."

The illumination bothered him. They were in a cave, yet the light was everywhere. The cave provided even light everywhere and Jared was perplexed over that. He heard a gasp from Rowena. "There!" she said.

He noticed how her chest tightened as she looked through the spyglass. "Here," Rowena said. "My son." She handed him the spyglass, a worried look on her face.

"Show me normal," he said. And the spyglass responded. He inhaled deeply. "You're right."

Through the spyglass, he saw a plateau rise up, and on one end of the plateau was a boy tied to a stake. There was a cut on his cheek, with blood smeared across his face.

They were too late to stop whatever Christina had already done, and they were too far away to run across the distance, and yet maybe they could get there in time to stop what other madness Christina was planning to unleash.

The dragon stone was the answer.

The boy's welfare was in jeopardy and they had to act.

He turned and found Rowena holding the dragon stone in her hand.

She held onto the stone firmly, her slender fingers spread out over the rough surface of the stone. "Grab hold because I'm not waiting for any harm to befall my son again."

The anger in her voice concerned him. He knew she would kick and punch and stab and even kill anybody who harmed her son and he didn't want to get in the way of a she-wolf's maternal instincts when it turned lethal.

Jared collapsed the spyglass and stowed it away in the satchel. His fingers curled around her waist and he held on.

"Take us there," Jared said.

When they reappeared, they were thirty feet away from the boy. His sister, Jared saw, was preoccupied by a gold and blue mass that floated in the air before her. All of her attention was focused solely on that mass. Whatever it was it must be important to her, he thought.

They crept forward, moving swiftly toward the boy. But when Rowena got closer and saw her son, she started to shout for joy. Jared slipped his hand over her mouth and brought her to the ground quietly.

"No noise."

Nobody noticed. The boy's attention was turned toward Christina who was speaking words in a language that Jared didn't understand. In front of Christina was a blue and golden mass, the rough shape of a man, suspended in mid-air before her.

They were still safe. The element of surprise was on their side.

Rowena nodded and closed her eyes for a moment. Tears leaked out from under her eyelashes. When she opened her eyes, there was a sheen to them.

Quietly, they moved toward the boy.

Jared crept next to him and placed a hand over his mouth. He faced him eye to eye. The boy's eyes grew wide as he started to struggle. Jared whispered, "You're safe, lad. Your mother's here. Be quiet. Understand?"

The boy grew still and nodded back in agreement.

Jared took out his knife and cut the straps that held the boy to the stake. Rowena hugged her son and they embraced for a couple of seconds.

"Time to get out of here," Jared said.

Rowena embraced her son again and, closing her eyes tight, she felt heartfelt gratitude for his safe return. It felt good to have him in her arms. She inspected him at arm's length, and noticed the cut across his cheek.

Panic surged inside of her: *Her son could have been killed!* If they had been a couple of minutes later, he could have been dead or worse.

She would have failed.

Then the avalanche landed on top of her with all the force of a landslide.

She couldn't breathe.

Her son, she realized, could easily have died and she had been powerless to stop it.

She remained still, letting her gratitude and anger circle each other ready to fight inside of her.

How could this have happened?

What gave them the right? He was safe.

She curled and straightened and curled her fingers again around the leather handled knife at her side. She gripped it in her raised hand and stared at the woman's back. Then she looked over at her son's blood-smeared face.

You bitch! she thought.

Jared heard the words bark out of Rowena's mouth. What was she thinking?

He motioned for her to be quiet. "Get the dragon stone and go." His back was to the abyss, and when he turned around large, dark eyes stared back at him.

"Sister, what are you doing?" He pulled the sword from his scabbard and held it by his side.

"Brother, you amaze me. I didn't think you'd ever find this place."

"Your birth place?"

"And more." She glanced at the vertical slab surrounded by a nimbus of gold and blue light. "Look."

"What evil is that?"

"No evil," she said. "It's our brother. He's coming back."

"He died. That happened a long time ago."

"A sister can have family with her."

"This is unnatural," Jared said.

"This is blood. I will have father and mother with me. My old brother," she gestured toward the shape surrounded in the gold and blue nimbus, "and you."

Jared stepped forward. He gave Rowena a worried look and gestured for her to go. He had to give them time to escape.

"But I am already here," Jared said.

"I cannot," Christina said, "visit you during daylight hours. But if we were all together, then the night time would be so much better, don't you think?"

Jared's mind was spinning with all that had happened to his sister. He felt sorry for her and he blamed himself for her state. Even now, as a vampire, she was still thinking of her family and how they could all be together.

He stepped forward even more, his arms spread apart as he inched closer to her. He hoped giving Rowena and her son time to grab the dragon stone and leave would be enough. If she could get her son to safety then maybe it would all work out.

His sister stopped talking, and she looked under his outstretched arms. "You brought the boy's mother along. You have nothing to worry about from me."

"Then we'll leave quietly, sister."

"Leave? Why go? My old life was taken from me. *You* failed me. *You* turned me into this."

"I failed to protect you, and for that I am sorry. But I never forced you to kill people, sister. That is on your own head."

With unexpected animal speed, she leaped toward him and, knocking him to the ground, she swept the sword from his grasp. The speed was fast and deadly and caught Jared by surprise.

Jared, flat on the ledge, glanced up at his sister, who pinned him to the ground.

She smiled down at him and cooed. "Mommy and child left. Now how could they do that, I wonder."

Her cold slender fingers circled his throat, squeezing the breath from him, choking him. He tried to release her grip but he couldn't move her. Her strength was incredible. He used the points of his elbows against her arms to budge her.

A burning sensation grew in his chest. His lungs were on fire because he lacked oxygen. Jared knew it was only a matter of time and then it would be too late. He had to strike now or risk blacking out.

If he blacked out then she'd win and the children would lose. He couldn't allow that to happen. He wouldn't stand for the children being turned into vampire food or worse, turned into vampires. It was something he wouldn't wish on his worst enemy.

Jared renewed his attacks against her wrists and forearms, but the effort was wasted. She remained strong and he was getting weaker.

He tried to buck her forward and throw her balance high, so he could turn and twist under her and get free. But she just pressed herself even firmer to the ground, an added weight that he couldn't move.

He tried twisting and turning his back to her, but her grip on him was too tight and he was seeing star bursts explode in the periphery of his vision.

He started to lose consciousness, feeling himself getting light-headed. It was the end.

He had failed. He failed the children. He failed Nix and Naveen. He failed Christina, again.

He hoped at least that Rowena and her son had gotten free. He could take comfort in his death if Rowena and her son were safe. Maybe his death would be put to good use.

He turned and struggled and heard Christina laugh at him. "You were always the weak one, Jared. I could always play you, always two moves ahead of you."

The admission of truth slapped him in the face, and a slow burn quickly sped through his body, galvanizing him. A quick last burst of strength flowed through him and he twisted and turned and then he lifted up his hips and bucked her off of him, catching her by surprise.

He watched as she flipped over his head and landed on her back.

Jared gagged and choked and inhaled air into his lungs like a thirsty man drinking water from a bucket. He coughed even more because of the burning, noxious gases in the back of his throat.

There was a scream and Jared staggered to his feet. His sister gave him a malevolent stare and charged at him; a twisted evil glint shone in her eyes. He reached for the sword, but it was too far out of his reach.

His sister leaped at him. Jared braced for the impact when suddenly she fell down.

Naveen stood behind her, his staff in one hand, his other hand outstretched and the fingers converged to make a point. Behind Naveen stood Nix, who placed a second dragon stone on the ground.

"Your timing couldn't be better."

"Wizards arrive when we are least expected, but most needed."

Naveen stood next to Jared. "What now?"

Jared pointed to the blue and gold nimbus covered form over the abyss. "He goes back to where he came from."

"What is it?"

"My brother."

Naveen raised an eyebrow.

"He's dead. She was trying to raise him from the dead. I want to give him the peace he deserves."

From the ground came a chuckle. Jared turned and a tingling sensation went up his spine.

Christina supported herself on one elbow. But he watched Naveen stun her. What happened?

"He is the start," Christina said. "You won't kill him. First me, then your dear brother. What will father and mother say?"

Naveen raised his staff to the vampire and said, "You will abide by what he says, vampire."

She regarded him. "A wizard. Oh, what a piece of work you are." Christina slowly got up. "But I know *magic* as well." At the word magic, she shot a stun spell at Naveen and the wizard collapsed to the ground.

Nix rushed forward, a short knife drawn up to attack her. Jared followed him.

Two against one. Christina used magic spells to block Nix away and shove Jared back.

Then she aimed a spell at Nix and knocked him out.

"No!" Jared said.

Jared leaped toward Christina and grappled with her, but he immediately realized his mistake. She still looked like his sister, but she had the strength of two dozen men. Jared pushed her back and grabbed the sword that was nearby. With the point between them, he started driving her back to the ledge.

"Last chance, sister. Give up."

"Why should she?" a haughty voice behind him said.

Jared looked sideways and Grinbell the wizard was pointing a staff at him. Jared felt a tingling sensation as if fire ants were crawling over his body. His hand muscles relaxed and he watched as the sword fell out of his hand. He tried to move but felt a deep paralysis swarm over him. He tried to take a step but fell sideways onto the ground.

He was alert, but his muscles turned slack. He cursed and willed his muscles to act, but they ignored him. There was no connection between his will and his muscles. As far as his body was concerned, whatever Jared wanted was all gibberish to it.

Jared lay on his side and watched Grinbell, the wizard, stand next to his sister.

Jared said, "How long have you been helping?"

Grinbell looked down at him and considered the question for a moment. He laughed. "When I was shown magical items of interest, it piqued my curiosity, so now we have areas of mutual interest."

Grinbell stepped away and Jared could see him advancing on Nix and Naveen, both of whom were on the ground unconscious.

Grinbell looked down at the unconscious form of Nix and said, "You took my dragon stone, thief. Your disguise as an old man was impressive, but obviously, you're here on your back, and I am on my *feet.*"

Grinbell smashed his boot against the side of Nix's head. "Next time you steal something thief, don't steal anything of *mine.*"

Nix awoke from the spell and screamed in pain. He curled in a tight ball, cradled his head and sobbed.

Grinbell stood over Naveen and shook his head at the unconscious form. "And you have the gall to call yourself a wizard. The profession has gone downhill completely with you younger wizards."

Grinbell reached down and held Naveen's staff in his hand, inspecting the handiwork. "I see certain influences of the west and east on your staff. No matter, your staff is now mine, wizard."

Grinbell looked around. "Where are the woman and her child?"

"They got away," Christina said.

Grinbell shrugged. "Doesn't matter. Either now or later they will be captured and then they will be killed. Can't have loose ends, can we?"

Jared was glad that Rowena and her son got out of there. She could be anywhere right now and that was fine with him. They set out to accomplish what they wanted and that was to rescue the children from the vampires. They did that.

"We found the children," Jared said, his brain scrambling for a toehold. The top was in reach, if only he could delay the death sentence. "We discovered what was really going on."

Grinbell stepped lightly over the ground and bent low to Jared. If his arms could move, he'd be able to strike the wizard in the face, maybe even grapple him to the ground and draw a knife on him.

"Yes," Grinbell said. "Wheels within wheels. I love that best, don't you?"

"All that trouble?"

The wizard said, "On the surface it seems like one thing, but if you're careful and you twist it just so, a totally different picture emerges." He sighed and a look of contentment filled the wizard's face. "Too bad. You all die. Although you all got further than I expected."

"Not him," Christina said, pointing to Jared. "He is family."

"Idle tongues cannot go about and wag. It would be dangerous."

Christina moved toward Grinbell and showed her fangs, inching closer to him. The wizard, although taller, took a step backward.

"Of course," Grinbell said, "let me lift the death spell from him right now." The wizard looked down at Jared and remained silent.

Jared wondered if Grinbell could really remove the death spell, when the wizard pushed the red hair off his forehead and announced, "It's done."

"Good."

Jared sat up, and felt the muscles returning back to his control. He could flex his fingers, move his arms. He climbed to his feet.

He was outnumbered and outmatched. His sister could easily stop him with her own physical strength and the wizard just demonstrated how easily he could move Jared off the chessboard if he wanted to. Jared knew he'd have to come up with a gambit, especially with his unconscious friends on the ground at the wizard's feet.

In a loud and angry voice, Jared said, "I was *poisoned* by one of your vampires and left to die. Was that the plan?"

Christina frowned and shook her head. "That vampire was tracked down. A rogue one. When he finished telling me what I wanted to know, he was killed. A pity. Good vampires are so rare."

Jared watched as Grinbell touched a rune on his staff with his forefinger. He was too late. Nix and Naveen started jerking on the ground.

"What happened?" Jared asked.

"The Death Spell has been activated," Grinbell said, a tone of satisfaction in his voice.

His sister turned and walked to the abyss, her mind filled with what she was planning to do.

Jared saw his friends choking. He moved toward Christina. "Help them," he pleaded.

"That is out of my control. There is nothing anybody can do for them."

Christina ignored him and focused on the hovering mass in front of her.

Grinbell regarded him coolly when something snapped behind them.

Grinbell whirled around.

Jared was surprised by the sudden appearance of Rowena, a short sword in her hand. She had snuck up and was poised to strike the wizard when he turned and cast a spell.

Rowena flew backwards through the air. She landed on her back—a moaning sound escaped her lips—and she laid still. In her open hand was a short sword. By her head was a rock she had landed on.

Jared searched for an explanation for her sudden appearance. Rowena came back because her companions needed help.

There was movement. Out from behind a rock the boy Steen rushed to his mother's side and kneeled over her. He touched her face, and then gingerly padded her head with his small hands. His fingers came back bloodied.

Grinbell regarded the child for a moment and then turned and faced Jared. "I wouldn't try anything. Alive or dead doesn't matter to me. If you move, you'll be dead."

"You would chance that?"

"Your sister knows how to bring back the dead. She's calling him back right now. She could call you back as well, if you were dead. So, don't tempt me."

Jared saw the boy reach for his mother's sword and grip it tightly in his small hand. The boy looked up at the tall wizard's back with revenge in his eyes.

"Hey, Grinbell, what does a wizard do with all the magical items you've gathered? Are you going to overthrow the wizard council? Are you going to start a war?"

Grinbell chuckled. "Something like that, but it's no concern of yours."

Jared watched as the boy crept closer and, standing behind Grinbell, he raised the sword and jammed it sharply down into the wizard's leg, just behind the knee into the fleshy part of the lower leg.

The wizard screamed in pain. He whirled around. "You piece of dung! You will pay for that!"

Jared picked up a sword from the ground and rushed toward Grinbell.

His friends would be dead if he didn't do something.

He felt the handle of the sword in his hand. It felt good being there. He tensed and felt his will and muscle unite in his arm.

He raised the sword in a mighty arc and brought it down with all of his might. He swung down hard, striking at the spot where neck met body. The sword blade sliced into flesh and muscles and blood shot out from the front of the neck. Deep crimson fluid rained down on Grinbell. Grinbell pivoted and staggered and stared at Jared.

Jared swung again. The sword severed head from body.

As the head toppled end over end and fell to the ground, Jared let go of the sword.

Naveen stopped struggling and color returned to his face.

Nix rolled over on his back and started coughing, the air forcing his lungs to expand and then exhale.

Jared looked over his shoulder at his sister. She was oblivious to everything around her except for the rapidly changing body in front of her. With each passing second the body took on the shape and size of his dead brother. The energy around the body changed violently from blue to gold and then retreated back to blue again.

With the death spell broken, Naveen was on his feet, the color returned to his grim face.

Nix rolled over and braced himself on hands and knees, choking and coughing. Jared helped Nix to his feet, and picked up Nix's dagger and hid it from the thief.

Jared glanced at Rowena. "See to her, wizard. See what you can do for her."

"What about you?"

Jared said, "I have unfinished business."

Nix said, "Has anybody seen my dagger."

Naveen said, "It's probably on the ground. You can find it later."

"Both of you take care of Rowena, take care of her son."

Jared watched as they knelt by Rowena and he knew she was in the best hands possible.

Jared turned and sucked in air. The noxious smell made him grit his teeth. He stared at his sister's back, and then he looked at his brother's face, newly raised from the dead.

The eyes opened and there was instant understanding in them.

"Sister, let him go," Jared said, walking until he stood next to her, shoulder touching shoulder, looking into Honor's bright and beautiful face, It had been a long time.

"Why should I? I deserve family too."

"His time is past."

"His time is *now*. I have the means. I should use it."

Honor, engulfed in a nimbus of blue and golden light that swam around him, a cocoon of protective energies, seemed like a bittersweet gift, a forbidden and wasteful remembering, something unnatural and perverse.

"Remember our summers in the forest? Honor and I would play and you would carve ..."

"My initials in a tree. Mother would sing to us and father ..."

"Would teach us how to use the bow and arrow."

"It was the best time of my life."

"Mine too." He stepped back, away from the shining newborn Honor and whispered, "I am sorry." He turned to Christina. "I love you."

A tentative smile flashed across her face and then she stiffened.

Jared moved the dagger's blade even deeper into his sister, under the rib cage, hoping to damage her heart, so death would be quick.

Christina staggered and pushed Jared away. She pressed her hand over the wound, blood seeping past her slender fingers.

"You failed me, brother."

"I failed you."

"We could have been together as family."

"We'll always be together."

"You've killed quite a few." Christina inhaled deeply and the pain made her wince.

"I had good reason."

She coughed up blood and looked at her hand. "They know about you. Your reputation grows."

Jared said, "Our summers were the best. I remember them with great affection."

"Vampire Nation is so much larger than this castle."

"I killed the king of Vampire Nation because he was the one who changed you."

"I lied," Christina coughed. "There are several kings in Vampire Nation, but there is only one Overking. Vampire Nation encompasses much land to the south and east. You, my brother, have stirred up a wrath of trouble."

Christina glanced at Honor, about to say something, and then turned to Jared. An arrow flew by Jared and struck Christina in the chest.

Jared turned and saw two more arrows in flight.

He ducked.

The arrows landed with a sickening thunk sound into Christina's chest.

Christina staggered and looked down at the arrows sticking out of her body. Wild eyed, she hissed, looked at her brother and then turned and leapt into the fiery river below.

"Christina," Jared said, reaching out for her, but she was already gone.

Jared reached the ledge and looked over it but he couldn't see her body, the fumes from the river drove him back. He coughed and hacked and then straightened up and Honor was still encased in his blue and gold cocoon.

"Remember me, brother," Honor said.

The blue and golden nimbus of light broke apart in sections, spinning apart and fading away. Honor's body, not totally solid, reverted back. His body fell to the ledge; Honor looked up at him and then the body dusted away.

Stunned by what happened, Jared staggered away from the ledge. Anger filled him. He pushed past Naveen and Nix and stood in front of Rowena. The bow, he noticed, was still in her hand and her head was bloodied on one side, a small piece of cloth tied around her head.

"How could you?"

"How could she?" Her eyes met his and matched his anger flame for flame until Jared realized that she was right. He didn't like it, but she was right and that was all there was about that.

His sister had started the whole chain of events, had created panic and fear in families across the land that had gripped them for days and weeks at a time.

Nix pressed between them. "What about the children?"

"Let's take them back home," Jared said.

Naveen added, "With one stop along the way."

Chapter Twenty-nine

IT REMINDED JARED of gypsies or something out of the fairy tales he heard as a child. They entered the village, with a swarm of children around them, and the villagers came out and looked at them, pointing to the children and wondering where they had come from. People would stop and stare and then they'd come closer.

They'd been traveling for several days now, re-tracing their steps. He didn't want news of the dragon stones to get out to others, so it was better this way.

Nix and Rowena explained to the villagers that the children were rescued from the castle of vampires, and that they were safe from them.

Shouts and cheers went up in the marketplace.

The shouting and the huzzahs brought forth three wizards, eager to hear what the noise was all about. The crowd of people pulled back as the wizards strode into the market, as if they owned the place.

Naveen saw them approach and moved to head them off.

Nix spotted the gathering of wizards and poked Rowena in the side; he tugged on Jared's sleeve and pointed. A smile came across Jared's face.

Rowena frowned. "He'll be hurt. Is this necessary?"

Nix said, "Yes."

"Why?" Rowena brought her hand to her face, her eyes twin pools of worry.

"A man's honor is as strong as a woman's love for her son." Jared said, "Besides, I think it'll be a fair fight."

Rowena bit her lower lip. "Three against one?"

Nix laughed. "They'll never see what hits them."

Naveen leaned on his staff and faced the three wizards. "High and mighty wizards, I greet you."

Roloth, with a scar across his left cheek, faced Naveen, and next to him was a bearded wizard missing two right fingers on his hand. Behind them was the tall slender wizard. They all stood their ground and nodded politely at Naveen.

"And we you, sir. What is the meaning of all this noise? Why do you disturb the peace of this glorious morning?"

"Have you not heard about the defeat of the vampires?" Naveen asked.

"Defeat? That is news indeed," Roloth said.

"Yes, and never was a word mentioned about three wizards from this village participating in the event. I wonder why that is. Could it be that you had better things to do with your skills like terrorize shop owners? Or bully people by your own presence?"

"You do us a grave dishonor wizard; I would watch your tongue."

"I think not Roloth."

"Have we met before, wizard?"

Naveen said quietly, "How soon they forget." Then he raised his voice and said, "Rather, it is you and your cousins who do a great dishonor to wizards everywhere." Naveen stepped back, holding his staff in both hands. "I remember something: a lesson learned is a sorrow saved."

Roloth rubbed his scar and said, "He throws our words at us."

"Let us teach him a lesson," said the wizard with missing fingers.

The tall wizard said, "He probably has a hard head. We'll have to drum respect into him really hard."

Roloth pointed at Naveen: "You were the wizard we hung upside down!"

"That is correct."

The wizards spread out before Naveen.

Naveen focused on their hands, especially the weak part of their hands, focusing on their joints. The pain was intense, but brief. Almost in unison all three wizards gasped in pain and released their staffs because of the pain in their hands. Then, as if by magical means, a strong gust of wind collected up their staffs and deposited them at Naveen's feet.

With their staffs on the ground, Naveen smiled wolfishly and moved his staff in a decisive manner. Roloth was raised up into the air, and then suddenly he was turned violently until his head was where his feet should be and his feet were where his head should be.

Naveen swung Roloth head over feet a couple of more times, taking pleasure in hearing the unexpected yelps of surprise escape from the wizard's mouth.

Naveen motioned his staff and Roloth was carried to the nearest tree, as if by invisible hands. Branches and vines, moving by themselves, strapped Roloth to the tree upside down. Roloth's robe fell over his waist and covered his neck and mouth. Roloth's undergarments were exposed for all to see.

The villagers murmured and pointed, but remained silent.

The tall wizard stepped forward. "That is uncalled for. That is no way to treat a wizard."

"You are correct," Naveen said. "But you forgot that lesson."

"You don't know who you are dealing with," the other wizard said, standing next to the tall wizard.

"I'm afraid I know all too well who I am dealing with."

Naveen stepped closer to the two standing wizards and raised his staff and suddenly the wizards went rigid. Invisible forces slammed the wizards together and then separated them, then slammed them together again and separated them.

The two wizards fell to the ground unconscious.

Roloth, strapped to the tree shouted, "We'll get you for this. There won't be any place you can hide from us."

Naveen approached Roloth calmly. "If you three abuse others I will be back to administer further training in how to serve people properly. In the meantime, I will keep your staffs with me. Safely. If I hear reports that you have acted civilly toward people, then your staffs will be returned. If you continue to abuse people with your magic, then I will bring this to the attention of the wizard council. They will judge what should be done to you for your minor crimes and annoyances against the populace."

"And you, wizard, what about you?"

"Come anytime, Roloth. I can take care of me and my own."

The villagers were silent for a moment and then the children started pointing and laughing because they saw the wizard's undergarments. The villagers joined in the laughter, although they were nervous as well.

Naveen turned and picked up the staffs of the wizards and walked back to his companions.

Nix said, "Nicely done. But I think a couple of fire spells would have been better appreciated."

"Next time," Naveen said, "if they are still hard headed."

Word spread before them and excitement filled the lands. The vampires had been defeated, and children were marching out of the land unharmed. Everywhere they passed people came out to see them, shouting encouragement or offering them food and drink for their company. On the eighth day of the journey back they entered a familiar sight.

They were passing the fields and rode over the bridge entering the village.

Jared stopped and saw the village where it all started for him.

Steen turned on the horse and said, "Mom, can I go home?"

Rowena turned in her saddle. "Why not?"

Steen slid off the horse and said to the other children, "Come on, let's go."

The children raced across the field, their screams pealed in the air as workers looked up as the swarm of children ran laughing and shouting.

Other children from the village joined in and a throng of excited children moved through the village. Workers and adults and the Captain of the Guard looked on as children rushed into the arms of their families and parents and were bestowed with hugs and kisses.

Tears of gratitude fell down the cheeks of many families that day as children were reunited with their loved ones.

Jared waited on the bridge, watching families welcome their children. It reminded him of his own family as a child and how he wished it could all have been different. He glanced sideways at Nix and Naveen.

Nix said, "You did it."

Jared shook his head. "*We* did it."

"What now?" Rowena asked.

"I should be moving on," Jared said.

"Why?" She looked at him, her eyes never leaving his face.

The aroma of meat filled their senses.

"I didn't have a good experience here," Jared said.

"But you turned it around to our advantage," Nix said.

"They need to know how it ended," Naveen said. "And if anybody tries to harm you, they'll have to get through me."

"And they have to get past my arrows," Rowena said.

"And my knife, too." Nix added.

Jared relented. "The food does smell good."

Rowena said, "Maggie does make a good spread that sticks to you."

"Okay, let's go," Jared said.

They rode slowly into the village and Jared heard more laughter and crying as parents came out into the street with children hugged close to their bodies.

Soon the whole village had poured out into the street and it was a holiday. Families celebrated and laughed.

Parents hugged their missing children and tears of love rolled down the weathered faces and made their voices thick with emotion.

Jared dismounted and tied his horse to a stump. With the others by his side, he walked into Maggie's place. She brushed her hair from her face and said, "I've been expecting you. News travels fast. Heard about you three days now. Your food is over there. And there's food for your friends as well."

"What do I owe you?"

"We owe you, stranger. Just sit and eat."

And with abandon they each sat down and ate heartily, tearing into the meat and bread with gusto and relish and soon their laughter filled the place and tears streamed down the faces of some of them.

"I don't believe my eyes," said a voice.

Jared looked up and saw the Captain of the Guard approach them.

"I didn't think you'd ever be back here stranger. I thought you'd be dead."

Jared stopped laughing and nodded. He swallowed the last piece of meat on his plate and said, "I gave my word."

"Aye. And I hate to interrupt this occasion ..."

"Then don't interrupt," Nix said, his eyes boring directly into the Captain of the Guard.

The Captain gave Nix a hard look right back and continued, "but there is still the matter of murder."

Jared said, "Which I promised to clear up."

"Grinbell the wizard will be your judge."

"No, he won't," Nix said.

"What do you mean?"

Nix drew his finger across his neck and made gurgling noises.

"What's that supposed to mean?"

Rowena said, "Grinbell, the sword and shield, was in league with the vampires. He knew about the children being kidnapped, and he knew about the murder."

"And you can prove this?"

Naveen pushed his plate away and stood up, staff in hand. "A man's words and actions have always been a good measure, have they not?"

The Captain of the Guard nodded. "Yes, I guess."

"Here is Grinbell's staff. I will keep it until I can get this to the wizard's council for their administration in this matter."

"That is news," the Captain of the Guard said, his eyes sweeping over them, back and forth, and then he relented and relaxed.

Rowena stood up and placed a hand on Jared's shoulder. "He has saved many lives today, restored a village's hope and faith in itself and its future. He brought children and parents back together."

"But do you have proof?"

"Sit down and I will tell you my story, and then you can determine my guilt."

Jared sat at the table and told the Captain of the Guard the whole of the events that happened to him, starting with when he first came to this village until he returned, careful to keep vague the magical items of interest they had found.

When Jared was done telling the story, he looked about and was surprised to see the faces of men and women and children hunched nearby listening to his story.

A man dressed in fine clothes stepped into the business and said, "Everyone is gathered here and I wondered why," he said and his eyes scanned the faces of everyone. He saw the people seated at the table and then his eyes widened in excitement.

"My lord. Is it? My lord, it is!" The man rushed forward and stood before Jared and grabbed him by the shoulders. "Your father has been looking for you. Word has been sent for you to return to court."

Naveen pointed a finger at Jared and laughed. "Who are you really?"

"My lord?" Nix said, choking on the words.

Rowena shook her head. "I knew there was something more to you."

THE END

www.ingramcontent.com/pod-product-compliance
Lightning Source LLC
Chambersburg PA
CBHW021001150626
46549CB00012BA/284